THE DECOY

THE DECOY

Al Ramsay

Full Gas Books (Chorley)

Copyright © 2021 Al Ramsay

Cover design by: Scott Cockerham

ISBN: 978-1-7399045-0-0

To my lovely Louise

1

Oblivious to the traffic roaring past on either side, the girl crouched forward over the handlebars, head down, legs burning as she raced to beat the next set of lights. The drab grey of south London's Old Kent Road stretched out before her, sapping the little energy she had left. It had been a hard day - six drop-offs around the City and West End, then cast from the bright lights into grimy reality south of the river. And now on the long ride home, the radio clipped to the strap on her shoulder bag, crackled into life.

'Kefie, where are you, babes?'

She lifted her hands from the bars and sat up, clawing at the radio. Holding it to her lips, she spoke quietly. 'Old Kent Road, coming through Peckham - on my way home.'

'Nah, got one more for you, love. It's a pick-up - down Rotherhithe way.'

'Harry, it is seven-thirty - I have been working for nearly twelve hours. Please find someone else.'

'No can do, darlin'. The guy was most insistent you do the job. The Majestic on Suffolk Square - room six. One of your mates, I reckon.'

'And what do you mean by that?' she asked.

'It's just that, from 'is accent, I'd say he was probably of the... err… the African persuasion.'

The girl pulled up at the side of the road, pressing the handset to her ear. 'Africa is a very big place, Harry - why would you believe this man to be my friend?'

'Don't get me wrong, I'm not being racial or nuffing. It's just that he asked for you by name, didn't he? And then he said to mention this word and you'd know what it was about. Odd really - still sounds a bit stupid if you ask me.'

Seconds later she'd dropped the radio into the gutter and was sprinting away on what she knew would be her last ever job as a cycle courier.

Circling round to the back of the run-down, four-storey Victorian building, she clicked the latch on the rotting wooden gate and entered a rear yard littered with rubbish and split bin bags. She propped the bike close to a fire exit, smiling at the 'One Less Car' slogan stencilled onto its crossbar. When all this was over, she'd take it back to Dalston and leave it in exactly the same place she'd found it, all those months before. She'd always felt a bit guilty about taking it but in the overall scheme of things it was of little consequence.

She walked in through the hotel's main entrance, scanning the deserted reception area with a cool, professional detachment. Glancing at the CCTV camera high up on the wall above a solitary moth-eaten settee, she moved swiftly towards the lift. After pressing the 'call' button she changed her mind, heading for the stairs just as the lift doors opened. The three men who emerged never saw her. Powerfully built, their uniform jeans and tan leather jackets, dark slicked-back hair and Mediterranean complexions, looked oddly out of place in the hotel's seedy surroundings. As they filed out, one of them clambered up onto the settee and ripped the camera from its bracket.

'*Vamos, Xavier*!' the biggest of them, a thickset heavyweight with a terrifying scar running across his face, growled back from the door.

'*Está roto, Hernandez*,' replied his companion, flashing a gold-toothed grin. '*Quiero informar al director del hotel*!'

Laughing, the trio strolled out into the warm evening air without so much as a backward glance at the camera, now lying smashed to pieces on the floor.

Up two flights of stairs and the girl made her way along the dimly lit corridor. The door to room six was battered and scuffed, and after pausing to compose herself she knocked crisply on the dirty brown paintwork.

There was no response.

She tried again, banging with the heel of her palm, and this time the door creaked open a couple of centimetres. After glancing over a shoulder to make sure she wasn't being watched, she edged forward into the darkness, the lock clicking shut behind her.

The room had a heavy, humid atmosphere and with eyes still adjusting to the gloom she had to feel her way forward, stumbling over an upturned chair and nearly falling across a chest of drawers that had been flipped onto its side. After making it to the window she threw caution to the wind and heaved the curtains apart.

Light streamed in on a scene of total devastation. It was as if the room had been picked up, shaken furiously then dashed to the ground. Clothes and furniture were scattered like confetti while the badly stained mattress propped against the wall, looked like a slasher movie victim, its cover ripped open, entrails oozing out across the carpet. Someone had got there before her and the girl's heart sank as she realised that whoever had done this had probably found what they were looking for - what she was looking for.

She'd barely begun her search when she heard voices in the corridor outside.

BOOM!

The door buckled under the impact of the blow, its lock rattling in protest. Cycle courier bag still slung across her back, she darted into the en-suite. She heard men's voices - English accents. They were in the room now and from the sounds of it the demolition job was back in full swing. Alone in the pitch-black of the windowless bathroom, she steadied herself, slowing her breathing as best she could.

Moments later, the door banged open. The girl looked down from her new vantage point, perched high on the end of the bath, back pressed to the wall. The broad-shouldered lummox with the shaved head peered into the darkness, ducking back out again after the most cursory of inspections. The door swung-to behind him.

She pulled a cycle light from her bag, clicking it on to illuminate her cramped surroundings in crazy, strobe light bursts. The shower curtain had been ripped from its rail and was lying in an untidy roll along the full length of the bath. She could just about make out a sink and toilet crammed in against the far wall. And then something caught her eye.

Seconds later she was down on her knees, face just inches from the foul-smelling toilet pan, hands searching across the wall tiles. The screws holding the service panel in place were swiftly located but there was no time to tackle them with the multi-tool in her bag. Feeling for cracks in the crumbling asbestos boarding, she set to work, easing away loose fragments, the flashing light now clenched between her teeth.

4

She laboured with painstaking care and in no time had removed a corner section big enough to thrust an arm through. Her hand groped blindly into a tangled undergrowth of rusty pipes and ancient cabling. Sensing the waft of cool, stale air blowing onto her face, she pictured the fire escape at the back of the building and prayed that this service duct might eventually lead her to it.

As she drew her arm back, her hand brushed against something solid and square-shaped. Eager fingers locked onto a small oblong box in a plastic wrapper, taped to one of the pipes. With beads of sweat forming on her brow she prised it loose, pulling it into the bathroom and only narrowly stifling a yelp of joy as she stuffed it into her bag.

What remained of the service panel was swiftly dismantled, the gaping black hole offering just enough space for her to squeeze through. Maybe. Lying motionless on the floor, the strobe light flickering away, she glanced back towards the bathroom door.

That was when she saw it.

The bloated face, smeared with a livid scar of congealed blood, seemed to be floating above the end of the bath. Bulging eyes stared down at her, the swollen dark-blue lips of the half-open mouth curled into a leering rictus smile.

Welling up from deep within, came an unstoppable, involuntary cry. And then all hell broke loose.

As he ambled past the shops on Fishergate, heading towards Preston station, Felix Haythornthwaite's mind was somewhere else altogether. If you'd asked him what he wanted out of life, just a few months earlier, the answer would have bounced back in an instant - GCSEs. It wasn't like he was hoping for straight A* grades and finishing top of his class. No. He just wanted them over and done with. He'd have given anything to jump in a time machine and leap effortlessly past the exam nightmare that lay ahead.

Of course, there was no time machine - he'd had to grind his way through them like everyone else - but now he was out on the other side, things hadn't turned out to be quite as fabulous as he'd hoped. Thanks to his former head of English, he'd secured a summer work experience placement, three days a week on Lancashire's third-favourite daily newspaper - the evening edition *Lancastrian Bugler*. His commute to Bugler House - located on a nondescript business park, deep in Preston's northern suburbs - was a killer, but for someone who'd always wanted to be a journalist, who'd been the editor of the school magazine, it was the best break ever. And yet...

'Cheer up lad - might never 'appen.'

'Oh, sorry.' Felix smiled absent-mindedly at the passer-by, wincing as he caught sight of his reflection in the polished glass of the department store window. His mum always said he'd grow into his gangling six-foot-three-inch frame, but he knew she was just trying to make him feel a bit better about himself. His school uniform had been consigned to the bin only a month earlier, but now it was the ill-fitting brown suit with the dated flared trousers that made him stand out from the crowd. The oversized shirt collar and charity shop tie merely added to his awkwardness. At least the gelled spike-top wasn't too bad, he thought. It made his mousey-brown hair look darker, contrasting with his lilywhite complexion, although when he saw himself shorn of the chaotic frizz he'd sported throughout his entire school life, he couldn't help thinking his head looked just that little bit too small for his body.

Oh well...

He dumped his rucksack on the pavement so he could take a closer look at his reflection. The unseen shop assistant who'd been crouching down to adjust something at the bottom of the lingerie display, looked up and gawped as he worked through the highlights of the 'robot' routine he'd been practising in his bedroom at home. He nearly jumped out of his skin when she got to her feet to offer him a round of applause. Mortified, he scurried off towards the station.

Trudging across the footbridge that spanned the grimy Victorian platforms, he headed for his usual spot by the Pumpkin Bar. Half a roll of wine gums later and the departures board flashed up a five-minute delay. A further ten minutes crawled by before the announcer confirmed what most of the unhappy passengers had already guessed:

'Due to an incident at Chorley, the 5:15 Trains4U service to Slaidforth Sands has been cancelled. Trains 4U apologise for any inconvenience caused.'

Some of the commuters dug out their mobiles and began making calls while others gazed back down the track or stared blankly at the information display, like extras in a zombie film. Felix groaned - he was tired and fed up, and he wanted to go home.

He'd survived his third week at the *Bugler* but it had been a close-run thing. He now knew that the chairman of the Slaidforth Sands Conservative party was Alderman Dennis Greenhalgh, and not, as the yellow Post-It note left on his desk had suggested, Councillor Hugh Janus. He'd found out the hard way, after a call to the alderman had quickly spiralled out of control. But the endless practical jokes of his work colleagues were just the half of it.

Shadowing his boss, Howard Brake - 'HB' as he liked to be called - an obnoxious bully in his early twenties, was the toughest gig of all. The week's big stories, such as the Leyland allotment society's giant marrow competition or the crowning of the Adlington carnival queen, were all, apparently, way beneath a reporter of HB's talents, and he delighted in taking out his frustrations on his new assistant.

Felix had wanted to work on a real newspaper for as long as he could remember but the whole thing had become such a nightmare, he was seriously considering jacking it in.

With time on his hands, he decided to make use of the station's toilet facilities. He wandered into the whiffy, white-tiled gents, determined to do what he needed to and get back out into the fresh air as quickly as possible. Once he'd been, he turned to rinse his hands. Try as he might he couldn't get anything out of the single, cold tap. He should have left it but it had become a point of principle and he leant forward, pressing down on the tap head with all his weight. The ominous gurgle from the ancient Victorian plumbing heralded the arrival of a pulse of water so forceful that almost all of it ricocheted back out of the basin, completely soaking the front of his trousers.

'Aw, man!'

It was bad, worse than bad, and the lack of a dryer made an emergency clean up a non-starter. Staying put until things had dried off was not an option so he shuffled back onto the crowded platform, clutching his rucksack to his groin. There was a space on the metal bench just outside the toilets and he squeezed in next to an elderly lady, who had to move up to make room.

'Oh dear, had an accident have we?' she asked in a loud voice.

'No, not at all,' he replied. 'The tap on the sink was faulty.'

'It's nowt to be ashamed of, love. My Arthur used to suffer something terrible from his waterworks. The poor dear was under the doctor for it but that didn't stop him having his little mishaps.'

'I'm sorry to hear it,' he said, 'but it's not that…'

She grabbed the rucksack from his lap and dropped it by his feet. 'You need to let the air get to it if you want things to dry out, proper-like.'

Embarrassed, he turned away, suddenly finding himself face to face with a young black woman - slim, tall, in her early twenties, and with a bag very similar to his own at her side. She was wearing a pair of faded blue jeans, a bright green T-shirt and a denim jacket. A multi-coloured headscarf completely hid her hair. He smiled at her, awkwardly.

'It's… it's not what it seems,' he mumbled. 'There was this plumbing problem… in the toilets.'

She looked up and it was if a jolt of electricity had run through his body. Her brown eyes were like deep warm pools that sucked in his startled gaze, so much so that he barely registered the effortlessness of her beauty. The perfect sheen of her complexion, the high cheek bones and the warmth of her smile, meant he was talking to the most stunning woman he'd ever met in real life.

'Are you unwell?' she asked.

'I'm fine,' he replied, amazed to be talking to someone so unbelievably gorgeous. 'Really good, actually. When I said there was a plumbing problem, I didn't mean…'

She smiled again and he could feel himself beginning to melt.

'So, where are you heading?' he asked, doing his best to distract her gaze from the damp patch on his trousers.

'I am travelling to Edinburgh, in Scotland. I hear it is a very beautiful city.'

Her voice was deep and rich, and while her English was perfect, she spoke in a way that made him think it might not be her first language. He'd visited Edinburgh once before, many years back, and his Scots accent always got a laugh from his mates. So, keen to impress, he threw himself into it.

'Och! It's a fandabidozey wee city, right enough!' he began brightly. 'Some say there's nae better place to go a-rroaming in the gloaming.'

She looked at him like he was mad. 'Why do you speak in this strange dialect? And what is this "roaming in the gloaming"?'

He came crashing down to earth with a bump. 'It's… err… it's Scottish,' he replied hesitantly. 'From an old song. My granddad was from up there and he used to sing it to us, back when we were kids. I think it's to do with going on a date with your girlfriend.'

'That is not the purpose of my trip,' she replied, frostily. 'But I am most interested in your local northern traditions. Would you sing this song for me now, please?'

Felix could feel his face beginning to flush. 'Sorry but I… I can't really remember the words.' The pause that followed seemed to last a lifetime. 'So, why are you going up there?' he eventually asked.

'I am visiting because I want to see the Edinburgh Fringe. My friends tell me that as a cultural experience, it is not to be missed.'

He didn't know anything about the Edinburgh Fringe but at least he was back on safer ground. 'Hey, if it's culture you're after, you don't have to trek all the way to Scotland!'

She gave him a quizzical look.

'No - just catch the Slaidforth Sands train then jump on the number 27 to Frecklesall-on-Sea! It's where I live - about forty-five minutes from here, all in.'

The line normally got some kind of reaction, but the woman had been distracted by something. Felix noticed her eyes searching through the milling crowds, an expression of concern flashing across her face for just an instant.

'Seriously, though,' he continued, 'we've been shortlisted for this year's UK City of Culture award. We're down to the last five and...' His words dribbled away as it became obvious she wasn't listening. 'Is everything alright?' he asked.

'Take my bicycle,' she said, quietly.

'What bicycle? What do you mean?'

'Behind me, locked to the sign. Do not look around!' Her attention was focussed on the two burly men in dark suits, striding towards them.

'Very kind of you, but I couldn't possibly.'

Waving him away, she stood up and greeted the new arrivals like they were old friends. 'Good afternoon, gentlemen.'

She picked up her bag and one of the heavies grabbed it from her while the other held her roughly by the arm. Suddenly, they were frog-marching her along the platform towards the footbridge. It took Felix a second to realise what was happening.

'Hey! What are you doing?' he shouted after them.

The men ignored him, continuing to bundle the young woman towards the exit. He gave chase, grabbing one of them by the shoulder.

'You need to clean yourself up, son,' the man said, looking down at Felix's trousers. 'You'll get yourself arrested looking like that.'

The woman glanced back over her shoulder and he instantly understood the words she mouthed.

Leave it.

He looked around at the bored, expressionless faces of the commuters. Why hadn't they done something? He wanted to shame them by shouting the question across the platform but seeing the looks he was getting, headed back to his seat instead.

Felix waited a good ten minutes while things dried off, eventually getting up and sauntering over to check out the bike. He felt the key in his pocket - the one she'd pressed into his palm just before they'd led her away.

The lock opened, with a satisfying 'click'.

As it happened, he was on the lookout for a new bike. He'd had a fantastic vintage racer a couple of years before but that was long gone, and his old mountain bike was way too small for him now. The woman had seemed insistent and he guessed that if she'd said it was his, he could just wheel it away - no questions asked. Then he thought of the two heavies and decided he'd better check.

'I can take it in to lost property if you want, but you'll not see it again,' said the first platform assistant. 'I'll tell you what though, mate - if some gorgeous bird presented me with a smart set of wheels like this, I wouldn't be complaining too much!'

'Track set-up by the looks of it,' added his older colleague as he crouched down to examine the frame. 'It's a fixy - no gears, no brakes or owt like that. All the rage in London, I've 'eard - especially with them cycle couriers.' He looked up at Felix and grinned. 'It'll still want some pedallin' though, lad!'

'So, do you think it's OK for me to take it home?' asked Felix.

The older man ignored the question. 'London, definitely - look at that rubbish on the crossbar: "One Less Car". Bloody tree-huggers!'

2

Inspired by the success of the European Capital of Culture award, the government had launched its own second-rate domestic version of the competition and with rules verging on the non-existent, it was decreed that just about anywhere could apply to become UK City of Culture. The result was a tidal wave of no-hope entries from towns, villages, a couple of motorway service stations and even a prison - all keen to raise their profile and be featured in the grand finale, which was to be broadcast live on national TV.

A management trainee at the town council had decided to give it a go - more as a joke than anything else - and when Frecklesall-on-Sea was declared one of the five short-listed finalists, everyone assumed it was a mistake. But everyone was wrong and the delighted local authority seized its moment, launching its campaign under the catchy slogan:

Frecklesall: It's Got it All!

And for a couple of weeks, it seemed Frecklesall was up for it. A public meeting attracted all of eighteen residents and members of the local Scout troop threw themselves into rehearsals for their annual gang show with uncharacteristic gusto. Predictably, the excitement was short-lived and in no time, had fizzled out altogether - the town's collective attention turning back to the more pressing issues of the miserable start to the summer season, and who was going to win that year's *Love Island*.

In truth, Frecklesall was, and still is, something of a black hole. Yes, there's the fortnightly karaoke (with meat tray bingo) down at the Pig & Whistle, and the occasional northern soul night for the oldies at the town hall, but beyond that you'd be pushed to find anything that might, even loosely, be described as cultural.

The council's website, www.visitfrecklesall.com, does its best to big-up the resort's visitor attractions ('…beautiful one hundred-metre stretch of golden sand'; '…spectacular vista offered by the stunning seafront promenade'; '…former glory of the 1920's art deco lido.') but the truth is a million miles away. There's the scabby beach, teeming with squabbling seagulls, the dingy brown slop of the Irish Sea and of course, the town's lido. Once a brilliant, elegant outdoor swimming pool, the lido had been transformed into an abandoned, burnt-out wreck following a fire a couple of years earlier.

Felix had been right there when it happened, chasing a story for his school newspaper. All he'd been trying to do was expose the truth and stop some really bad stuff from going down. Not that the locals believed a word he said on the subject, the vast majority still blaming him for the catastrophe. He was innocent - or at least he thought he was - but that didn't stop him feeling responsible for the way things had turned out. All of which meant that in the unlikely event that the winning

EuroMillions ticket ever came his way, he was pretty sure that fixing up the lido would be one of the first things on his shopping list.

The platform assistant had been right - the bike was a death trap. With no gears, no brakes and no way of freewheeling, the pedals kept turning as if they had a life of their own. The five-mile ride from Slaidforth station had been like an episode of *Casualty*, with every traffic light and junction becoming a near-death experience. By the time Felix was slogging his way around the Big Lamp roundabout, the decrepit gateway to his home town, he'd fallen off three times. So, it was with oil-stained trousers and grazed knees that he dumped the bike in the back garden of the cramped, 1980s-built family home at 21 Scundale Chase, and hobbled into the kitchen.

'Where have you been?' his mum greeted him grumpily. Four plates were set out on the counter, ready to receive their dollops of tinned stew and oven chips.

'Sorry,' he mumbled. 'My train was cancelled, and then things got a bit weird. I was waiting on the platform and this random woman gave me a new bike…'

They were joined by his dad and his eleven-year-old sister, Flo. It wasn't often they all sat down for a meal together these days. Over the past six months Felix's mum had glammed herself up and was out most nights, strutting her stuff with Frecklesall's Salsatastic Sensations Dance Academy. Meanwhile, Felix's dad was heading in the opposite direction. With his expanding waistline and thinning hair, he'd taken to spending his spare time locked away indoors, watching TV and shuffling around the house in his slippers.

Felix's parents' diverging interests did not make for a particularly happy home life, but the way he saw it, if there was a problem with their marriage - which he very much doubted - they could sort it out for themselves. Unfortunately, his little sister had a different take on things.

'I'm out at the dance club again tonight,' their mum announced as she cleared the plates away. 'Ramón's organised a partners' evening to bring in some new faces and we're working on this routine for the culture festival. So I'll be back late.'

'Does that mean you'll be going too, Dad?' asked Flo, hopefully. 'You've been talking about it for weeks.'

'I'd love to Florence, really I would,' he replied. 'You know how I like a bit of the old cha-cha-cha action.' He grabbed the salt and pepper pots from the table, shaking them over his shoulder, maracas-style.

'It's *salsa,* you idiot!' snapped his wife. 'You said you were going to come along, Brian.'

'Gutted, Christine - absolutely. The thing is, Mart will kill me if I don't get this paperwork sorted by Monday and anyway, you know how I like to listen to our Freddie's show on a Friday night. He needs all the support he can get.'

Felix's mum sighed. 'I'm sure he's really grateful, Brian.'

Felix's older brother, Freddie, was nineteen and had spent the three years since leaving school in a series of dead-end roles. He'd left home a few months earlier, moving into a grubby bedsit above Mustafa's chippy in town. Currently 'between jobs', Freddie spent his days hanging with his mates, chatting up the girls and hosting the local community radio station's *Metal Mania* heavy metal slot on Friday and Saturday nights. There was talk of a career in broadcasting but Felix knew better. *Mental Mania* as he called it, was a lame excuse for 'Full-On' Freddie - AKA 'DeeJay FoF' - to crash the airwaves with his heavy metal mash-ups before heading to the Pig & Whistle to get plastered with his lame, loser mates. Felix knew that no one listened to his show and the idea of their dad tuning in was a complete joke.

'Sorry love, I nearly forgot. There was a call for you just before you got home,' his mum announced, later, from the depths of the washing-up. 'It was this odd-sounding man from the *Bugler*. He said he's double-booked on Sunday morning and wants to know if you'll cover for him.'

Felix glanced down at his suit trousers and checked the spikiness of his freshly gelled hair, knowing he'd never before looked this sharp, this early on a Sunday morning. It was his first solo assignment and nothing had been left to chance. Marching down the slimy green slipway onto the smooth, damp sand, he ignored the gaggle of children gathered around the Sandcastle Competition sign, under the Frecklesall: It's Got it All! banner, heading instead for the group huddled around the large rowing boat by the water's edge.

Rear Admiral Sir Hubert Montague-Dunk (Retired)'s plans were set out in the single sheet press release handed out to all in attendance. Some general blurb about the old boy's service in the Royal Navy was backed up with a photocopy from a Collins world atlas, featuring a crudely drawn biro line which started at Frecklesall-on-Sea, on England's north west coast, skirted around Northern Ireland, then headed a mere three thousand miles westwards to the bright lights of New York City.

The Navy veteran had the uniform, the full-on beard and the seafaring track record, but he was well into his seventies and to Felix's eye, didn't even look like he had the muscle to row his boat, *The Diamond Queen*, across the leisure lagoon at Slaidforth park, let alone half way around the world.

'Rear Admiral!' the crumpled-looking journalist in his mid-fifties, with the piggy eyes and soggy roll-up tucked behind an ear, kicked things off. 'Dave Heptonstall, *Frecklesall Journal*. I've got to ask the question, sir - is this really such a good idea?'

Sir Hubert laughed. 'My good man, this vessel represents British craftsmanship at its very best. She's capable of withstanding whatever Mother Nature can throw at her, and with a superb watertight sleeping compartment, provides all the comforts an ancient mariner, such as my good self, could possibly need.'

Felix gave *The Diamond Queen* a nudge with his foot. 'But this isn't about the boat, Sir Hubert,' he said. 'It's about *you*. The coastguard have already tried to have you sectioned under the Mental Health Act.'

There was a murmur of disapproval from the crowd.

'And you are?' the old sea dog asked.

'Felix Haythornthwaite, *Lancastrian Bugler*... err... sir.'

The Rear Admiral glared at him from under the thatch of his bushy eyebrows. 'I see. So let me ask you about these historic sea battles, *Mr* Haythornthwaite - Jutland, the Falklands, Trafalgar - any of them ring a bell?'

Felix shrugged his shoulders. 'Not really.'

The naval man shook his head, sadly. 'My dear boy, let me respectfully suggest you re-boot your wireless hooter and do a download onto Goolie or Face-ache, or whatever it is you young 'uns waste your time on these days. Perhaps then you might appreciate the significance of my mission.'

'But why would you risk your life doing something like this?'

'Because it's there, my boy, because it's there! My great chum Eddie Hillary conquered Everest way back in '53, the year of dear Queen Elizabeth's coronation, and now I, Sir Hubert Montague-Dunk, offer my own humble tribute!' He turned to salute the flag hanging limply from the vessel's mast. 'Oldest man to row the Atlantic - a venture dedicated to Her Maj's glorious reign! God bless you, Ma'am!'

The applause was cut short by shouts from further up the beach. Felix turned, along with everyone else, trying to work out what was going on. Moments later, he'd stuffed his notepad into his rucksack and, realising he could move more quickly without it, dropped the bag onto the sand next to Sir Hubert's boat. And then he was sprinting off in the direction of the sandcastle competition.

Barging onlookers aside, he stumbled breathlessly into a full-blown row between a silver-haired man in his late sixties, and Frecklesall FM's finest - his big brother, Freddie. They were squaring up over a partly demolished sandcastle and a screaming four-year-old boy.

'You should be ashamed of yourself!' yelled the older man. 'Maurice was *so* looking forward to this event. Look at the state of him now!'

'The kid attacked me!' Freddie shrieked.

'You frightened the wits out of him. He thought you were dead!'

'Guess what? I'm not!' Freddie gurned and waved his arms around to demonstrate the ongoing nature of his mortal existence. 'I was... err... meditating, wasn't I? There's no law against that, is there?'

'From the state you're in, I'd hazard you've been out on the beach all night,' the man snapped. 'I think you'll find there most certainly *are* regulations and by-laws against that sort of thing and I've a good mind to report you to the authorities.'

Freddie always looked rough the morning after *Metal Mania* had aired but this was something else. Wearing a filthy pair of jeans and a ripped T-shirt, he'd managed to lose a shoe somewhere. His face was ashen-grey, the matted shoulder-length mess of his hair coated in wet sand. Felix was in no doubt that his brother *had* spent the night out on the beach and to make matters worse, was nursing the mother and father of all hangovers.

'Grandpa!' wailed the child. 'That man squashed my sandcastle!'

Freddie jabbed a finger at the toddler. 'I'm the one with the beef here, Maurice - back off, willyer!'

The older man grabbed him by the shirt. 'Don't you dare talk to my grandson like that! My God, I can smell alcohol on your breath. You've been drinking, and it's only ten o'clock in the morning!'

Freddie shoved him away. 'Get your hands off me, you old duffer!'

The wrestling match that followed ended with the two of them collapsing on top of the small pile of sand that had once been little Maurice's pride and joy.

Felix and another onlooker jumped in to separate them. 'What do you think you're doing?' he screamed into his brother's face.

But Freddie wasn't listening. He was looking out across the beach at the lone policeman striding purposefully towards them. Turning on his heels, he sprinted off up the slipway.

In the end, Felix had to spend the best part of fifteen minutes grovelling to the constable and the old man. He was eventually allowed to go, although only after he'd spent an age helping Maurice rebuild his sandcastle. By the time he'd made it back to the water's edge, Sir Hubert was a good fifty metres into his journey. He took a few shots on his phone but when he reached into his jacket for his notepad, it wasn't there. After a moment of panic, he remembered he'd left it in his bag, but that was nowhere to be seen.

'Anyone found a blue rucksack?' he asked forlornly.

There were shrugs and shakes of the head from all around, and then an elderly lady approached him.

'Actually, I think Sir Hubert might have picked it up just before he set off,' she said.

'It's got my notes in. I'm with the *Bugler* and this is my first ever assignment. I can't write up the story without my notes.'

'So why not do something about it?' she replied, snippily. 'The water's not that deep on this part of the beach at low tide. I'm sure a strapping lad like you can manage.'

He groaned, and then he was stripping down to his undies, dumping his suit on the damp sand. 'Sir Hubert! Wait! I think you've got my bag!' he yelled, wading into the shallows to peals of laughter from the onlookers.

Monday was one of Felix's days off and he was so excited at the prospect of his story appearing in the paper that he hung around in the hallway all morning, waiting for the *Bugler* to arrive. It plopped through the letter box just after two o'clock and he flicked through the pages, punching the air at the sight of his article on page seven. It was his piece - all his own work - although the 'Naval Nutter's Nautical Nightmare!' headline wasn't quite the way he'd have played it.

It was during the second read through that he noticed HB had changed one thing, and it was the most important thing of all:

By Bugler Special Reporter Howard Brake

The byline, complete with cheesy mugshot of his boss, made him want to scream. It was his article - he was the one who'd put in the graft, who'd ended up freezing his bits off when he'd waded out to rescue his bag, yet HB was taking all the credit! He stewed on it for the rest of the day and by the time he arrived in the newsroom the following morning, was spoiling for a fight. Setting off for the kitchen on the brew run, he bumped into one of his colleagues.

'Hi Sharon - you seen HB?'

'He was in earlier,' she replied, 'but then he got the call to go and see Grindrod. Wasn't too chuffed about it either, the idiot.'

Felix didn't rise to the bait - his views on HB had to be shared on a strictly face-to-face basis. It was midday before his boss made an appearance, stomping around the open plan office, looking like he'd swallowed a wasp.

'I was reading my piece in yesterday's paper,' Felix remarked, as casually as he could. 'Can I have a word with you about it, please?'

HB glowered at him from over the top of his computer screen. 'Breakout, now!' he barked.

Felix grabbed his bag, the sniggers from the newsroom team following them on their way out to the brew room.

HB was a scrawny five-foot-six and his baggy pink shirt, always worn with gleaming silver sleeve garters, a loud tie and red braces, meant he stood out from the other journalists - and not in a good way. His head was shaped like a lightbulb, crowned by a patch of straggly gel-smeared hair, the back and sides were clippered to the faintest stubble. There was a pinched meanness about his face, the thin lips of his tiny mouth almost permanently pursed in an expression of disapproval.

'You've let the *Bugler* down, Haythornthwaite,' he began in his whiney voice, which had the faintest of Liverpudlian twangs. 'Worse still, you've let *me* down.'

'Hang on a minute!' spluttered Felix. 'I'm the one who should be upset. I helped you out with that story on Sunday, and then you go and stick your name on it!'

'It's dog-eat-dog out there, so deal with it. Mind you, if I could turn back the clock, you'd be welcome to take the credit for that piece - every last, lousy word of it.'

Felix had expected more of a fight. 'Oh… right. Well, as long as we're clear on that for the next time.'

'You just don't get it, do you?' HB slapped down a copy of Frecklesall's weekly rag, the *Journal*, which had come out earlier that morning. 'Same time, same place, but while you were mucking about with Captain Pugwash and his stupid rowing boat, you missed the real headline.'

Felix glanced at the *Journal*'s front page, instantly recognising the photo of the elderly man with the silver hair, pictured with his grandson at the sandcastle competition. His heart all but stopped as he read on from Dave Heptonstall's screaming headline:

Culture Chief Slams Frecklesall Bid!

U.K. City of Culture Chief, Sir Derek Heffner OBE, today told the *Journal* that Frecklesall's bid for the prestigious award was 'dead and buried' following a shocking incident that took place during the Got it All! International Sandcastle Competition, last Sunday.

After making the two hundred-mile trip from his home in Hampshire, to check out the town's artistic credentials, the boss of the UK City of Culture judging panel fell victim to a mindless assault on Frecklesall beach, while all around, excited families took part in an event described by council officials as, 'demonstrating the very best the resort has to offer'.

'My four-year-old grandson, Maurice, was innocently building his sandcastle when he spotted something against the sea wall,' Sir Derek told the *Journal*. 'Thinking it was an old bin bag, the little chap toddled over to investigate and was horrified to discover what appeared to be the dead body of a rough-sleeper.' The distraught culture guru (69) went on to describe a shocking twist to this gruesome story. 'In the next instant, the "corpse" miraculously sprang to life and we were confronted by an abusive, drunken half-wit, who destroyed my grandson's sandcastle. When I remonstrated with him, I was subjected to a vicious assault.'

Eyewitnesses confirm that the incident involved the host of Frecklesall FM's cult, *Metal Mania* show, DeeJay 'Full-On' Freddie ('FoF') Haythornthwaite (19). A spokesman for the radio station denied any involvement on the part of the DJ, adding that, 'The FoF was unavailable for comment due to hair washing commitments... and stuff.'

A representative from the town's Got it All! Bid Team said Sir Derek's experience was 'deeply regrettable', but that Frecklesall's pitch for the top prize had 'bouncebackability'.

The Culture Chief's response was damning: 'I've never been treated so shoddily in my life. As far as I'm concerned, Frecklesall-on-Sea's bid is dead and buried.'

HB broke the silence. 'This DeeJay FoF guy - are you related to him, by any chance?'

'No,' replied Felix. 'That is to say, well yes, kind of.'

'I thought so. Is he one of the gang who helped you burn down Frecklesall lido a couple of years ago?'

'It wasn't me! Why would you think that?' he took a deep breath to try to calm himself down. 'But...but anyway, what did Mr Grindrod want you for?'

HB leant back in his chair, smirking. 'Our glorious leader hates it when the *Journal* gets one over on us, so he just spent the last hour yelling at me. The upshot is, he's launching a formal investigation.'

'What?'

The reporter produced a stick of Pepperami and began chewing on it, noisily. 'That generally means someone's for the chop, Haythornthwaite. All I know for sure at this stage is that it ain't gonna be me!'

Felix felt his blood run cold. 'I was only trying to help. I'm just here on a work placement - you can't blame me for this.'

'That's always the way with you, isn't it? Nothing that goes wrong is ever your fault. Well, wake up and smell the coffee, my friend! I just hope you learn from this experience, although I'm guessing it won't be in a newsroom round these parts. Everyone knows I've been carrying you since you arrived - you're a waste of space!'

Felix only narrowly suppressed the urge to thump him. Eating lunch with his boss was the last thing he wanted to do, but he was desperate to find out more. He reached into his bag for his sandwiches, and things went from bad to worse.

'Aw man, I don't believe it!' he groaned. 'My mum made me some butties but I forgot to take them out the fridge this morning. I haven't got the money to buy–'

HB's laughter echoed around the brew room. 'I'm not subbing you, Haythornthwaite, and that's mainly because you won't be around here long enough to pay me back! Once that investigation kicks in…'

A look of confusion spread across Felix's face as he dug deeper into the bag. 'Hang on… none of this is my stuff.' He pulled out a brightly coloured headscarf and a wallet. 'That's totally weird.'

HB stopped chomping and snatched the wallet from him.

'I don't think you should touch that,' said Felix.

His boss flipped it open, emptying its contents onto the table. 'Let's see now - ferry ticket from Stranraer to Belfast for last Saturday morning, a few quid… and a photograph.'

A business card fell out and fluttered to the floor. Felix shot out a foot and covered it with his shoe.

'Some old guy in fancy dress,' continued HB, who hadn't noticed. 'Looks like it was quite a party.'

Felix bent forward, pretending to check his laces while he stuffed the card into a jacket pocket. Straightening back up again, he studied the dog-eared black and white photograph. The man looked African - probably in his late seventies. With bare shoulders and arms, he was wearing what appeared to be a leopard-skin toga and clutching a large spear and surf board-shaped shield. It was a great fancy dress outfit, Felix thought, although the black slip-on shoes and ankle-length socks didn't really fit the look. Staring grimly into the camera, the old man's shoulders were pushed back, his chest puffed out proudly.

'Any other surprises?' asked HB.

Felix had almost turned the bag inside out by this time. 'That's the lot, I think... No, wait a minute... There's something stuck inside the lining. I can't quite get to it.'

'Give it here, you loser.' HB snatched the bag from him and ripped noisily into its stitching. After rooting around for a few moments, he plonked a small wrap of white material, about twelve centimetres by six, onto the table. 'Interesting,' he remarked, stroking his chin. 'Open it up, Haythornthwaite.'

'I shouldn't. I mean, it could be anything - like drugs.'

HB smirked. 'Yeah right. Sometime today would be good.'

Felix began opening the package with the care of an army bomb disposal expert.

'Just like pass the parcel!' HB's laughter stopped abruptly as the last layer of material was unfolded.

3

Felix had seen diamonds before - tiny pinpricks of light winking out from a ring or a necklace - but these were monsters by comparison. Rectangular and lozenge-shaped, there were six of them all in, the biggest the size of a box of matches, the three smallest like a glittering trio of boiled sweets. He picked one up and felt the cool sharpness in his hand. The brilliance of the light reflecting from hundreds of perfectly polished facets, almost took his breath away.

'These can't be real,' he said. 'They're way too big.'

HB had been stunned into silence.

'Even the smallest is about a zillion times bigger than the one my mum has on her engagement ring,' Felix continued. 'We need to call the police.'

'Don't even think about it,' said HB, as the door to the brew room opened and Sharon wandered in to retrieve her sandwiches from the fridge. 'We'll talk about this later, OK?'

Felix spent the afternoon retracing his steps from the previous few days, so preoccupied, he forgot all about missing his lunch. He went over it in his head again and again until things eventually clicked. The girl at the station had a bag just like his - she must have picked up the wrong one. The last time he saw it, one of the heavies had it tucked under his arm and was marching off up the platform with the girl in tow. They looked like the kind of guys you wouldn't want to meet in a dark alleyway, he thought, suddenly beginning to feel very nervous.

His growing sense of unease was interrupted by the ring of the telephone, and HB's nasal tones.

'Get yourself down to the caretaker's store, now, Haythornthwaite.'

Clasping the rucksack to his chest, Felix trudged across the office towards the service staircase.

The caretaker's store was deep in the basement of Bugler House - a stifling, windowless cell with walls of rough, grey blockwork, stacked on all sides with cleaning gear. Sitting on a plastic chair behind a small table, HB greeted his assistant with uncharacteristic warmth.

'Pull up a seat, my friend!'

Felix was taken aback by the welcome but he knew what he had to do. 'We've got to call the police, HB. If these diamonds are for real there's bound to be a reward. Tell you what - how about we split it 50:50?'

'A most generous offer,' his boss replied, eyes lighting up as the trainee reporter spread the six glittering stones across the table, 'but what I have in mind isn't a small change handout.'

'But–'

'No way! Tell me, Haythornthwaite, who's the most talented reporter on the *Bugler* payroll at this particular moment in time?'

Felix shrugged.

'Who's the guy who can get right across our little find and shape it into something compelling - award-winning, even?'

Felix reporter continued to look blank.

HB spread his arms wide. '*C'est moi!*'

'Oh…'

HB pressed the palms of his hands together, forefingers resting on his lips. 'So, here's the direction of travel, comrade. We run it up the flagpole and see who comes sniffing. After we've weeded out the timewasters, we size up the nature of the beast and take it from there. Teamwork is critical - you'll be heading up the admin, catering, typing etcetera, giving me the headspace to work my magic. Once the clay is on the table and I've weaved it into top quality copy, we float it through an agency - *Reuters*, probably - then sit back to enjoy the bidding war. I'm seeing a four-page spread in a top national, but better than that, I'm seeing our golden ticket.'

'What? Like Willy Wonka?'

'Yeah, but you can forget the chocolate factory! The *Times*, the *Egalitarian*, even the *Scorcher* - they'll be queuing up to offer me… I mean us, top jobs after we break this one.'

'But if we're not going to the police, surely we have to take this to the *Bugler*?'

HB reached across the table and grabbed him by the lapels. 'Listen up, Haythornthwaite - we have to go strictly sub-radar on this project. Work with me and I'll get you off the hook with Grindrod. Better than that, your career goes stratospheric in six weeks, max. But hey, if you'd prefer to hang around for the witch hunt, be my guest! "Dead man walking" - that's what they're saying about you, up in the newsroom.'

They stayed in the tiny room for another ten minutes while HB took shots of the diamonds on his phone and quizzed him about the bag. Felix played dumb - things were bad enough without more fuel being poured on the fire.

'Word to the wise, Haythornthwaite,' HB said as they got up to leave. 'Shape up and get your act together. I might just about have enough ammo for the two of us to shoot our way out of this hell-hole, but if I do, it'll be no thanks to you.'

Felix sat there, fuming.

'And one other thing,' his boss continued, caressing the largest of the stones. 'Lavish these beauties with all the love and attention they deserve. And don't even think about going to the police - if you want to hang onto your job, that is.'

He handed over a business card as they walked out. 'Be sure to visit this website later on tonight, my friend. It's highly likely you'll come across an extremely interesting posting.'

It had been a traumatic journey home, Felix clinging grimly to the rucksack, his mind in knots. He'd been wrong to agree to HB's stupid plan and first thing the next morning he was going to sort it out. If he really did have a fortune in diamonds in his bag, they had to be handed in to the authorities, whatever the consequences.

Navigating around the mobility scooter parked across the driveway, he dumped his new bike in the back garden before stumbling in on the heated discussion taking place at the kitchen table.

'He's as much use as a one-legged man in a bum kicking competition!' his aunt Doreen announced loudly. 'I couldn't give a monkey's about this City of Culture nonsense but I do care about our Freddie's future. We can't have the *Journal* printing front-page stories saying what a loser he is - the lad'll never get a proper job.'

Even though Doreen had retired from running Frecklesall's donkey attraction, following a heart attack a couple of years earlier, she was still a force of nature. In her late seventies, she was short, wiry and determined, her eyes sparkling from beneath a tangle of steel-grey hair. Living on her own at the Paddock, a rundown bungalow on the edge of town, she was well known as a local eccentric. But in spite of her bag-lady appearance, she was as sharp as a tack and anyone crossing her was likely to get back much more than they'd bargained for. It looked as if her eldest great nephew was next in the firing line.

'We were so pleased when he got the job on that radio show,' said Felix's mum. 'It's been such a good start. Broadcasting seems to suit him down to the ground.'

'Broadcasting? Don't make me laugh!' Doreen exclaimed. 'That programme's bloody awful! You'll have heard he's doing a live show at OT's on Friday night? God knows how that's going to end up!'

'We all need to do our bit for the culture bid, Doreen. Anyway, Brian's going to have a word with him, aren't you Brian?'

Her husband grunted, barely lifting his nose from the newspaper he was reading.

Doreen rolled her eyes and turned to greet the new arrival. 'Everything reet with you, Felix lad? Only, the way you're clinging to that bag, anyone would think you'd got the crown jewels in there.'

'No... err... hi everyone,' he mumbled, placing the bag on the floor and pulling up a chair.

'How's it going down at the *Bugler*? You managed to persuade them to run that story on the lido, yet? It's just what's needed to put some pressure on those idiots at the council. The place is a disgrace!'

Felix shrugged. 'My boss isn't interested. I mentioned it to him a few times and he blamed me for burning it down.'

'Unbelievable! Anyway, your mum said you had your first article in print, yesterday. Have you got a copy? I'd quite like to see what you've been up to.'

He fished the previous day's *Bugler* from his bag and handed it over.

'Reads well,' she said, after scanning the piece, 'but how come someone else's name's at the top?'

'My boss insisted on taking the credit. There was nothing I could do about it.'

Doreen checked out the byline picture of HB. 'He looks a bit of a plonker if you ask me. Do you get on with him?'

'Not really.'

'That's alright then, because you've sold him a right pup, here!'

'What do you mean?'

Doreen laughed. 'You do realise, this Sir Hubert Montague-Dunk character is as nutty as a fruit cake?'

'A bit confused, maybe…'

'More than that, lad - he's completely off his trolley. And he's never been in the navy in his life!'

Felix couldn't believe his ears. 'Are you sure? He had the uniform and the medals, and everything.'

'Oh aye! His real name's Anderton - Colin Anderton - and I had the misfortune to be at school with him, back in the day. He was always a bit of a rum 'un and things didn't get any better after we left. He fell in with some dodgy characters and drifted into thieving. The police got on his case so he eventually upped sticks and moved to Blackburn. I heard he's worked all sorts of scams down there over the years, and he's been inside a few times as well. Mind you, he's harmless enough now he's lost his marbles. Last time I saw him he was down on Slaidforth pier in that stupid uniform, cadging change off the day-trippers,'

'So, he's not an Admiral then?'

His great aunt laughed so hard she nearly lost her false teeth. 'Cheer up lad, it's your boss who'll be getting it in the neck, not you. It serves him right for nicking your work.'

Felix felt physically sick - not only had he missed the real story on the beach that Sunday morning, but the one he had written was complete rubbish. He was turning into a lousy journalist and the way things were shaping up, he wasn't even going to get the chance to put it right. He shoved a ready-meal in the microwave, made his apologies, and headed upstairs to eat it in his room.

After polishing off the lasagne straight from the plastic tray, he sat on his bed trying to make sense of what had happened. The whole thing was a disaster but at least the thought of handing the diamonds over to the police made him feel a little bit better. It was definitely the right thing to do, although losing his *Bugler* placement was a high price to pay for something that wasn't his fault.

A few minutes later there was a tap on the bedroom door and his little sister walked in. With everything that had been going on, he'd completely forgotten about the promise he'd made her the week before.

'Well?' she said from beneath her fringe. 'Have you talked to Dad yet?'

Felix groaned. He'd never understood how such a slight, angelic-looking little girl, could be so terrifying. What she lacked in size she made up for with brains, common sense and an ability to cut straight to the heart of the matter. She was already running her own business, selling home-made jewellery at school, and doing very nicely out of it too by all accounts.

'I'm sorry Flo, I've been really busy,' he replied. 'I'll speak to him in the next couple of days, I promise.'

She looked downcast. 'Come on Felix! If we don't do something soon, it'll be too late. You can't keep avoiding awkward situations like this.'

'Things seem fine between them if you ask me,' he said, knowing that if avoiding awkward situations ever became an Olympic sport, he'd be nailed-on for the gold medal. 'Anyway, I don't want to talk about it now, I'm totally wrecked.'

She smiled sweetly. 'So, I should tell Naz to go home? Only, he's waiting downstairs for you.'

After shooing her out of the room, he greeted his unexpected visitor. He'd known Naz - Naz Hussein - since primary school and they were great friends. Immaculately tidy and stick-thin, he lived above his family's DVD and Vape shop in the centre of town. He was sensible, steady and so cautious, he made Felix look like a reckless, dangerous-to-know maniac.

Naz greeted him with a smile. 'How's it going, mate?'

'Been better,' he replied, 'Bernie not with you, then?'

'I called round, but he was out and his mum wouldn't say where he'd gone.'

Felix smirked. 'Maybe he's got a hot date and he's keeping it quiet!'

They both laughed. While neither of them had enjoyed much (indeed any) success in the girlfriend department over the past year, knowing that their friend Bernie's prospects were even more non-existent than their own, always cheered them up.

Felix flipped open his laptop. 'Something a bit odd happened at work today,' he said. 'I need to check out this website that came up.'

'It's not another of your Freddie's recommendations, is it?' Naz asked, nervously. 'Only… I'm not sure that stuff we looked at last time is actually legal.'

Felix rolled his eyes and switched on the computer while Naz skimmed through his *Bugler* article.

Felix grimaced as HB's mugshot appeared on screen, the centrepiece of his very own *Braking News* website. Taking a deep breath, he clicked on the 'Rolling News - Real Time' tab, and recoiled at what he saw:

Braking News: Lancashire, U.K. 21:03**hrs**

Huge Lancs Monster Diamond Stash Mystery

'What are you looking at?' asked Naz, peering over his shoulder to check out the shot of the diamonds HB had taken on his mobile that afternoon. 'Blimey!'

Felix shushed him and they both read on:

The Braking News Corporation (BNC) can today, exclusively reveal the recovery of a priceless diamond hall in the city of Preston, Lancashire, earlier today. The six sparklers - the biggest ever seen in the county - with a street value, valued at 'unpresidented', were secured late this afternoon and are now being held at a top secret, secret location.

'The discovery of these beauties comes after months of intelligence work, spreading over all six continents,' BNC Chief Executive, Howard Brake told me this evening. 'The truth is, there are times when it's not enough to just 'Brake'

the news, sometimes you just have to darn well go and 'Make' the news, as well!'

Ownership of the diamonds, the biggest of which matches the approximate dimensions of the popular biscuit, popularly known as the 'custard Cream' biscuit, remains a mystery. 'Someone somewhere must be missing these stunners, and the team here at BNC would love to talk to you,' Mr Brake said as we went to press.

Anyone with intelligence of a bony-fido nature should contact me, Howard Brake, C.E.O. on the Braking News, Right Here – Right Now web porthole.

ENDS

'What the hell is the Braking News Corporation?' Naz asked.

'It's my boss from the *Bugler* - that numpty I've been telling you about. And it looks like this is his own private website.'

'That's ridiculous! He can't write to save his life, he can hardly spell - and who'd be daft enough to believe you could get a diamond as big as custard cream?'

Felix pulled out the wrap from the rucksack and placed it on his desk.

Naz eyed the package warily. 'What have you got there?'

'You'll see - just open it really carefully.'

The diamonds had been stowed beneath the loose floorboard under the spare bed in his room - the former home of Freddie's porn stash. They were safe, no one knew they were there, yet still Felix was unable to sleep that night, his heart beating with the rhythm of a galloping horse.

His commute to work the following morning was awful - the train was late so he missed his bus connection, meaning it was nearly half-past-nine by the time he made it into Bugler House. He was exhausted and could barely think straight, but he was on a mission. No matter what HB threw at him, the diamonds were going to be handed in at Frecklesall police station that evening and nothing would make him change his mind. But when he arrived at the newsroom, his boss was nowhere to be seen.

'HB? I've not seen him, love,' replied Sharon, pulling a face. 'Probably out getting his fangs sharpened.'

He didn't know whether to laugh or cry - he was primed and ready for a fight, but he also wanted to talk to his boss before he did anything. Deep down he hoped he might still be able to make HB understand, and maybe even persuade him to put in a good word for him in the Grindrod investigation.

In HB's absence he was dumped on the *Bugler's* Features Team, which consisted of Dan Pickles, a grizzled old hack in his early sixties. With his shock of white hair, a nose like a cauliflower and a nice line in saggy, elbow-patched cardigans, Dan ran the 'Lifestyles' offering, churning out articles on health & wellbeing, cooking tips, the daily horoscope and the crossword - to say nothing of the monthly fashion supplement. Felix marvelled at how one journalist could do so much, until Dan explained that most of the pieces were syndicated - bought in from agencies and slotted into the paper wherever they had space to spare.

Felix was kept busy with some filing while Dan sat hunched over his keyboard.

'You have my sympathy, Felix,' he said, not even lifting his eyes from the computer screen. 'Getting lumbered with that idiot Brake is enough to put anyone off journalism for life.'

'He's not the easiest of bosses,' Felix agreed.

Dan laughed. 'He's bloody useless, as well! Grindrod's still seething about what happened up at Frecklesall beach last Sunday.'

It was all getting a bit too close for comfort and Felix glanced around the cluttered office looking for something to help him change the subject. His eyes alighted on the contents of a tray on the journalist's desk. 'Those photos,' he began hesitantly, 'the ones of the girls. What's that all about, then?'

Dan laughed. 'It's not what you might think!'

'I didn't mean it like that - honestly.'

'It's our *Bugler Belle* feature,' said Dan. 'Not exactly PC these days, I know, but it's a bit of a tradition on the paper. Local lasses send their shots in and we feature one of them each month in the fashion supplement. I get inundated.'

Felix flicked through the first handful of pouting images. 'Wow! How do you decide?'

'Grindrod pops down sometimes, otherwise I just pull one out of a hat. Actually, you'd be doing me a big favour if you'd pick August's *Belle* from that lot. I'm a bit pushed today.'

Felix spent the rest of the morning sifting through the pictures. All of the girls looked impossibly gorgeous and by lunchtime, he still hadn't made up his mind.

'Come on lad, get a move on will you?' Dan chided him, good-humouredly. 'We work to some really tight deadlines in this department. The fashion supplement goes to print in, ooh, let me see.' He checked his desk-calendar. 'Yes... that would be midnight, a week this Friday. We're in danger of missing it, the rate you're going on!'

Lunch came and went and Felix got as far as the stairs on the way back to Dan's office when his mobile rang. Moments later, he heard a familiar scouse whine.

'Haythornthwaite - listen up. There's something I need you to do for me.'

Felix breathed a sigh of relief. 'Where the hell have you been? I was getting worried.'

'Everything's... err... it's all good,' HB replied. 'I just need you to bring the package into town. I'll meet you down at the docks by the swing-bridge in thirty minutes.'

Felix caught the urgency in his boss's voice. 'Are you sure you're alright, HB? You sound a bit stressed.'

'I am NOT stressed! I've hooked up with these guys and they've agreed to give us the backstory on the diamonds. They just need to check out the goods first.'

Felix tried to contain the wobble in his voice. 'Actually, I wanted to talk to you about that. I've been thinking it through and we really shouldn't be messing with stuff like this. So I've decided to take them in to the police.'

'DO NOT DO THAT!' HB yelled so loudly, the speaker in Felix's handset started buzzing. 'You can't! I mean, you mustn't! It's really, *really* important. Once these guys have seen what we've got, we're cooking on gas!'

Felix was beginning to get annoyed. 'Well I've not got them on me, have I? And I can't just stroll out of here and go and get them. Anyway, I've made my decision - I'm taking them in, whether you like it or not.'

'Do *not* go to the police - that's an order!' HB shrieked. 'You must promise me - on your life!'

Felix could hear voices shouting in the background.

'Do this one thing for me,' wailed HB, sounding like he was about to burst into tears. 'I'm begging you, Haythornthwaite - I can't tell you how important it is. I've got to go now but I'll be in touch soon, on this line - so keep your mobile on you.'

The phone went dead.

Felix sat down on the stairs, feeling like his head was about to explode.

4

Felix spent that Wednesday at home in a state of high anxiety. Trawling through precious-stone websites had done little to calm his nerves, and calls to HB's mobile had drawn a complete blank. He knew he should go to the police but after hearing the fear in his boss's voice, didn't have a clue what to do for the best. So, panic-stricken and paranoid as he was, he whiled away the hours staring out the window for signs of hooded gunmen scurrying across Scundale Chase, and checking beneath the floorboards in his bedroom to make sure the diamonds were where he'd left them.

By late afternoon his mum had returned from her shift at the Spar and, fed-up with his bizarre behaviour, had kicked him out of the house with instructions to visit his brother. Felix complained but deep down he knew it was for the best. Staying cooped up indoors was doing his head in and he needed something to take his mind off his worries.

He cycled down the hill into town and landed at the back of the chippy. Lifting the bike, he crunched across the glass-strewn yard, heading for the narrow gap between two huge and rather smelly paladin bins. The outer door to Freddie's flat was unlocked, so he nudged it open with the bike's front wheel and wandered in to the dank communal lobby, clicking on the timer-controlled light switch. He was struggling up the rickety stairs with the bike slung over his shoulder when the light timed-out, leaving him to grope his way up the last few steps in total darkness. Breathless from the effort, he hooked the handlebars over the balustrade rail on the tiny landing and, noticing that the door to the flat was slightly ajar, headed inside.

The entrance led directly into a narrow galley kitchen, his arrival sending a cluster of cockroaches scuttling for cover under the fridge. Something was cooking in the oven and a family sized can of baked beans was bubbling away on the hob, still in its tin. It looked as if Freddie had guests.

The living room door wouldn't open when he tried the handle, so he forced the issue with a hefty kick.

'WAAAAAHHH!'

The door banged open, sending three shadowy figures diving from the settee - one scrambling over the back, another darting into the bathroom and a third, crouching on the floor clutching two crossed wooden spoons to his chest. Something gruesome was playing on the TV - a young girl with a very bad complexion was directing a stream of lime-green projectile vomit towards a couple of priests, who were cowering at the bottom of her bed.

'Everyone alright in here?' asked Felix, choking in the fetid atmosphere.

A white-faced figure, shielding its eyes like a vampire caught out in the sunrise, screamed back at him, 'You idiot - you scared the life out of us!'

Felix smirked. 'Sorry, Fred - you really should get Mustafa to have a look at that door.'

He glanced around the bombsite that was his brother's home - unwashed plates scattered across the floor, empty beer cans littering the windowsill and half-empty takeaway cartons ground into the carpet. Dirty clothes were draped over the back of the settee and screwed up in untidy piles where they'd been dropped.

'Panic over!' Freddie announced to his guests. 'It's only my doofus brother. You've met him before, guys - he's just started as a newspaper boy at the *Bungler*.'

'Trainee reporter, actually,' Felix corrected him, acknowledging the grunts from Trellis and Honker - hard-core members of Freddie's *Metal Mania* posse. 'So what are you lot up to?'

'Pre-gig briefing,' replied his brother, clicking the 'pause' button on the remote. 'Film, scran, then down to the Pig to work out how we're gonna blow the roof off OT's on Friday night.'

Felix picked up the DVD case from the arm of the settee. '*The Exorcist*? Isn't that, like, the scariest film in the world?'

'*Legally Blonde 2* was out,' replied Trellis, fiddling self-consciously with his long, greasy ponytail. 'The lad down at Hussein's said this was one of the greatest movies ever made.'

Felix chuckled. It was classic Naz - the more obscure the film, the better, in his book.

'Hey, you gonna be there on Friday?' asked Freddie. 'It'd be good for an *uber*-nerd like you to see some genuine "creatives" at work. You should do a feature on us.'

'As if!' Felix snorted. 'To be honest, Fred, I'm amazed they're letting you anywhere near the culture bid after what you got up to on the beach last Sunday.'

'The kid and the old guy should be locked up after dissing me like that,' Freddie replied. 'But hey - I've never been one to bear a grudge. I dropped in to see the town hall suits this morning and they're saying Friday's gig is gonna be a cult-fest re-boot, but with the FoF-*meister* at the controls!'

'Awesome!' chimed Honker.

'Full-on!' exclaimed Freddie. 'How about it, Felix? Play your cards right and there could be a VIP pass pinging your way.'

Felix agreed, setting off a round of cheers. He'd already planned on being there but if he could get in for free, so much the better.

'Nice one!' said Freddie. 'Fancy a beer?'

Felix caught the can, which exploded in his face as he opened it, white froth spewing out and soaking his jeans. The three Metal Maniacs sniggered uncontrollably when he dropped it, still fizzing, onto the carpet. After a quick clean-up he settled in to watch the end of the movie and despite another case of damp trousers, was soon enjoying himself. *The Exorcist* may have been a terrifying tale of satanic possession but it was a welcome distraction from giant diamonds and missing scousers.

'Honk, dude, the pie should be done by now,' Freddie announced, checking his watch as the credits rolled at the end of the film. 'Time to get the fries in, mate.'

Honker winced. 'To be honest, FoF, I'm a bit strapped.'

'Don't look at me, mate,' added Trellis. 'I bagged the DVD and the benny don't pay out 'til tomorrow.'

All eyes turned to the new arrival.

'You're on Bro,' said Freddie. 'Nip down to Mustafa's and snag us some chips, willyer? Payback for that ice-cool beer I just gave you.'

Felix shook his head. 'Yeah right, Fred - my trousers really appreciated that.'

Trellis and Freddie fell about laughing but Honker just sat there, his face a picture of concern.

Freddie elbowed his friend in the ribs. 'Whassup, Honk - why the long face?'

Honker held a finger up to his lips. '*Shhh… I think someone's out in the kitchen, FoF.*'

'Come on man, you gotta do better than that...' Freddie's words faded away as they all caught the sounds of shuffling footsteps on the other side of the kitchen door.

Honker scooped up the wooden spoons while Freddie grabbed a tennis racquet from beneath the settee. Felix could barely move, his stomach tying itself into knots, a cold sweat instantly forming on his brow.

'Let me talk to them, Fred,' he mumbled, distractedly. 'I… I think I might know what this is about. Y'see, I found these, well… they're like, diamonds.'

His brother gave him one of his 'don't be stupid' looks and moments later the four of them were crammed in, side by side, backs to the wall next to the kitchen door - Freddie wafting his Andy Murray Pro-shot, Honker trembling so much he could barely hold the wooden spoons to his chest, while Trellis mouthed a Latin incantation he'd picked up from the film.

'*What's going on out there?*' whispered Trellis.

They strained their ears, trying to make sense of the noises which had morphed into weird metallic plinking sounds, like nothing Felix had ever heard before.

'They're tooled up,' Freddie said in a low voice. 'Knives, machetes - axes probably. Listen guys - sit here doing nowt and we're dead meat. The way I see it, if we're going down, we might as well go down fighting.'

'No,' pleaded Felix. 'It's too dangerous!'

A grim smile played across Freddie's lips. 'Overruled, Bro. On my count, dudes... One... Two...' The four of them glanced at each other one last time, the countdown momentarily interrupted by another loud 'PLINK!' from behind the kitchen door.

'THREE! Go! Go! GO!!'

Before the words had even left his lips, Freddie was hurtling towards the bedsit's only window. Clearing the settee in one giant leap, he hauled at the ancient sash, the rusty Victorian pulley mechanism squealing in protest. Eventually realising what their leader was up to, his two friends followed suit, albeit with far less panache. Honker slipped on the slimy remnants of some week-old chicken chop-suey, upending Trellis in the process.

'Get up you idiots!' yelled Freddie. 'Help me open–'

Plink! KLUNK! WHOOOOMPH!!

The expansion of the blast was followed by an almighty 'KLANGG!!' as something heavy and metallic clunked to the kitchen floor. In the next instant the door blew open, slamming around on its hinges and catching Felix square in the face. Suddenly, the living room was engulfed in choking black smoke.

Face buried in his hands, he slid down the wall while the *Metal Mania* trio piled out through the window, their terrified screams drowned by the piercing shriek of the smoke alarm.

Felix stared at the 3.00am display on his alarm clock, having failed miserably to block out the noises rumbling from Freddie's bed. It was like sharing a room with a camel suffering from dodgy adenoids, and the worst of it was that the whole thing had been his fault! He wanted to wake his brother up, to smack him around the head and ask him why he was such a total plank, but instead he just lay there fuming.

It turned out that Satan had not stopped by to make a personal, *Exorcist*-style, appearance at Freddie's flat, nor even had HB's kidnappers made an unexpected house call to retrieve their diamond stash. No. The explanation was much more mundane.

As the tinned variety go, the Meaty Munch Family Size Steak and Kidney 'Classic' is a prince amongst pies. Beloved for its 'succulent chunks of meat and delicious beefy gravy, topped with the famous Meaty Munch signature puff-pastry', it comes with easy-to-follow cooking instructions. Freddie had managed the gas mark eight bit - even remembering to preheat the oven before popping the tin in for the recommended twenty-five minutes. Sadly, he'd not got as far as reading the final, all-important warning, even though it was printed across the top of the can in large capital letters:

IMPORTANT! REMOVE LID BEFORE PLACING IN OVEN

At least, that was the explanation offered by the nice female fire fighter who'd helped Felix out onto the landing after he'd crawled through the kitchen, past the smouldering remains of the oven. The shards of pie tin embedded in the ceiling, the steak and kidney splatter-fest up the walls, and the oven door, twisted off its hinges and dumped to the floor, left little room for argument. Even so, the emergency gas team arrived to cap off the supply, sealing the flat and declaring it out of bounds until it had been fully checked for leaks.

Felix would have happily seen his brother walking the streets for the next few nights but predictably, his tearful mother had taken pity and made up the spare bed in his room.

Freddie appeared completely unfazed by the drama of the evening and had fallen asleep before his head even hit the pillow. In contrast, Felix's mind had gone into overdrive. The fire service's explanation added up - the metallic sounds had clearly come from a distressed pie tin on the verge of rupture, the loud 'Klangg!!' marking the moment the oven door was blown off its hinges. But that didn't quite cover the footsteps they'd all heard beforehand... And when Felix had eventually made it into the kitchen, the front door to Freddie's flat was open, which was odd, as he clearly remembered closing it when he'd arrived an hour earlier. The door swung inwards, so the effect of the blast would have been to slam it shut. There was no reason for it to be ajar - unless, someone really had been lurking out there and had left it open as they'd made their getaway.

And there was something else - something much more sinister. He saw it, or thought he saw it, on the kitchen floor as he was crawling out through the tiny, smoke-filled room. There, tucked away down the side of the fridge, nestling in the filth, was what looked remarkably like the bloody, severed tip of a human finger.

'Here's the thing, Felix,' the slight figure of Jeremy Grindrod, Editor-in-Chief of the *Lancastrian Bugler*, announced from the depths of his black leather executive chair, the next morning. 'Life in these parts is *steady* - a smattering of juvenile nuisance cases, the occasional political row on the council, maybe a mobile phone mast petition or two - it's never going to make the *News at Ten* but it's what our customers want to read about. Brake never really understood that.'

Felix checked out the editor's office, trying to get his head around how he'd come to be sitting there amidst the leather settees and smoked glass coffee tables, talking to the surprisingly small man behind the surprisingly large desk, who ran Lancashire's third most-read regional newspaper.

'I'm sure that's right Mr Grindrod, sir,' he replied, admiring the editor's neat grey suit and scrupulously trimmed moustache.

'Good lad! Suffice to say, Brake will never darken the *Bugler's* doors again. I had to let him go. Not something I particularly enjoy doing but I'll tell you this much - when you're at the top, it's not about being popular, it's about being respected.'

Felix knew that if the celebrations he'd witnessed down in the newsroom earlier that morning were anything to go by, sacking HB was the most popular decision the editor had made in years, but he kept the observation to himself. 'I totally respect your decision, sir, but I'm really worried about Howard. He was working on this big story.'

Grindrod chuckled. 'Ah yes, the custard cream diamonds! We've run the checks, of course, and there are no reports of anything like that going astray. Let's face it, if someone really had lost a fistful of diamonds that big, don't you think the whole world would know about it by now?'

'I suppose so, but he went into town yesterday and when he called–'

'Never did get that "Pork scratching shaped like Jesus" piece he promised me. Really annoying - always shifts copy, that kind of thing.'

'He told me he'd met up with some contacts,' Felix said. 'He sounded terrified. He said not to go to the police.'

'Listen lad, the only person who should be calling the boys in blue, is me. I'm reliably informed that Brake has been running his own private news agency while he's been on our books and *that* is gross misconduct, whichever way you look at it! Even worse, he's a useless journalist. I still don't understand how he missed that story on Frecklesall beach last weekend.'

'Actually, Mr Grindrod–'

'And the piece he did write,' the editor added, 'the one about the old boy rowing across the Atlantic? Complete bloody nonsense, every single word. The guy hasn't even been in the sea cadets let alone the Royal Navy!'

'That's terrible, sir.'

'Caused considerable upset amongst my friends at the British Legion, I can tell you. I'm going to have to grovel for England if I want to hang onto my VIP slot on their annual pro-am down at St Annes.'

Felix offered him a sympathetic look.

'But enough of my woes,' Grindrod continued. 'You live out Frecklesall way, don't you, lad? What's all this about an explosion at the chippy last night? '

The words came pouring out before Felix even knew it was happening. 'They thought it was a gas leak at first, Mr Grindrod, sir. Actually it was… well, never mind. The point is, I think there might be some kind of link between those diamonds and the explosion. I was there when it happened and I saw this… this *thing* on the kitchen floor and it looked a bit like…' But he'd lost the editor's attention before he'd even begun.

'OK Pauline, love,' Grindrod shouted through to his PA, who was waving at him from the other side of the glazed partition. 'Fresh pot of coffee and best biscuits please, sweetie.' He turned back to the trainee reporter. 'Ten o'clock's due any minute now lad, so I'll cut to the chase. We've never really got across this City of Culture business - never taken it that seriously, if I'm being honest. We urgently need to up our game in that particular department and I'm thinking you might be the man to help us out.'

Felix could hardly believe his ears. 'Wow! Are you sure?'

'Absolutely. I want you working out there in the field, *embedded*, as it were. I need your copy on everything that's going down in Frecklesall, culture-wise. Dave Heptonstall at the *Journal* got one over on us last weekend and I simply cannot allow that particular scenario to repeat itself.'

'You won't regret this, Mr Grindrod,' Felix gushed. 'You can count on me! Maybe the *Bugler* could do a piece on the lido - relaunch the fundraiser to sort out the repair works as part of the City of Culture campaign? I mentioned it to Howard a few times but–'

The editor interrupted him. 'Rest assured, I'll give that due consideration in due course. In the meantime, I need you to squirt everything you get, in on this channel. You can leave the rest to us.' He handed Felix a scrap of paper as he got up from behind his desk.

The trainee reporter looked at it, his brow furrowing. 'Isn't this the webmail address we give out to the readers for their news tipoffs, Mr Grindrod? We never do anything with the stuff they send in. Aren't you going to let me have a proper newsroom contact?'

The editor grabbed his hand and shook it vigorously. 'All the best for the future, son, it's been a pleasure. And, err… leave your accreditation with security on the way out, would you? Best to be on the safe side, eh?'

Felix was shunted out with such force, he almost collided with the elderly military man in full uniform, who marched past him into the office.

'Ahh, Major, an honour as ever!' Grindrod greeted his new visitor with a salute. 'And how's the handicap coming along, sir?'

He felt like one of those sad, middle-aged businessmen who'd lost his job but couldn't admit the terrible truth to his wife - leaving the house early each morning and returning at tea time, briefcase in hand, having spent the day feeding the ducks at the local park. But he hadn't been sacked - or at least, he didn't think he had - and with HB off the scene, he clung to the hope that he could pull things around. So, he continued to write - about anything and everything - sending his articles in to the *Bugler* on a daily basis. Not that he got any kind of response.

Predictably, sharing a room with his brother was a total nightmare. Freddie had quickly made himself at home, scattering his dirty clothes across the floor (with the exception of a single pair of badly soiled Calvin Clines, left hanging from the ceiling light shade) and sprawling over his bed chugging cans of lager into the early morning hours. The *Metal Mania* DJ had brought something else with him, as well. Even with the window permanently propped open, the room had taken on the gagging stink of a hamster's cage and there was nothing Felix could do to shift it.

He was still in Flo's bad books, of course. She'd given up asking him to speak to their dad and had instead, turned her attention to some of their mum's extravagances. The manicures, new outfits and expensive perfumes, were all evidence, in Flo's eyes, of their mum's plans to trade her husband in for a younger model. Felix still couldn't see it - their parents had been together forever and while the flame of passion was clearly spluttering a bit, he was pretty sure that's what happened with all couples when they got old. And anyway, the one thing he knew for sure was that if he ever got around to raising the subject with his dad, it would only make matters much, much worse.

Felix was in the bathroom that Thursday morning, hunting for his toothbrush, which wasn't in the mug on the windowsill with all the others, when he came across an unusually curvaceous, blue bottle. 'Svelte, *pour Femme*' - the French labelling lent a splash of sophistication to the family's Poundland toiletry collection, standing out from the discount anti-dandruff shampoo and Freddie's long-abandoned 'Rampant' aftershave box-set, which he'd won in a raffle.

'Thirty pounds that Svelte cost her,' Flo had told him, the day before. 'I know the Hollywood stars are supposed to use it but it was *thirty pounds*, and all it is, is a depilatory!'

'*Delapidatory*?' he'd asked, not having a clue what she was talking about.

'Depilatory, you moron! Look it up. And while you're about it, why not try getting your stupid head around why Mum might be spending so much money

55

pampering herself. Even an idiot like you should be able to work that one out.'

Not wishing to show his ignorance, he *had* looked it up, and now knew that a depilatory was a cosmetic cream or lotion used for the removal of unwanted hair. He opened the bottle and had a sniff, only just managing to resist the urge to rub some onto an armpit to see what happened.

He eventually spotted the missing toothbrush as he was easing the Svelte back onto the windowsill. Nestling in the U-bend of the toilet bowl, its bristled head poked bravely above the waterline.

There were no prizes for guessing who was responsible.

Rolling up a pyjama sleeve, he reached into the murky depths, vowing revenge that would be both swift and decisive.

Throughout those long days and even longer nights, the diamonds lay in their hiding place beneath the floorboards, a dark presence gnawing away at the back of Felix's mind. He was desperate to discover the truth, desperate to hear HB's nasal tones telling him it was all a wind-up. But there was one very good reason why that was not going to happen - on his mobile, at least. He hadn't seen his phone in days and eventually worked out that he must have dropped it in the chaos of his escape from Freddie's flat. Until they got the green light from the Gas Board, there was no way of retrieving it and no way of receiving any more of HB's calls.

5

Freddie crunched into the gears of the family's vintage orange Fiesta, elbow resting casually through the open window. They must have only been doing about twenty-five but the rattle of the engine and the high-pitched whistle coming from the roof rack, left on from a trip to the dump the week before, made it seem much faster and much more dangerous. Felix glanced across at his brother with well-concealed envy. With his designer stubble and wraparound shades, Freddie always managed to scrub up well. Whilst he'd never have admitted it, Felix secretly regarded him as the essence of cool, but on this particular occasion his attention was focussed on his brother's full head of shoulder length hair. He'd set the trap in good time, raving about how their mum's ultra-expensive Svelte purchase was such an awesome hair conditioner the Hollywood stars used it on a daily basis…

Oh well - good things come to those who wait.

He checked his own reflection in the Fiesta's wing-mirror. Freddie had warned him about the strict dress code at OT's and, as clueless as ever over what to wear, he'd ended up following his mum's advice. The beige 'summer holiday' chinos met the required smart/casual guidelines, while the brown and cream diamond-patterned jumper, now screwed up on the back seat, looked tidy enough. But it was his orange and yellow sunburst shirt with the striking 'Born to Boogie!' motif that was going to knock them dead. Even Freddie had been impressed. 'Sharp!' he'd said, admiringly. 'Looks like I might have some competition in the babe stakes this evening.'

'We need to pick up some kit for the gig,' Freddie announced as he swung the car onto the high street.

'OK but can we get a move on? I'm supposed to be meeting Naz at nine,' Felix said, checking his watch, impatiently. 'Are we still good for the VIP passes?'

'No problem, you're with the talent now.'

They trundled down a side street and pulled over, just around the corner from the back of the chippy. Freddie squirmed about in his seat as he retrieved the keys from his jeans pocket.

'I'll need my laptop and there should be a couple of memory sticks in there as well,' he said. 'They'll be kicking around on the floor, somewhere.'

Felix looked at him, incredulously. 'What are you talking about?'

'Had to leave my gear behind the other night, didn't I? You're my roadie - it's your job to sort it.'

'But the place has been sealed off by the Gas Board. It might be dangerous.'

Freddie sighed. 'Just do it, you wuss.'

Grabbing the keys, Felix prised himself from the car and stomped around the corner into the back yard. An official looking 'Risk of Gas Explosion - DO NOT ENTER' sign had been pasted to the outer door but oddly, the yellow and black warning tape slung across the entrance had been broken and was hanging limply from the frame. He tried the lock and was surprised when the door swung open. Guessing it had been damaged when the fire service forced their way in, he took a deep breath and stepped over the threshold.

The door clicked shut behind him, plunging the lobby into darkness. Searching blindly for the light switch, he heard a noise coming from up on the landing, near where he'd dumped his bike a few evenings before.

Someone was up there.

As he turned to reach for the door handle, powerful hands grabbed hold of him, pinning him against the wall.

'Hey!' he shrieked. 'What do you think you're doing?'

The light clicked on and he was confronted by two solidly built men - olive-skinned and a good six inches shorter than he was. One had slick black hair and a droopy 1970s moustache, the other had a gruesome scar running diagonally across his face - as if he'd come off second-best in an argument with a meat cleaver. Wearing jeans and tan leather jackets, they were both sporting identical chunky silver chains around their necks, complete with triangular, wedge-shaped medallions.

Moustache-guy thrust a crumpled sheet of paper into his face. 'You know theeese-a *hombre*?' he asked, a glint of gold flashing from his front teeth.

It was a flyer for the evening's gig.

97.8 Frecklesall FM proudly presents:

Metal Mania!

Live and Kicking from OT's,

Frecklesall-on-Sea: Friday 24th July

Feat: DeeJay 'FoF' Haythornthwaite

Felix shook his head - even in his terrified state he knew it was probably best not to let on that the man they were looking for was just around the corner in the Fiesta, picking his nose.

The two foreigners launched into an unintelligible exchange - it sounded Spanish, although the accents were like nothing Felix had heard on the Haythornthwaite's recent summer holiday to Torremolinos. While they'd been there, Emilio, one of the more gregarious waiters at the Hotel Miramar, had gone out of his way to teach him a few useful phrases. Now seemed like a good time to try them out.

'*Hola senyoras*,' Felix began hesitantly. '*Grassyarsey por favoro. No hablo Espanyolo.*'

Pushing his compatriot away, Scarface glared at him menacingly. Petrified, Felix struggled to remember anything else Emilio had told him. '*It is a traditional Spanish greeting*,' the waiter had said, '*for when you are meeting someone for the first time and want to show great respect.*' The words came back to him in the nick of time.

'*Grassyarsey!*' he blurted. '*Me tire un pedo!*' Pleased with his mastery of the language, he thrust out a hand and offered up the cheesiest of smiles.

The gold-toothed moustache-guy lunged forward. Grabbing a fistful of Boogie! shirt, he almost lifted Felix off his feet. '*Donde está?*' he growled. '*Donde está el Saydoss Perdido?*'

Scarface pulled his sidekick away. '*Estás loco, Xavier? Nunca debes hablar del Saydoss!*'

'*No comprehendo!*' screamed Felix, as he sensed the contents of his lower intestine heading southwards. '*No comprehendo…* about this *Saydoss* or anything else for that matter!'

The pair stared at him, open-mouthed, seemingly taken aback by his use of the word, and at that exact same moment the light timer clicked itself off. Plunged into darkness again, there was a moment of confused silence - just long enough for them to catch the sounds of glass crunching underfoot, outside. Someone was heading across the yard towards the door.

Before Felix could cry out, a hand had been clamped over his mouth.

Whoever was out there was just inches from them now, having stopped to read the warning sign. There was an agonising pause... and then the footsteps were crunching away again.

BANG!

Felix jumped in fright as the lobby flooded with daylight and two burly men in dark blue boiler suits and yellow Hi-Vis vests, burst in.

'We're from the Gas Board,' growled the first guy, pointing to a badge on his jacket which announced: 'Hi! I'm Tony - Happy to Help with your Domestic Appliance Needs'.

'According to our records,' added his similarly labelled co-worker, Eric, 'the supply to this residence has been suspended under statute 16, subsection E of the Gas Act 1982, making it the subject of an evacuation order. What I'm observing here is a serious breach.'

'Their English is rubbish,' Felix shrieked, 'but thank God you're here - they were trying to kidnap me!'

The two foreigners exchanged glances and in the next instant, Scarface had pulled out a vicious-looking blade. Felix fell flat on his face as he tried to scramble up the stairs, but the gas men stood their ground. Eric raised his arms as if surrendering while Tony, almost casually, flicked open one side of his jacket. Felix couldn't see what was concealed in there but the effect was remarkable, the Spanish duo stepping back, eyes wide in fear.

Eric hooked the door open with his foot. 'Clear off scumbags,' he shouted, 'and don't you EVER mess with the Gas Board boys again!'

The would-be kidnappers careered across the yard, running as fast as their legs would carry them.

Felix was in a state of shock. 'What was that you just showed them?' he asked

Tony blanked the question. 'We need access to these premises, and we need it now. Do you live here?'

'It's my brother's place. He's outside in the car - I'll get him for you.'

Twenty minutes later, with Freddie's kit safely stowed on the Fiesta's back seat and Felix's bike liberated and locked to a nearby lamp post, the Haythornthwaite boys set off once more for OT's. Tony and Eric had taken some convincing that Freddie's bedsit always looked like it had been burgled but even then, they'd shown surprisingly little interest in the gas supply. After sifting through the debris in the living room, they'd pummelled Felix with questions about what had happened. It was only when he described his attempt at conversational Spanish that their stern expressions cracked for just an instant.

'I don't get it - when we were on holiday in Spain, I picked up a few phrases,' Felix said. 'It's a traditional greeting but it seemed to really wind them up. '*Me tire un pedo* means, "I throw you a hand", so I was only asking them to shake hands.'

'Except *pedo* means wind,' Tony corrected him, struggling to keep his face straight.

'That doesn't make sense.'

'Does to me, Bro,' said Freddie. 'I'm pretty sure you just told them dudes you'd farted.'

'Oh…'

Red-faced, he busied himself tidying up in the kitchen, eventually plucking up enough courage to check out the gap at the side of the fridge. But there was no sign of a severed human finger and he encountered nothing more sinister than a handful of mouse droppings.

'What's it got to do with them?' Freddie complained as they rattled along in the car, a few minutes later. 'The place wasn't looking that bad.'

Felix's head was still in a spin. 'One of them had a gun, I'm sure of it.'

'As if!'

'Well, that Tony had something under his jacket that scared them off. And before you tell me I imagined it, don't forget, it was *you* those Spanish guys were after.'

Freddie reached across and patted his brother on the head. 'Hey, it's no biggy, Bro - the FoF is a global brand these days. My fans are all over the place.'

They got out of the car, Felix pulling on his jumper as they headed around to the back of OT's. Naz was waiting for them there, looking even tidier than usual in his pressed trousers, zipped-up bomber-jacket and black school shoes. He greeted his friend grumpily.

'You're twenty minutes late.'

'Sorry Naz,' Felix said as they trotted along behind Freddie, who was closing in on OT's back door at speed. 'We had to pick up some stuff from the flat.'

'Oh. Right. Find anything interesting?'

'Well, I got my bike back at last, and my mobile as well - although the battery's dead. But something really weird happened while I was there. It freaked me out a bit, if I'm being honest. I'll tell you about it when we get inside.'

Freddie had already disappeared through the club's back door but when they tried to follow, their way was blocked by a dinner-suited bouncer.

'Sorry lads, there's no access this way.'

'We're with my brother - we're his roadies,' Felix pleaded.

The bouncer laughed. 'Tenner on the door at the front, but be quick about it - the place is filling up fast.'

'Fred!' Felix shouted over the bouncer's shoulder. 'You said you'd got some passes for us...'

His brother carried on up the narrow corridor without even breaking stride.

They queued for the best part of twenty minutes, convinced they weren't going to get in. At least it gave Felix the chance to update his friend.

'I'm pretty sure it was "*Saydoss*" they were talking about - at least that's how it sounded to me. They went ballistic the moment I mentioned it.'

'To be fair though, you'd already wound them up, hadn't you?' said Naz, trying not to laugh. '"*Me tire un pedo*"? That's priceless, that is!'

'I'd like to have seen you do better.'

'Oh... Sorry mate. So, you reckon they were wearing these medallions?'

'Yeah, it was bizarre - they looked kind of cheese-shaped. I mentioned it to the gas men and they said I shouldn't report any of it to the police. They don't cover gas regulations, apparently.'

Naz looked unconvinced. 'But if those Spanish guys really were after the diamonds, why would they bother looking for your Freddie. I mean, what's he got to do with anything?'

Felix shrugged. 'How would I know? If my Spanish went beyond "I don't understand" and "I've farted", I'd have asked them, wouldn't I?'

They stood together in silence as the bouncers counted their way back along the queue. For once they were on the right side of the cut and secure in the knowledge they were going to get in, Felix's mood began to lift a little.

'I didn't think anyone listened to Fred's show, apart from my dad - and that's only so he can moan about it for the rest of the week,' he said, looking back at the dozens of disappointed punters who'd been turned away.

'Heavy metal's always been big in Frecklesall, hasn't it?' Naz said, surreptitiously checking out the group standing next to them. 'Have you noticed, we're just about the youngest ones here?'

'And look at what they're all wearing,' Felix added. 'Actually, I'm not sure we've got this right, Naz.'

Ripped denim was the name of the game, grungy T-shirts featuring the names of bands Felix had never heard of, and long greasy hair - the pelmet ponytail favoured by the baldies. And there was a studded leather thing going on - from belts to waistcoats, even a few dog collars.

Felix watched on as a big guy with a giant spider's web tattoo inked on top of his bald head, made his way up the steps in front of them, complete with a live python draped around his neck. 'I dunno, Naz,' he said. 'I'm thinking perhaps we should nip home and get changed.'

'If we leave now we've got no chance of getting in,' his friend replied, unzipping his bomber jacket.

Felix turned towards him, and his face froze in horror. 'I don't believe it…' he mumbled, as if in a trance. 'We can't go in looking like this… we just can't.' He began to walk away.

Naz hauled him back into the line. 'Are you mad? We'll lose our place.'

Felix pulled his jumper over his head and a cheer went up around them. It seemed there were at least two *Metal Mania* fans heading into OT's that night, who'd been 'Born to Boogie!'

'We look like a couple of talent show rejects,' Felix muttered, as they handed over their money and shuffled into the club. 'That idiot brother of mine said–'

Naz interrupted him. 'Stop moaning, will you? People probably won't even notice after a while. We can still have a good time.'

But people were noticing. The matching shirts were getting some very funny looks and it was a relief when they got to the main dance floor where they could merge into the crowd. Looking about the place, Felix's mood plummeted still further as it dawned on him that men outnumbered women by a ratio of about ten to one.

Neither of them had been inside a nightclub before and they gazed around in awe at the glamour of their surroundings. There was a stage at the top end of the room, decked out in Frecklesall FM and Got it All! banners, while the bar was tucked away to the side of the main entrance. Next to it was a staircase, leading to an upper mezzanine platform that cantilevered out over the crowd. The punters up there had a great view of the dance floor and were at eyeball level with a giant, mirror-encrusted glitter-ball, suspended from the ceiling by a huge chain.

'Ay up - it's the Boogie Brothers!'

The pair were greeted by their long-time friend and partner in crime, Bernie Devaney, who was carrying a fully loaded drinks tray. Felix's level of discomfort ratcheted up another notch as he realised that even Bernie, who was wearing jeans and a black Spinal Tap T-shirt, had picked up on the evening's dress code.

'Where have you been hiding, Bernie?' Felix shouted over the noise. 'I haven't seen you in ages!'

'Been missing me then?' said Bernie. 'Hey - lovin' the shirts, guys!'

Felix laughed, forgetting his awkwardness for just a moment. With his razor-sharp wit and evil sense of humour, Bernie could be a total pain at times, but that's how he got by. Even at the age of sixteen, he still weighed in at a mighty seven stone and at just under five-foot-four, still had the same high-pitched squeak of a voice he'd had from primary school. Not that it seemed to bother him, in the least.

Felix tried again. 'Seriously, Bernie, what have you been up to?'

'Just hanging with some new mates,' Bernie replied, eyes twinkling from behind the battered metal frames of his glasses. 'Why not come over and meet the guys?'

He set off, barging his way through the crowd, his friends following on behind. Approaching the table, Felix was shocked by what he saw.

'Bernie, are they *your* mates?' he asked.

'Yeah, what's the big deal?'

Felix was struggling for words. 'But… but…'

Naz helped him out. 'They're *girls*...'

Bernie laughed. 'Hey, you lads are on fire tonight!' He put the tray down on the table and elbowed his way in amidst the group with a shout of, 'Come on ladies, make room for a little 'un!'

It was difficult to tell how old they were - maybe eighteen or nineteen - but from where Felix was standing, they all looked impossibly attractive.

Bernie did the introductions. 'Zoe, Neesha, Dannii - these are my mates, Felix and Naz. I know they look like a pair of dorks but believe me… they really are!'

'Hi!' Felix greeted them, waving self-consciously while Naz just stood there looking petrified. There were more shocks in store as Bernie swung an arm around Zoe's shoulder and suddenly, they were all over each other like a rash.

Felix didn't know where to look. He decided some small-talk was called for. 'Danni's an odd name, for a girl,' he said to the nearest of the trio.

Wearing tight-fitting denims, knee-length leather boots and a white Harley Davidson T-shirt, she looked at him like he was stupid. 'Not when your name's Daniella, it's not, is it?' she replied.

She was quite a bit shorter than him, with wide-set eyes, lush lips and a tiny button-nose. Her long blonde hair was swept around to one side, her face plastered with orange foundation. With false lashes so mega, it was a wonder she had the strength to pull her eyelids open. She was most definitely not his type - maybe two or three years older, shapely, attractive, and way out of his league. Any one of these things would normally have sent him running in the opposite direction, but for some inexplicable reason he found himself drawn to her, whilst simultaneously finding it impossible to string together even the simplest of sentences.

'Oh, right then,' Felix mumbled. 'So Daniella, how do you know Bernie?'

'Dannii,' she corrected him, a white blob of gum squirming around in her mouth as she spoke. 'Like, through my best mate Zoe, actually. They've been seeing each other a few weeks now. I always thought people who worked in IT were, like, *so* boring, but Bernie's such a laugh, ain't he?'

Felix was taken aback, although not by the news of his friend's fictitious career. 'What? He's going out with Zoe? Her, over there?'

Dannii bristled. 'Yeah. What's your point, *actually?*'

He looked across at Zoe - she was gorgeous, too. 'It's just that, well it's Bernie isn't it? Look at the state of him.'

'Some mate you are,' she said, turning away, huffily.

They sat together in awkward silence for what seemed like an age. Felix tried to attract Naz's attention but his friend was too busy chatting with Neesha to notice, the two of them looking as if they were getting on like a house on fire.

'So, what is it you do for a living, Dannii?' he asked, eventually.

'This and that,' she replied. 'Style and fashion, mainly.'

'Oh…'

'I'm working up my portfolio at the moment and my sister Portia's like, "Your look is so *now*, Dannii, babes, you've got to get it out there". The thing is, it's all about the platform these days, innit?'

'Wow, that's interesting,' he lied. What he knew about fashion would fit comfortably onto the back of a postage stamp with room to spare, but as he gazed into her eyes none of that seemed to matter.

'So, like, have you had any hits over here then?' she asked.

He gave her a puzzled look.

'Y'know - the charts. So Bernie's like, "These guys are totally mint" and I'm like, "Well I never even heard of ToyBoyz2, Bernie, are you having a laugh, or what?" and Bernie's like, "Well you wouldn't of 'cos they've only made it big in Moldova so far" and I'm like–'

'It's a wind-up,' he interrupted her. 'We're not in a boy band. It's just Bernie trying to be funny.'

'Seemed kind of random to me, but I suppose it's the formula, innit?'

Felix gawped at her.

'What with you and Naz being twins,' she added.

'We look nothing like each other!' he spluttered.

'Didn't say identical, did I?'

'And he's Asian!'

'Oh... I thought it were a sun tan. Anyway, it's your fault for wearing those *stoopid* shirts.' And with that, she got to her feet and stomped off towards the toilets.

Felix sat there with his head in his hands. He was useless at this stuff. Dannii was drop-dead gorgeous, and as usual he'd just blown it - big style. And then the voice of an unseen announcer boomed out across the PA system.

'Coming to you right here, right now, live from OT's: 97.8 Frecklesall FM, in association with the Bulgy Burger Corporation UK, proudly present the man you've all been waiting for. Give it up now, please, for *Metal Mania's* very own DeeeeJaaaay FoF!!'

Felix had to climb up onto his chair just to see what was happening as Freddie surfed onto stage on a wave of dry ice.

70

'Helllllooo Maniacs!' he yelled. 'Are you ready to GET! IT!! ON!!!?'

Moments later, OT's had been transformed into a seething mass of head-banging insanity. Felix was stunned. He'd pictured Freddie's listeners as a handful of 'Billy No-Mates' with nothing better to do on their Friday nights than tune into his rubbish radio show, but he couldn't have been more wrong. The effect of cramming these guys onto a dance floor while their favourite grooves were blasted out at brain-melting decibels, was pure dynamite.

Suddenly, the place was heaving with middle-aged men thrashing air guitars, tinkling on non-existent keyboards and pummelling imaginary drum kits. With nothing to lose, Felix plunged into the action, throwing himself around like a lunatic. Even the arrival of the first commercial break ('*Get your gob around a Bulgy Black-Pudding Burger - hand fried in 100% lard: Because you're worth it!*') did little to dampen the energy in the room.

After a couple of numbers he was drenched in sweat, so he headed back to the table to cool off. As soon as he sat down, Dannii smooched up beside him, a syrupy expression on her face.

'OMG! That was, like, totally awesome! Was it one of your ToyBoyz2 routines?' she asked breathlessly. 'Listen, I'm *so* sorry about before, Felix babes, only, my friend Neesha, she's like, "Dannii, you can be such a *stoopid* mare at times" and I'm like, "What you talking about, babes?" and she's like, "That Felix is a total sweetie and you just bit his head off" and I'm like–'

He was getting a headache just listening to her. 'It's not a problem, Dannii - honestly.'

'Awww, thanks.' She leant across and gave him a peck on the cheek.

He had to pinch himself to make sure he wasn't dreaming.

She moved in close, whispering in his ear, 'Bernie said when you're not gigging in Moldova with the ToyBoyz, you've got this top job at the *Bugler*.'

Felix recoiled.

'You OK, babes?' she asked.

'Absolutely… err… *babes,*' he replied, going with the flow.

'Fancy coming upstairs?'

'Oh… I'm not sure. I mean, we've only just met.'

She gave him a funny look. 'Up there - on that balcony thingy. I can't see owt from down here.'

What he really needed was a trip to the toilet - he hadn't been since lunchtime - but there was no way he was letting this girl out of his sight. From what he could see of the chaos on the upper level it didn't seem like the view would be any better, but if that's what he had to do to get a snog he'd sling her over a shoulder and carry her up there himself.

'OK, let's go for it.'

They worked their way to the stairs where a massive logjam had formed on the half landing, the crowd peering through the window at something that was kicking off in the street outside.

'What's going on?' asked Dannii as they got caught in the crush.

'I don't know,' he replied, craning his neck to try to see. He could just about make out a handful of bouncers squaring up to a couple of beefy guys with short haircuts, wearing jeans and brightly coloured shirts. He assumed they must be drunken squaddies back on leave, but when his eyes adjusted to the street lighting, he did a double-take. It was Tony and Eric - the men from the Gas Board.

Dannii tugged at his arm. 'So what is it, then?'

'Nothing really,' he replied, struggling to make sense of it all. 'Just a couple of numpties looking for trouble. The bouncers are sorting it.'

Eventually they made it up the stairs, and were able to work their way across to the balcony railing, overlooking the dance floor.

'That was the Verminators of Anthraxion, with their latest hit, *Total Oblivion Overload!*' Freddie's voice boomed out.

'It must be *so* cool having a famous brother,' Dannii shouted over the din.

Felix grimaced. 'Right. Yeah. Totally awesome.'

She gave him that look again. 'Actually, I reckon you're pretty awesome as well, Felix.'

She hoiked the gum from her mouth and flicked it over the rail. Their eyes met and then, unbelievably, she was pulling him down towards her.

He was losing himself in the moment when he spotted something out of the corner of his eye - something that nearly stopped his heart in mid-beat. Untying Dannii's arms from around his neck, he straightened up to his full height.

'What's up with you?' she complained.

Felix was staring, open-mouthed, towards a lone figure who'd appeared near the top of the stairs. Clearly visible above the sea of balding heads and multi-coloured bandanas, he'd climbed up onto a chair and was checking out the crowd. The dark slicked-back hair and tan leather jacket told Felix everything he needed to know before he'd even picked out the livid crease carved into the man's face.

'Dannii, I'm... I'm really sorry but I've got to go,' he said, urgently. 'There's this Spanish guy back there who's after my brother. He tried to kidnap me this afternoon and he's got a knife! I need to warn our Fred.'

'That's the lamest excuse I ever heard,' she snapped. 'If you don't fancy me, at least have the guts to say so.'

'That's not true! You're absolutely gorgeous. It's just that, well, I think he might actually want to *kill* him.'

With the music still blasting out, they were suddenly distracted by the dazzle of the spotlight illuminating the grinning figure down on the stage. Freddie was standing behind the sound deck, his long hair swept back, hands cupped behind his ears. In the next instant, bullets of light pinged around the room like something from a *Star Wars* film. The diamond earrings were massive - each as big as an Everton mint - and the effect of the spotlight's beam was amazing. Felix glanced back to check on Scarface, but he'd already abandoned his vantage point and was battling his way down the stairs.

'You're pathetic, you!' yelled Dannii. 'I've had better offers this evening, y'know. And good luck with the Toyboyz2 thing - you're *so* going to need it, you loser.'

It took her a moment to realise she was talking to herself. Confused, she looked around to see where Felix had gone.

That's when she started screaming.

6

Inching along the narrowest of ledges, on the wrong side of the rail, Felix gazed down onto a sea of upturned faces. He'd seen them do this kind of thing on the telly plenty of times and it had always looked pretty cool. Now he was the one teetering on the brink, he wasn't so sure.

'Oooff!'

An unseen figure shoved him from behind and he toppled forward. Springing away from the ledge in an attempt at a graceful swallow dive, he instantly found himself on a collision course with the giant glitter-ball suspended high above the dance floor. There were screams as he grabbed at the mirror-encrusted globe, his momentum sending it swinging forwards then back again, like the pendulum of a novelty clock. He clung on for a few brief seconds, the glitter-ball's steady three-hundred-and-sixty-degree rotation providing him with an unrivalled view of the mayhem below.

And then he let go.

Buoyed by a mighty roar he landed flat on his back onto countless upturned palms, yelping as a wayward fist caught him in the kidneys. And then he was on the move, passing over the heads of the crowd, hands poking and prodding, ruffling his hair and tearing at his shirt. The balcony plunge had given him the jump on

Scarface, but he was now heading in exactly the wrong direction - away from the stage and back towards the knife-wielding gangster.

'I'm going the wrong way!' he shrieked over the cheers, as another body plummeted from the balcony, high above. 'I need to get up to the stage! Take me to the FoF!'

He never knew whether it was the mention of his brother's handle or just a random outcome of the crowd's collective will, but his momentum began to slow. Moments later he'd been flipped onto his front and was being propelled at speed, back the way he'd come.

It was painful but weirdly brilliant. Surfing above the crowd it looked like he'd be up on the stage in no time and with a bit of luck, could grab Freddie and make a sharp exit through OT's back door. But his elation was short-lived. Suddenly, he was being dragged down - his right arm locked in a vice-like grip. He twisted around to complain, finding himself up-close-and-personal with a grinning, gold-toothed gangster.

'Help! Somebody help me!' he screamed, but all eyes were focussed back on the balcony, where the next Metal Maniac was preparing for his leap of faith.

Being a lanky featherweight with the body mass index of an oversized stick insect, Felix had sailed through his first ever balcony dive with relative ease. Alas, for the next in line, things were to prove a bit more of a challenge. Fuelled by eight pints of lager, 'Wee Malky' McNulty, the twenty-five stone Glaswegian in the kilt, Scotland football shirt and tartan bandana, paused only long enough to punch the air and yell, 'Fae Bonnie Scotland!' before hurling himself off the balcony onto the revellers below.

One moment, Felix was being dragged, kicking and screaming towards the exit, the next, he caught a flash of lilywhite thigh from the very large tartan object now plummeting towards him. He only just managed to wriggle free in time.

Wee Malky landed on top of the gangster with a floor-shuddering 'BOOM!'

Before Felix knew it, he was riding high above the heads of the crowd once more. Seconds later, he'd been dumped onto the stage in an untidy heap.

Freddie greeted him enthusiastically. 'Awesome plunge, Bro! You might just have started something out there!'

Felix struggled to his feet. 'Those Spanish guys are back, Fred, and they're after us. We've gotta get out of here!'

'Like, that's gonna happen!' his brother replied, gesturing towards the crowd. 'These are my people. Why would anyone want to spoil this full-on vibe?'

'I don't know - maybe it's got something to do with those diamonds you've got hanging off your ears, you plank!'

Grinning, Freddie pulled back his hair to reveal the sparkling earrings. 'Glad you took the time to notice, Bro. I found them under the bed this morning. I thought they looked pretty cool so I glued some clips on from Flo's jewellery kit. Neat job, eh?'

'Nice work,' remarked Felix as he pointed out the leather-jacketed duo now battling towards them through the madness of the mosh pit. 'You see that guy with the scar for a face? He's the one who pulled the knife on me round at your flat. I'm pretty sure he thinks those diamonds are the real deal. You can hang around to explain things to him if you want, but I'm out of here.'

Shielding his eyes against the spotlight's glare, Freddie looked out across the crowd. Face suddenly turning a ghostly white, he snatched up the microphone. 'Competition time, guys!' he yelled. 'Frecklesall FM wristbands for the first Maniacs to de-bag them two *bandidos* down here at the front! They've come all the way from sunny Spain, so let's be sure to give 'em a proper Lanky welcome!'

The spotlight swivelled around to the dance floor where the two foreigners instantly disappeared under a tidal wave of Iron Maiden T-shirts.

The brothers jumped from the back of the stage, bouncing along a corridor and crashing through a couple of fire doors before coming to an emergency stop by the club's rear entrance.

'Get 'em off!' Felix barked.

Freddie pulled up his jeans, defensively. 'No way man. I've gone commando tonight!'

'Not your kecks, you numpty - the earrings.'

'Oh...' He unhooked the diamonds and passed them over.

Felix ripped the clip from each stone, shoving one in his pocket and handing the other back to his brother. 'Better if we split them up, just in case. Stash it somewhere safe - quick!'

'Okey-dokey!'

Before he could stop him, Freddie had flicked his diamond high into the air, catching it, peanut-style, in his mouth.

CLACK!

'Oww, maan!' he shrieked, holding his mouth and cursing.

It was only a short dash to the Fiesta but it felt like the longest sprint of Felix's life. They arrived at the car, gasping for breath, Felix glancing over his shoulder to see two figures stumbling from the back of the night club. One of them wasn't wearing any trousers.

'They're onto us!' he shouted. 'C'mon Fred, let's get out of here!'

Freddie fumbled with the keys, the driver's door creaking arthritically as he hauled it open. His brother jumped in on the passenger's side.

'Let's do one - now!' shrieked Felix.

Freddie tried the ignition.

CLICK

The devastating awfulness of the sound was accentuated by the silence which followed it.

'Houston, we have a problem,' Freddie announced.

'Stop messing, Fred - they're nearly here!'

CLICK

He tried again, pumping the accelerator while Felix rocked back and forth, willing the ancient engine to start. Eventually, they heard an unhealthy noise coming from under the bonnet.

RURRR…RURRR…RURRR

'Battery's dead!' yelled Freddie. 'Get out and push!'

Felix looked back down the road at the men running towards them. 'I'll never manage it on my own!'

THUNK!

Suddenly, the car was rocked on its suspension, a pair of ghostly faces looming up at the rear window. It was Bernie and Naz, shoving for all they were worth. Felix jumped out to help.

'Got here as fast as we could,' gasped Naz. 'We came down the backs, just in case.'

'You owe us a drink for this!' added Bernie.

'Shut up and push!' Felix shouted.

After an agonising few seconds the car began to gather momentum.

'Now!' yelled Naz.

A cloud of choking black smoke belched from the Fiesta's exhaust as the mighty 1.1 litre engine stuttered into life. Bernie and Naz scattered into the shadows but naked fear kept Felix's hands welded into place. As the car picked up speed, he was faced with a stark choice - hang on and take his chances, or let go and get scraped off the tarmac by Scarface and his gold-toothed mate.

It was a no-brainer.

Muttering a silent prayer, he jumped up onto the back bumper, fingers locking onto the rusty roof rack. He did his best to crouch down, half-expecting bullets to come fizzing past his head, but a few seconds later he was mightily relieved to see the two men doubled over in the middle of the road, gasping for breath. They'd done it! Cruising along at a steady twenty-five miles per hour, the wind whistling around his ears, Felix threw his head back and laughed.

The ear-piercing squeal of rubber on tarmac was the first indication that things hadn't gone quite as well as he'd first thought. A big black Lexus had pulled up next to the two foreigners, a door swinging open to scoop them up. Seconds later, it roared up the road in hot pursuit.

'Go! Go! GO!' screamed Felix, banging on the Fiesta's roof with his fist. He clung on for dear life as the car thrashed down a side road, leaving a trail of broken wing mirrors and wailing car alarms in its wake. Crashing on through a herd of stray wheelie bins, they burst back onto the high street, the Lexus closing all the time. Felix's puny arms were burning with the effort - he couldn't hold on much longer - but the Lexus would not be shaken. Glued to the Fiesta's tail, it followed every swerve and acceleration Freddie threw at it.

'Get out of the way!' Felix yelled, waving frantically at the group of drunks staggering across the zebra crossing in front of them. The startled pedestrians scattered at the last moment, cursing and swearing as they tumbled onto the footpath. He had to duck to avoid a blurred white package flung at him by one of the disgruntled revellers. The newspaper-wrapped missile flew past his ear but the Lexus was not so fortunate, a soggy 'SPLAT!' marking a direct hit to its windscreen.

Even going like the clappers, the Japanese precision-engineered wipers were no match for the devastating impact of the chippy bomb - a heady cocktail of mushy peas, chips and curry sauce (mild). Moment later the gooey mess had been smeared over the tinted glass, completely obscuring the driver's view. Felix watched in amazement as the Lexus slewed across the road, mounted the kerb, and slammed head-on into a post box. The Fiesta screeched away, skidding around another couple of turns before chugging down Marine Drive towards the seafront. With no sign of their pursuers, Felix banged on the roof once more.

'Fred!' he shouted. 'Stop, for God's sake! I can't hold on much longer!'

The car squealed to a halt, Freddie's arm emerging from the open window, fist pumping. 'We did it Bro! That was awesome!'

Felix dropped to the tarmac, his legs suddenly turning to jelly. In the excitement of the chase, he'd completely forgotten about needing to go to the toilet but standing there in the chill night air, the urge suddenly hit him, big time. They'd pulled up outside the town's derelict lido complex and with its overgrown landscaped frontage, it was too good an opportunity to miss.

'I'm bursting, Fred - I just need a minute. Wait for me, will you?' Felix said, diving off into the undergrowth.

'Get a move on willyer? We shouldn't be hanging around out here!' Freddie shouted back from the car.

Now well into the bushes, Felix patted the pocket of his chinos to check on his diamond. 'Have you still got the dia... I mean, that *thing* you were looking after for me, Fred?'

His brother grinned at him through the open car window, the reflected orange glow of the street lights glinting from the gemstone clamped between his front teeth.

'Nice one,' said Felix. 'We'll drop them off at the police station on the way home.'

'No way, man!'

'You saw what happened - those guys will be back, and next time we might not be so lucky.'

But Freddie's attention had been grabbed by something else - something he'd spotted in the Fiesta's rear-view mirror. 'Come on Bro, we gotta split. They're onto us!' he screamed.

Felix was still in mid-flow. 'I can't. Just a few more seconds...'

Revving the engine furiously, Freddie pulled out into the middle of the road and accelerated away. Felix could only watch helplessly as the Lexus, complete with partly detached front bumper, gave chase.

The Fiesta must have been doing forty when it hit the speed bump.

BANG!

A shower of orange sparks flew up from beneath the car. Somehow, it kept going, but the engine was now emitting an ear-splitting squeal and its front end had dropped down, as if the suspension had collapsed.

'Brake, you idiot - BRAKE!' yelled Felix.

A group of late-night drinkers dived out of the way as the car careered across the Prom and slammed up onto the pavement. There was a sickening 'CLANG!' as it smashed through the rusty cast-iron railings and disappeared over the sea wall.

The Lexus slowed momentarily before speeding off with a screech of tyres.

Felix felt a deathly chill spread over his body, and then he was scrambling through the bushes and running down Marine Drive faster than he'd ever run before. Twenty seconds later he caught a final glimpse of the Fiesta's tail-lights as the car slid into the inky blackness of the Irish Sea.

He'd always been a lousy swimmer - coughing and spluttering after a couple of widths of wonky breaststroke was as good as it got - yet here he was, shivering on top of the sea wall in his trollies, preparing to throw himself into the icy depths. He could see the bubbles rising to the surface about ten metres out. It didn't look that far but he had no idea how deep it was or whether he'd be able to get Freddie out of the car, if he could even find it.

After pausing to mutter a silent prayer he took a deep breath and launched himself into the abyss. The icy chill hit him like a ton of bricks. Arms and legs near-paralysed with shock he spluttered to the surface, disorientated and coughing up sea water by the gallon.

Even though his brain issued the clearest of instructions to his limbs, they refused to cooperate - the manly front crawl he'd envisaged, instantly turning into a whimpering doggy-paddle.

A well-oiled group had gathered up by the broken railings to watch the entertainment. 'Bit late for a skinny dip, pal!' one of them shouted.

Felix struggled to get the words out through chattering teeth. 'My b…b…brother - trapped in the c…c…car. Call the p…p…police!'

'As if!' yelled another. 'Hey, look out for that shark!'

And then something distracted them. There were wolf-whistles and shouts of 'Gerr'emoff, love!' Moments later there was an almighty kerfuffle and one of the guys had crumpled to the deck, clutching his face. His friends gathered around him, roaring with laughter.

Felix spotted the silhouette of a tall, slim figure, on the sea wall. After executing a perfect racing dive, whoever it was, was ploughing past him with the most powerful stroke he'd ever witnessed.

'The car's over there, somewhere…' he spluttered, just about managing to point vaguely into the darkness. His words were cut short by the wave that slopped over his head. Struggling back to the surface, he completely missed the white, circular object spinning through the air towards him, like a low-flying UFO.

CLUNK!

The hefty plastic buoyancy aid smacked into the side of his head and he grabbed for it through a haze of dizziness.

7

It had been a busy night for Police Constable Terry
Plimsoll. The phone lines had been red-hot since OT's
had shut its doors, with incidents kicking off across the
town. And now some idiot had nosedived his car into the
sea. The attending officer had dropped off one of the
prime witnesses and PC Plimsoll's job was to take a
statement - oh, and with the entire night shift out on
patrol he also had to keep the police station afloat,
single-handedly. Conducting the interview in the
reception area was far from ideal but he'd had no choice.
They'd already been interrupted three times and tempers
were starting to fray.

'So, you can confirm he'd not been drinking?' asked
the policeman.

Now fully clothed and with a blanket wrapped around
his shoulders, Felix tried to keep the frustration out of
his voice. 'I've already told you - he may be a complete
idiot but–'

'And what about drugs - was he acting strangely?'

'Hey, this is Fred we're talking about. Acting
strangely is pretty much business as usual for him.'

'I think what he meant to say, officer,' Felix's dad
intervened, 'is that our Freddie is most definitely *not* on
drugs. I've known him for many years - since he was a
baby, in fact - and there's no way he'd go down that

particular road. As for alcohol, the lad never touches the stuff.'

Felix looked at him in amazement.

'OK then, maybe just the odd glass when the occasion demands it,' his dad added.

The policeman clicked away on the keyboard of his desktop computer. 'Interesting,' he remarked, 'because according to our records, Mr Haythornthwaite, your eldest does have something of a track record in that department.'

'Nonsense. He's pursuing a career in broadcasting, y'know.'

PC Plimsoll pointed at his computer screen. 'There's quite a lot to go at here so I'll just give you a bit of an executive summary, if that's OK?' He took a deep breath. 'On June nineteenth we had a late-night callout for noise nuisance near the town hall. The attending officer's report cites Queen's *Bohemian Rhapsody*. The subject was singing it - murdering it more like, from what it says here. On June twenty-third your eldest was cautioned and warned as to conduct at 2.35am, down on the Prom. He had a traffic cone on his head and a flashing road works lamp stuffed up his jumper. June thirtieth - reports of a man seen urinating–'

'Actually, we don't see that much of him these days, officer,' Felix's dad jumped in. 'You know what kids are like - do the best you can for them, set a good example, and this is how they repay you. It's no wonder the country's in such a mess.'

The policeman turned to Felix. 'So lad, we're sticking with this giant diamond and kidnapping story, are we?'

'Definitely,' Felix replied. 'And you can check with Tony and Eric from the Gas Board if you don't believe me.'

A wry smile crept onto the constable's lips. 'I might just leave that particular line of enquiry until the morning, if you don't mind. I don't think I can handle any more abuse, after calling your boss.'

Felix groaned. Cajoling PC Plimsoll into waking Jeremy Grindrod from his slumbers to confirm his story had not been the smartest of moves. The grumpy editor's revelation that HB had sent the *Bugler* newsroom a postcard from his holiday on the Costa Brava and was having a lovely time, had not exactly helped his cause.

'I advise you to think *very* carefully about what you say next,' Plimsoll continued. 'I could easily do you for wasting police time and frankly, that's unlikely to end well, given what happened with that lido fire a couple of years back.'

'It was a set up!' spluttered Felix. 'You of all people should know that. Anyway, I'm the one who should "doing you" for accusing me of something I didn't even do!'

'All right, let's calm things down, shall we?' his dad said. 'The constable is only trying to do his job.'

Felix rolled his eyes. 'So how do you explain the diamond, then? I've five more of them at home - well that's four now, actually, seeing as Freddie's still got his one on him. That's why those Spanish guys were chasing us. That's why he crashed the car.'

'The hospital staff have checked his things and there are no reports of anything like this among his possessions,' said the policeman as he studied the precious stone, now resting on the reception desk.

'He must have lost it in the crash… OK then, so what about that woman at Preston station - the one I switched bags with?'

PC Plimsoll eased himself away from the desk and turned to Felix's dad. 'Mr Haythornthwaite, with your permission I'll take this so-called "diamond" through to the back office and get some photographs for our files. And then I'm going to make us all a brew. Try to talk some sense into the lad while I'm away, will you? I'm sure you appreciate the seriousness of the situation.'

'Absolutely,' he replied. 'Leave it with me, officer.'

'And we still need to clear up the matter of that assault, out on the Prom. The victim may have been drunk and abusive, but that's no reason for someone to break his nose.'

'Had it coming to him, if you ask me,' muttered Felix.

PC Plimsoll disappeared into the back office, leaving father and son in the grip of an awkward silence. Felix stared at his feet while his dad paced around the room holding his mobile up to the lights in an effort to read the message he'd just received.

'Mum's texted to say, Freddie's fine,' he eventually announced. 'They're keeping him in overnight but it's only for observation.'

Felix breathed a sigh of relief.

'And the girl who rescued him is with them now,' his dad continued. 'Turns out she's visiting town and has nowhere to stay, so Mum's invited her back to ours. We'll have to shuffle round a bit but it's the least we can do.'

'She was awesome,' Felix said, 'although I didn't see that much of her, to be honest. By the time she'd fished Fred out, there were police and paramedics everywhere. They wouldn't let me through.'

His dad pulled up a chair and sat down facing him. 'Now then, Son,' he began. 'You and your brother have clearly got yourselves into a bit of a pickle over this "diamonds" business. How about you tell me what really went on.'

'Typical! Even you don't believe me.'

'We all make mistakes, Felix. Drink, drugs, girls - I was young once, y'know.'

'Really, Dad? Tell me more.'

His dad spluttered. 'The point is, it's two in the morning and PC Plimsoll isn't going to let us go until he's heard something vaguely believable from you.'

'But I've already explained what happened. I've not made any of it up!'

His dad sighed. 'I'm just trying to help, Son. Me and your mum have always been there for you, whatever the problem. So, if there *is* anything you want to tell me - anything at all - now would be a pretty good time.'

Felix's insides folded in on themselves. He sensed the shutters coming down and was about to offer the blank, disengaged response he usually trotted out in these situations, when something clicked inside his head. 'Actually, Dad, there is something. I've been meaning to talk to you about for a while now.'

'Excellent! This is how it should be - father and son, sharing problems, man to man.'

Felix took a deep breath. 'It's… err… a bit awkward.'

'Don't hold back - we're family!'

'Well, if you're sure… It's about you and Mum. Flo's worried you might split up, what with all that dancing she's doing and… well, Flo thinks maybe you're not that bothered.'

'Not bothered?' His dad looked like he was about to explode. 'That's ridiculous! Why would she think that?'

'Do you remember what you gave Mum for her birthday last year?'

'Oh, but it wasn't like an ordinary frying pan, was it?' his dad replied indignantly. 'It had one of those NASA-approved coatings *and* a heat-resistant handle. Cost quite a bit I'll have you know. Anyway, don't you forget what she gave me for my birthday!'

The nasal hair trimmers had not been the most well received of gifts, remaining unused on the bathroom windowsill until Freddie discovered they were ideal for doing his eyebrows and some other unmentionable areas.

Felix was beginning to wish he hadn't raised the subject. 'It's not me, Dad. Flo's the one who's been getting herself into a state over this.'

'It's nice your mum's got a hobby she enjoys,' his dad said. 'I'd be out dancing with her myself if it wasn't for this hernia.' He pointed to his groin and winced. 'Anyway, when you've been together as long as we have, you learn to trust each other–'

The discussion was interrupted by the bang of the police station doors and suddenly, a giant whale of a man sailed into the reception area with a worried looking police officer in tow. Wearing a kilt and a huge pair of boots laced to just below the knee, the man was shirtless, the blue of his Glasgow Rangers tattoos the only respite from the bulk of luminous white flesh which rippled and wobbled as he staggered towards the desk. There was something familiar about him but in his exhausted condition, Felix couldn't quite place it. On the other hand, Wee Malky McNulty was clearly overjoyed to see a familiar face.

'Hey, Birrrdy Boy! How yiz doin'?' he yelled.

'Excuse me!' Felix's dad jumped to his son's defence. 'The lad's had enough excitement for one night - leave him be.'

'By the way, I wasnae aware I was speaking to you, pal,' replied the Scotsman. 'And just so's you know, me an' Birrrdy here, are auld buddies.'

'McNulty, get over to the desk, now!' barked the arresting officer.

'Och, wheesht man!' Wee Malky waved him away. 'See him - Birrrdy Boy, there - he can really fly. We were doon at OT's before and he just kind of... took off. It was a total belter!' Suddenly, he was cantering around the reception area, arms outstretched, shouting at the top of his voice, 'I can fly too! I can fly, like a wee chookie birrd!'

The arresting officer attempted the interception on Wee Malky's third circuit. Spread-eagled across the giant Scotsman's shoulders, he was being twirled around, helicopter-style, at the precise moment PC Plimsoll came back into the reception area carrying a tray loaded with mugs of tea and an oversized diamond.

Caught by a flailing limb, the tray was smashed high into the air, tea splattering up the wall, the diamond sent bouncing off across the floor. Oblivious to the mayhem he'd just caused, Wee Malky thundered on until PC Plimsoll jumped on board. The extra burden was too much for the Glaswegian man-mountain and after a couple of faltering steps, one of his boots landed directly on top of the precious stone. There was an awful scrunching sound as his right foot slid forward, stranding the Scotsman in a near-perfect execution of the splits. The two policemen dived in and handcuffs were quickly snapped into place.

After collecting the bike from the lamppost at the back of Freddie's flat, they began the long walk home. Felix was embarrassed - humiliated, even - but at least the events following Wee Malky's tearful departure to the cells had shed some light on the chaos of the past few days. Felix's dad had eventually found the diamond, nestling in the grime beneath some plastic seating. He wiped it on his sleeve and handed it over to the policeman who produced a small magnifying eyepiece, switched on a desk-lamp, and invited them both to take a closer look.

Neither of them spotted it at first but once their eyes had got used to the lens, the tiny abrasions across any number of the stone's facets confirmed what PC Plimsoll had taken great delight in telling them - real diamonds don't get scratched or scuffed, they're too tough, so this one, while nice to look at, was clearly a fake.

After everything that had happened, Felix was mightily relieved to discover he didn't have a fortune in precious stones stuffed under the floorboards in his bedroom. The news that HB was alive, in rude health, and enjoying a holiday in the Spanish resort of Tossa de Mar, was even more welcome. That still left the puzzle of Scarface and Gold-tooth, but the more he thought about it the more he realised that it wasn't him they were after, or even the diamonds - it was Freddie. He didn't have a clue what his brother had done to wind them up, nor what the mysterious *Saydoss* connection was about, but it came as no real surprise. Freddie was such a monumental pain in the backside he'd have driven even the Pope to violence.

Trudging up Scundale Chase, his bike at his side, Felix, glanced over a shoulder at the dishevelled figure, shuffling along a few steps behind.

'Cheer up, Dad,' he said, feeling a bit guilty about their earlier conversation. 'Things will sort themselves out with Mum. I'm sure it's nothing to worry about.'

'Everything's fine between us,' snapped his dad. 'And you can tell your sister that, as well.'

'Oh. You looked a bit down and I thought…'

His dad groaned. 'It's the car, isn't it? Freddie's written it off and I've got to get to work in five hours. Mart will kill me if I don't turn up.'

Felix dumped his bike in the garden and they came in through the back door. The kitchen light was still on and he made straight for the fridge, his dad plonking himself down at the table to read the note that had been left for them.

Felix,

Back from hospital at 2.30 and gone straight to bed. Sorry I can't wait up for you love, but I'm on an early shift in the morning. I'm so proud of what you did for your brother - it was very brave.

Mum XXXX

PS: Brian, I've moved Florence in with me so Themba can have her own room. You can stay on the settee in the living room for the time being.

*

The next morning, he awoke with a start and lay in bed, staring at the ceiling. After a few minutes he sat up, pulling back the curtain to peek at the new day. He wanted to believe that the night before hadn't happened, that it had all been a bad dream. The oil stain on the driveway where the Fiesta was usually parked told a different story.

He grabbed his laptop from beneath his bed and switched it on, more out of habit than anything else. Nothing new on Facebook but when he checked his emails he was surprised to see a message from Jeremy Grindrod. Fearing more bad news he slumped back into his pillow and opened it up:

Felix,

Been mulling how best to support you in the new role and wanted to run this by you. We're stretched, resource-wise, following Brake's departure, so direction of travel is this: we keep you embedded in Frecklesall, as per our little chat, but I'm outsourcing your line-management to an old friend of mine - Hugo Mulholland from NewsKwest International. Hugo's a top guy and NKI are one of *the* cutting-edge agencies. Squirt everything you get in his direction and he'll give you all the advice and backup you need.

You remind me of myself when I was starting out, Felix: energy, passion and raw talent to burn - you're definitely going places. This is a great opportunity, so don't let me down.

Jerry Grindrod
Editor in Chief
The Lancastrian Bugler

'Energy, passion, raw talent…' He read the words over and over, scarcely able to believe his eyes. HB's long-distance wind-up had driven him to the brink, but now he was the one having the last laugh. Just the thought of running his copy through an international news agency was way beyond his wildest dreams. It was the perfect start to his career and would make a brilliant addition to his CV. He punched the air in celebration.

Mind buzzing, he headed downstairs to get some breakfast. His sister was already at the kitchen table.

'What went on last night?' she asked, looking up from her iPad. 'Mum wouldn't say.'

Felix groaned inwardly. With his head crammed full of a fast-track route to a top job with a national broadsheet, he'd completely forgotten about Flo and the grilling she was duty bound to give him. 'Well…' he began. 'I went to Fred's gig - which was lame by the way - and we were heading home along Marine Drive when he lost control and ended up driving the car into the sea.'

'So you were with him when it happened?'

'Not quite. I got out just before.'

'Why did you do that?'

'I needed a wee - y'know those bushes by the lido?'

His sister screwed up her face. 'Gross! But why would Freddie set off without you? And going *down* Marine Drive towards the Prom takes you away from our house–' She was cut off, mid-sentence, as the kitchen door opened and suddenly, everything got a lot more complicated.

She was tall, probably in her early twenties - long-limbed, graceful, and black. Her face was stunning - lit by a brilliant smile and fabulous cheekbones, it was framed by a stylish, short-cropped afro. But it was the deep, warm, pools of her eyes that really took his breath away.

The same eyes.

The smile remained frozen on Felix's face as their guest extracted herself from Flo's embrace. And then she was holding a hand out towards him.

'Themba!' shrieked Flo, bouncing up and down with excitement. 'How are you? Mum and Dad are out at work so you've got me to keep you company. Oh, and this is my other brother, Felix.' She jabbed an elbow into his ribs. 'Felix… wake up, you idiot!'

8

Felix had experienced lots of awkward moments over the course of his sixteen and a bit years, but that morning's encounter with his brother's heroic rescuer was up there with the best of them. He'd eventually come-to, offering his thanks and listening to their guest's story in a state of barely concealed torment. Her name was Themba Kigelle and she was a student - London based - visiting because she'd read about Frecklesall's City of Culture bid and thought it sounded interesting. She'd not long arrived in town and had been looking for somewhere to stay when she'd witnessed the Fiesta's dramatic plunge. Being a strong swimmer, she didn't think twice.

Flo was in raptures and he should have been too. This woman had risked her life to save his halfwit brother, but try as he might he couldn't get past their previous encounter - the one that had ended so abruptly on platform six at Preston station, just a few days earlier. Behind the fixed smile his mind was doing somersaults, and lurking in the back of his head was the realisation that the truth might not now be anything like as convenient as the explanation he'd cobbled together for himself. As for Themba, either she'd forgotten about their earlier meeting or she was a brilliant liar. Neither option made him feel particularly comfortable.

He headed up to his bedroom, knowing that coincidences like this didn't happen in real life. Themba was in town for a reason and he was certain it had nothing to do with Frecklesall's non-existent cultural offering. His laptop was still switched on and, desperate to take his mind off the nightmare unfolding downstairs, he tapped in a NewsKwest International Google search. There were dozens of links and he settled for the official website with its swish, high-tech graphics and images of NKI's gleaming LA headquarters. Navigating his way to the profile of Senior Investigative Correspondent, Hugo Mulholland, he found himself gasping in amazement.

Mulholland couldn't have been more than thirty-five but his record was stunning. Embedded with special services in Iraq and Afghanistan, he'd also led on countless high-profile domestic stories. With his Next Catalogue looks, winning smile and sharp suit, Felix couldn't begin to imagine why NKI's top man would be interested in what was going on in a dump like Frecklesall, let alone helping out a useless trainee reporter whose only published work had turned out to be complete and utter rubbish.

He jumped into his crumpled chinos from the night before and pulled on a clean T-shirt, grabbing his jacket and mobile. The phone had been charging overnight but he was completely out of credit. Deciding that a stroll into town to top up his card would help clear his head, he tip-toed down the stairs and out through the front door. He made it half way along Scundale Chase before realising he had company.

'Excuse me, Felix,' Themba said, slightly out of breath. 'I would like to walk with you, please.'

He turned, trying to think of a nice way of telling her to mind her own business but instead, found himself grinning like an idiot. Outside, in the morning sunshine, she looked even lovelier than before.

'Not a problem!' he replied, brightly.

They strolled along together, Felix doing his best to calm down.

'It is very nice to see you again, Felix,' Themba began. 'I am sure you remember our first meeting?'

He gave a wry laugh. 'I won't be forgetting that day in a hurry. Everything's been totally mental since then.'

'Oh, I hope this is not my fault. When I discovered I had picked up your bag, I felt very bad.'

'It's not been great for me either, to be honest. Do you still have it?'

'No, I am sorry - I mislaid it soon after we met,' she replied. 'I will pay for a new one, and the contents of course. You must tell me how much I owe you.'

Felix knew that the old ice-cream tub with the mouldy remains of the day's lunch and a copy of that evening's *Bugler* were hardly going to set the compensation lawyers drooling, but she wasn't to know.

'No worries,' he said. 'It's not important.'

'And my bag?' she asked, casually. 'Is it still in your possession?'

'Yes, as it happens.' He pictured the blue rucksack with the ripped lining, now stuffed into the bottom of his wardrobe

'And the contents - do they remain intact and undisturbed?'

'Yeah. Absolutely,' he replied, surprised by her choice of words. 'I had a bit of a poke around to try to find a contact number but I put everything back where I found it. I even thought about taking it in to the police.'

He paused, waiting for a reaction, but she was giving nothing away. 'To be honest, I was worried about you, Themba. When those guys grabbed you, I didn't have a clue what was going on.'

She fixed him with her beautiful eyes. 'I owe you an explanation. We must find somewhere to talk.'

They continued into town, Felix stopping off at the Spar and narrowly avoiding an audience with his mum as he paid for the phone top-up. As usual, it wasn't a great investment - his network's mobile signal was dodgy at the best of times and on this particular morning, non-existent. After trying a few times he gave up, shoving the phone back into his jacket pocket as they made their way down to the Prom.

The sight of the ancient orange Fiesta balanced precariously on its nose, midway between the sea wall and the incoming tide, dominated the scabby stretch of sand. A handful of day-trippers had gathered outside the cordoned-off area to get a closer look.

'I bet they think it's some kind of art installation for the culture bid,' said Felix, laughing. 'Hey, how about a photo - heroic rescuer with stricken car? It'll set off my piece, perfectly.'

Themba shook her head. 'I am sorry, that is not a possibility.'

'But it's such a great story - just the sort of thing the *Bugler* readers would be interested in.'

'No photographs. And if you do decide to write about this, you will make no mention of my name.'

Felix was surprised. All he knew was that if he'd been the hero of the hour, he'd have milked it for all it was worth, even if it was only Freddie who'd been saved.

*

'No wonder you ditched Dannii last night,' Bernie said, from behind the ketchup bottle on the corner table in the Full Monty Café. 'That Themba's a top bird!'

Felix followed his friend's gaze and found himself gawping at the shapely figure of the stunning young woman who was getting the teas in at the counter. Just at that moment, she turned and smiled. They both waved back, sheepishly.

'Stop drooling,' hissed Felix. 'You know it's not like that.'

Bernie smirked. 'Well if you're not interested, you won't mind if I give it a go.'

Felix grabbed a fistful of sweatshirt and hauled him across the table. 'In case you've forgotten, she saved my stupid brother's life last night. Disappointing, I know, but it means we owe her. The last thing she needs right now is a little squirt like you hassling her.'

'Hey, chill out, reverend!' Bernie said, laughing. 'I can't help the effect I have on women, can I? Did you see the way she was looking at me just then?'

'Maybe I should mention it to Zoe, next time I see her.'

Bernie sat back in his chair looking worried. 'You… you wouldn't do that, would you?'

Felix chuckled. 'Dunno, mate - I'll have to think about it… Tell you what, why not come around to ours this evening? We could do with catching up. Some really crazy things have been going on.'

His friend pushed back from the table. 'Sorry mate, I'm out with the girls tonight. Hey, you should join us - Dannii'll be there.'

Felix felt his face flush. 'I can't - I'm kind of busy.'

'This isn't about last night, is it? Only, I talked to her and she's totally cool with the whole thing. She actually said she'd like to meet up with you again - reckons you're quite sweet.'

'Yeah, right. Half the problem was you telling her me and Naz were in that boy band.'

Bernie grinned. 'Sorry, it was the shirts. I couldn't help myself.'

'Well, thanks but no thanks. I've got loads on at the moment, what with the *Bugler* job and minding Themba, and everything.'

'Minding Themba...' Bernie said, wistfully. 'Nice work if you can get it, eh?'

Felix shooed him away and his friend turned at the door to blow Themba a kiss as she headed back to the table.

'Just ignore him,' Felix said, reaching for his jacket, which was slung over the back of the chair. 'Can I pay for the teas?'

'No, it is the least I can do,' she replied. 'We will speak now but it must be in the strictest confidence. When I tell you my story, you will understand.'

She leant forward across the table. Up close like this, he found it extremely difficult to concentrate.

'You asked me about those men at the station,' she began in a low voice. 'The truth is, they had been following me for some time. They are from your immigration police.'

He nearly fell off his chair. 'What?'

'The Border Force, I think it is called.'

'What did they want with you?'

'I have outstayed my welcome in your country. They intend to deport me - to send me home.'

Felix thought back to that afternoon at the station - the dark suits, the no-nonsense haircuts - he'd never met anyone from the Border Force before but guessed that's what they might look like.

'After the arrest, they took me to a detention centre for questioning,' she continued. 'Fortunately, I was able to escape.'

'So you're on the run?' He said it as casually as he could, but didn't quite manage to conceal the excitement in his voice. 'But why would they want to throw you out of the country?'

Themba took a deep breath. 'My home - my *real* home - is in Lesotho.'

He looked at her, blankly.

'It is a small African nation state - landlocked and completely surrounded by South Africa. My parents died when I was young, so I was brought up by my grandfather. When I was a little girl he used to tell me stories about his time in London and how, when I grew up, he would send me to England to complete my studies. Many years later, when I secured a place at the School of Law in the University of London, he was extremely proud.'

'Your grandfather - is he the old man in that black and white photo from your wallet - the guy in the fancy outfit?'

Themba laughed. 'Indeed that is him, and the "fancy outfit" you talk of is traditional dress for a tribal chief.'

'Blimey!'

'Do not be so surprised. The tribal system still plays an important role in many parts of African society. It is based on tradition, honour and respect - principles that have remained unchanged for centuries. You must appreciate that my grandfather is both an honourable and highly respected man, which in many ways makes my problem worse.'

'So, what happened then?'

She hesitated for a moment, her eyes beginning to well up. Felix reached across to offer her a paper napkin from the table.

'Thank you,' she said, dabbing her tears. 'Things started to go wrong after the second year of my studies, when I failed my examinations.'

'It happens to the best of us,' he sympathised. 'Our Fred's made a career out of it.'

'My visa was dependent on the successful completion of my degree. Once I lost my university place I had no right to remain in the UK and should have returned home, immediately.'

'So why didn't you, then? Oh… not that you should have. I mean, if you hadn't been around last night, God knows what would have happened.'

'I knew the humiliation my failure would cause my grandfather, so I decided not tell him,' she replied. 'I thought that, perhaps, I could enrol on another course and cover things up, but in reality I was putting off the moment. Now a year has passed and it is too late.'

'You saved Fred's life. We could write to your granddad telling him what happened. Surely he'd be proud of what you did, whatever else has gone on?'

'It is more complicated than that,' she said, her eyes downcast. 'I fear I may have revealed too much, already. All I ask is that you respect the confidentiality of this conversation and allow me to remain with your family until things have calmed down a little. Sooner or later I must tell my grandfather the truth. I'm sure you agree that this will be easier if I am not in prison, awaiting deportation, when the conversation takes place.'

Wally Nockles, the Full Monty's owner, sidled up to the table. In his mid-fifties, with his bony frame, greasy comb-over and weaselly face, he was not the best advert for his establishment's fine dining experience. He did like to gossip, though.

'Oreet, Felix, lad,' Wally greeted him with a thin smile.

Felix grunted, hoping he'd take the hint and clear off. No such luck.

'It's just that we had a couple of likely lads in 'ere yesterday, askin' after your Freddie,' Wally continued. 'Foreigners, I reckon.' He turned to Themba. 'No disrespect, love. Might have lost a bit in the translation, but they wanted his address.'

'What did you tell them?' Felix asked.

'Nowt!' Wally replied. 'I didn't like the look of 'em at all.'

'That's probably for the best.'

'So what's he been up to this time?'

'Haven't got a clue, Wally, but thanks for letting me know.'

'That's your dad's car out on the beach, isn't it?' the café owner asked, smirking.

After waving him away, Felix made his excuses and headed for the toilet. Sitting in the grubby cubicle he allowed himself a moment of self-congratulation. He was well on the way to gaining Themba's trust and she was beginning to open up to him. All he needed to do now was steer the conversation towards the diamonds and things were bound to start falling into place. He felt the slightest pang of guilt - she'd saved his brother's life, after all - but this was his big chance. If he was going to make a good first impression with Hugo Mulholland he needed to get across the diamond story and feed it through to the NKI correspondent with as few loose ends as possible.

He shuffled back into the café, still preoccupied with how best to nudge the conversation in the right direction. Themba had something in her hand and it was only as he got closer that he realised what it was. It looked like the back had come off his mobile and she was in the process of a hasty reassembly job. She fixed him with a penetrating glare.

'I have some questions,' she said, in a tone that sent a chill down his spine. 'Who is this man, HB? And what is this package you are holding for him?'

Bloody mobiles - one minute they're dead as a dodo, the next, they spring back into life, generally at the most inconvenient of moments. With the whole deception spelt out across the screen, there was no way he could deny it. There were texts from Naz and Bernie, from earlier that morning, but Themba had found HB's message from a couple of days earlier - the one he hadn't been able to read because his phone had been glued to the carpet in Freddie's flat.

HB's instructions had been crystal clear - Felix was to meet him at the furthest seafront shelter at the north end of the Prom, and he was to bring the 'package'. If that wasn't damning enough, Themba followed up by playing him a wailing voicemail from his ex-boss, bemoaning his non-appearance. If Felix hadn't known that HB was conducting a long-distance wind-up from a Mediterranean sun lounger, he'd have been straight round to the police.

Sadly, Themba wasn't buying his explanation. After dragging him out of the café, she frog-marched him down to the Prom, rounding on him as soon as they got there.

'You people are all the same,' she said. 'You act as if you are concerned for the welfare of others, yet all the time you are plotting - trying to gain advantage. I would not be surprised to see the immigration police here, right now. You were probably calling them when you were in the conveniences.'

'How could I?' he replied indignantly. 'You had my phone, didn't you? Anyway, what were you doing reading my texts and listening to my messages?'

She ignored his question. 'I have been foolish to trust you, so now it is time for the truth. When I asked before, you said my bag was undisturbed - that everything was still intact and in place. This is a lie. Your friend HB mentions a "package". I believe you have removed this from my bag. Tell me what it contained.'

'Why do you need to ask? It's your bag - surely you already know what's in it?'

She fixed him with a cold, hard stare. 'You are assuming it belongs to me.'

A look of confusion spread across Felix's face.

'Has it occurred to you,' she continued, 'that I might have been acting as a courier, transporting the bag and its contents on behalf of another person?'

Suddenly, his mouth felt very dry. 'Well… no, but if that really was the case you'd be pretty useless at your job. Picking up the wrong bag at the station wasn't the smartest of career moves, was it?' It was a cheap shot but all he could think of.

'You are wrong, Felix,' she replied. 'You are wrong, because I picked up the *right* bag.'

9

'They were closing in,' said Themba. 'I was left with no choice.'

Felix's head was in a spin. 'You mean, you switched bags on purpose?'

'Our rucksacks looked similar, so yes - it was a deliberate act. It was a most fortunate coincidence that I arrived in Frecklesall at the same time as your brother's accident, but my real purpose in coming here was to find you, or more specifically, to find my bag.'

They continued their walk along the Prom, ending up on a bench in one of the seafront rain shelters overlooking the beach.

'So I will ask you again, and you will give me an honest answer this time,' she continued. 'Do you still have my bag?'

'I do, really. Like I told you, I've got it at home and I didn't–'

She put a finger to her lips. 'Then it is of vital importance that you understand the danger you now face. The man I have been working for, the man who owns the bag and its contents, is a ruthless criminal going by the name of Harry Carey. He became aware of my illegal status and has been blackmailing me - forcing me to work for him as a courier.'

'That's awful.'

She waved away his sympathy. 'Do you still have my bike?'

He nodded, although he was pretty sure that if the question of ownership came up in a court of law it would now be more accurate to describe it as *his* bike.

'That is good because I owe it my life,' she said. 'Some day, when this is over, I will tell you that story.'

Felix was dying to find out more, but he had to stay focussed on the diamonds. 'What kind of things did this Harry guy make you deliver?' he asked.

'I think you already know that.'

He shrugged. 'Sorry, but–'

'You would not play such games if you had met him!' Glancing around to check no one was eavesdropping, she continued in a low voice. 'Harry Carey is a vicious and dangerous man. I have seen him do the most *terrible* things.' Her emphasis of the word sent a shiver down Felix's spine. 'Two weeks ago, he sent me to a pick-up in south London. I was too afraid to ask him what was in the package - all that mattered was that when I brought it to him, he was very happy. He told me the contents were of immense value - so much so that once I had completed the onward delivery to his associates, it would conclude his last ever deal in this country. At that point he would be leaving the UK and my obligation towards him would finally be at an end.

'A few days later he gave me the bag, with the package sewn into its lining. The delivery address was in Belfast, Northern Ireland. I asked him what I was carrying but he would not say. He did give me a warning, though. He said that if the lining of the bag became disturbed in any way, or if I failed to make the drop-off, I would be killed.'

Felix gasped.

'I should have completed the job the day before yesterday,' she added. 'I have tried to call Harry to offer an explanation but he is not answering his phone.'

'You... you didn't leave a message saying where you were, did you?' Felix asked, nervously.

Themba ignored his question. 'We are both in danger. Now that you know the truth, will you help me?'

His gut instinct was to offer up an apology and run for his life, but he knew his future career depended on seeing this through. 'OK,' he replied. 'What do you want me to do?'

'I need the bag, and the package of course. With your assistance I may still be able to get across to Belfast and complete the delivery.'

'No way! It's too dangerous. You've got to report this to the police.'

She looked him straight in the eye. 'You do have them, don't you? If you have sold them it would mean the end for us both. There can be no hiding place.'

'What are you talking about?'

'The drugs, you fool! Where are they? Tell me, now!'

Felix reached into the pocket of his chinos, feeling the fake diamond still nestling there from the night before. 'There are no drugs, Themba,' he said, slowly opening his hand. 'Just six of these.'

Her eyes widened in amazement. 'That is so beautiful... It must be priceless!' She grabbed the stone and held it up to the light. 'My God, it is no wonder the pick-up was so hazardous. Do you still have them all?'

'Well, sort of. Our Fred's got one - at least he did up until his accident last night.'

'I have never seen anything so perfect... so pure,' she said, breathlessly.

'Actually, when I showed it to the police, they threatened to arrest me for wasting their time.'

Themba looked stunned.

'After the accident, me and my dad ended up at the police station,' he continued. 'I was sure the diamonds were connected to what had gone on but they just didn't seem that interested. I had that one on me and they checked it out. There are these tiny scratches on one end - difficult to see without one of those magnifying eyepieces, but believe me, that stone is a fake. I reckon they're all fakes.' He paused, waiting for the news to sink in. 'So how about *you* telling *me* what this is all about, Themba?'

'This is not possible,' she said, her voice tensing. 'One person has already died. And Harry's reaction when I brought the package to him was… remarkable. He is not a man who smiles easily - not unless he is in the process of inflicting pain on someone else.'

'Maybe Harry did the switch,' said Felix. 'Maybe he's pocketed the originals and sold you down the river.' The breath was knocked out of him as he was slammed up against the wall. 'S…S…Steady on, Themba!' he gasped. 'I was only trying to help.'

'Or maybe it is *you* who has sold *me* down this river,' she snarled. 'My bag has been in your possession for many days now - you could easily have had replicas manufactured. This HB - is he your *fence*? Is he the intermediary who will sell the real diamonds and cut you in on the proceeds?'

'Themba, please - you're frightening me. Think about it - what would someone like me be doing with a stash of precious gemstones worth thousands of pounds? And if I had done the switch - which I haven't, by the way - why would me and Fred be wandering around town with the fakes in our pockets? And why would I try to hand mine in to the police?'

She loosened her grip, allowing him to slump back onto the bench.

'You do believe me, don't you?' he asked.

She shrugged. 'What *I* believe is unimportant, Felix. The fact is, the real diamonds are missing and *they* will be coming here to find them, if they are not here already.'

'But this is Frecklesall! It's beyond the back of beyond. It's like the land that time forgot!'

'So what was that ugly man talking about in the café, earlier?' she asked. 'Who are these "foreigners", so keen to find your brother? And what was it that made him drive his car into the sea last night?'

Felix sensed chasms of uncertainty opening up before him. 'It's… it's Fred isn't it?' he blustered. 'He'll have done something to wind them up - it's just the way he is. It can't be to do with the diamonds.'

Themba shook her head.

'It's true!' he continued. 'If they'd found out about this from HB and his lame *Braking News* website, it's me they'd be after, not my stupid brother. I've actually spoken to them and he's the one they're looking for. Oh, and there's that *Saydoss* thing, whatever the hell that is.'

He knew the instant the word came from his lips that he'd said too much.

'You must tell me everything,' she said calmly, her expression making it absolutely clear it was time to come clean.

She listened in silence as he ran through the edited highlights of his nightmare week, although he steered clear of his connection to Hugo Mulholland and NewsKwest International. There was still the chance of a cracking story to write up from this, after all. When he explained how Freddie had raided the diamond haul beneath his bed to cobble together a set of mega-earrings for the OT's gig, he heard a sharp intake of breath.

'So he is the one,' said Themba.

'What do you mean?'

'You may have shown the diamonds to others but only your brother knows of their hiding place.'

'Come on Themba, you've met him!' pleaded Felix. 'He's way too thick to pull off a stunt like this.'

'I must talk with him. At the very least he should know of the danger he now faces. As for your friend HB, I fear it may already be too late.'

'He's no friend of mine. Anyway, he's off on his jollies - the police told me that, so it must be true.'

Themba gave a hollow laugh. 'Believe what you wish, Felix, but I would have expected more from a journalist.'

'Why would they lie to me? Anyway, they love their wind-ups in the *Bugler* newsroom. Getting him to send me those texts and voicemails from his holidays is a classic.'

'You do not talk of this HB as someone who commands your respect. Maybe we should leave him to his fate - to finish off his break, or not. It is unimportant to me, either way.'

Left with the cold, stark choice, and the alarm bells now clanging noisily in his head, Felix knew he couldn't let it lie.

A couple of hours later, Felix was scanning the handful of 1960s-built, maisonette blocks on the edge of the council estate, wondering how he'd got himself into such a mess. He hadn't wanted to come here, to the concrete brutalism of Preston's eastern suburbs - hadn't even realised that this was where HB lived - but once he'd handed over his ex-boss's *Braking News* business card there could be no turning back. He'd never seen a smartphone quite like the one Themba had pulled from her pocket, and he'd certainly never come across an app that could transform a website reference into a postal address at the touch of a button. He'd tried to look over her shoulder as the high-tech handset had worked its magic, ending up with a clip around the ear for his troubles.

They walked along the footpath carved into the scabby, low-level planting that surrounded Sir Tom Finney Heights, Themba striding on with purpose, her reluctant companion mooching along behind. She stopped to look at the list of residents on the intercom display next to the block's main door, and beckoned him closer.

Bloody Hell!

Flat 12: Mr Howard Brake – C.E.O.
Braking News Corporation (Global) Ltd

They tried the door and rang the intercom but there was no response. And then an elderly lady, weighed down with some huge shopping bags, came struggling along the footpath. Themba stepped forward, armed with a charming smile.

'Excuse me madam. We are visiting our dear friend, Mr Howard Brake. He lives on the second floor but the intercom does not appear to be working. Would you be so kind as to let us in?'

The old lady was only about four-foot-eight, her prune-like face creased with the deep-set wrinkles of a career smoker. 'Brake, eh?' she replied, in a deep, gravelly voice. 'Is he that idiot what works for the *Bugler*?'

Felix's smirk was cut short by a stern look from his companion. 'That'll be Howard!' he replied brightly.

'He's not home,' the woman said. 'I bumped into him t'other day, with a couple of his pals. He said he were off on his 'olidays.'

Felix breathed a sigh of relief. 'Great. Thanks for clearing that up. I told my... err... my girlfriend here that he was taking a break but she didn't believe me.'

Themba intervened. 'Madam, please - did you notice anything unusual when you spoke to him?'

'Spain - that were it,' the woman replied. 'It's funny because he never normally talks to me, the nowty bugger. And as for his pals, they didn't look like they needed any more sunshine.'

'Why is that?' Themba asked.

'They already had these lovely tans. If they were any browner they'd have been your colour, love.'

A couple of minutes later, Felix dumped the shopping bags outside the old lady's third-floor flat and they slipped down the stairs to HB's front door. Themba pressed an ear to the chipped turquoise paintwork, listening intently.

Felix crouched behind the bannisters, a few steps up on the half-landing, watching as she leaned forward to knock on the door. When a second knock went unanswered, he drifted down to join her and was about to suggest they call it a day when he saw her pull something from her pocket. He thought it was a pen-knife at first but when she flicked it open, the blade turned out to be what looked like an oddly shaped corkscrew. Before he could stop her, she was poking it into the lock.

'What are you doing?' he asked. 'You can't break in, it's against the law.'

Themba ignored his protests. 'Do you have a credit card?'

He pulled out his wallet and began flicking through its contents. 'Let's see now - American Express Platinum, Diners Club International, Barclaycard? Take your pick!'

Ignoring the gag, she snatched the wallet from his hand.

'Hey, that's mine!' He tried a half-hearted grab but she shielded it from his reach.

'This will have to do,' she muttered, her face cracking into a smile as she clocked the frizzle-haired photo on his bus pass.

'It was a few weeks ago, before I got the haircut for the *Bugler* job,' he said defensively.

'You should grow it like that again,' she remarked, sliding the card down the edge of the door. 'It hides much of your face, which in my opinion is a considerable improvement.'

Nudging the door open, she slipped inside. Felix hesitated, dreading to think what they might find in there. After taking a few deep breaths and checking to make sure the coast was clear, he followed on.

They'd walked into a disaster zone. Furniture had been upended, cupboards and drawers emptied onto the floor, packets of food ripped open, their contents strewn about the place. And there was a terrible smell - a putrid, gagging stink which caught in the back of Felix's throat. He stood in the doorway, knowing all too well that this did not look like the home of someone who'd popped off on their summer holidays for a fortnight - not unless they'd booked the Bash Street Kids to give the place a makeover while they were away.

The main room was a bleak space with a low ceiling and peeling orange wallpaper. It was divided between an open kitchen and a living area, dimly lit by a single naked bulb. Any doubts Felix might have had over whether this really was his former boss's home, disappeared the moment he spotted the poster on the wall above the TV. The Blu Tack had come unstuck from one corner, leaving it flapping down. He walked over and pressed it back into place.

The futuristic shot of the planet had HB's grinning face photo-shopped into its midst. The Saturn-like rings encircling the globe contained the cheesiest of mission statements:

The Braking News Corporation
Because the Global Village Never Sleeps

'What a plonker!' exclaimed Felix.

'And still you believe he is on holiday?' asked Themba.

'Maybe the place got burgled while he's been away,' Felix mumbled as he wandered through to the bedroom, where if anything, the mess and the smell were even worse.

'They have torn this flat apart,' she said. 'We both know the reason why.'

The sound of jangling coat-hangers coming from the wardrobe at the end of the bedroom, stopped him dead in his tracks.

Someone was in there.

Felix scrambled for cover behind HB's bed. Moments later, Themba appeared at the door and within three strides was pressed against the wall beside the wardrobe, armed with a broken chair leg. He could see the calm focus in her eyes. It was as if she'd been in this kind of situation before and knew exactly what to do.

The seconds crawled by. With his gangling frame scrunched into a defensive ball, his back was starting to ache and he used the cover of further coat-hanger jangling to change his body position. Midway through manoeuvring onto his hands and knees, he caught the sound of creaking hinges and looked up to check what was going on. Themba had eased the wardrobe door open and was poised to strike, the chair leg held high over her head like an executioner's axe.

A banshee-like shriek filled the room and suddenly, a blurred black shape was arrowing towards him. He'd barely made it to his feet when the thing slammed into his chest. Staggering from the impact, he only just managed to clamp his hands around its half-starved body.

Held at arms' length, fingers digging into its ribs, the furious animal hissed and spat, its claws slashing wildly. Felix lost his balance, throwing up his arms and launching the thing over his head as he toppled backwards. Legs flailing, the creature flew through the bedroom doorway before crash-landing onto the upturned settee in the lounge.

The bedraggled feline staggered to its paws, hissed venomously, then shot out through the half-open front door.

Felix lay groaning on the floor, feeling like he'd been flattened by a steamroller.

Themba offered him a wry smile. 'You must be sure to report this matter to the authorities. For your friend to go away on holiday and leave his cat locked in the wardrobe is animal cruelty of the worst kind.'

'Alright, I get it,' he said, struggling to his feet and examining the scratches on his forearms, which were now beginning to sting. 'Can you give me a minute? I need to clean these up.'

He headed for the bathroom while Themba went through into the lounge to close the front door. After putting the plug in the wash hand basin, he turned on the hot tap, jumping back as scalding water came spluttering out. She was right, of course - apart from everything else they'd seen, there was no way HB would have left the water bubbling away like this if he'd been off on a planned break. After topping the level up from the cold tap, he leant forward to wash his forearms.

Ouch!

The bathroom mirror was fogging with condensation and he shook down the sleeve of his sweatshirt to wipe it clear. Something made him stop, just centimetres from the glass.

The message began to materialise from the left side of the mirror, his ex-boss's spidery scrawl instantly recognisable - spindly capitals, dashed out with a greasy fingertip.

He yelped at the knock on the bathroom door.

'Felix!' Themba shouted through. 'Hurry, please - we must leave this place, immediately.'

His response was instinctive. 'Hold on, Themba, I'm nearly done!' He pulled out the plug and turned the hot tap full-on, all the time concentrating on the words, still forming in front of his eyes.

HELP ME

CALL POLICE

DIAMO

COL

She was hammering on the door now. 'Is everything alright in there, Felix?'

Reaching across to flush the toilet he did his best to memorise the message materialising just inches from his nose. And then the door banged open and she was standing directly in front of him.

'Felix, we have to leave!'

'That cat nearly killed me!' he complained, wafting a forearm in her face while managing to wipe the mirror clear with a sweep of his free hand. 'I should probably go to hospital for a rabies jab.'

It was obvious that her look of concern had nothing to do with his injuries.

'What's your problem?' he asked, angrily.

'Actually, it is *our* problem,' she replied. 'This apartment is being watched. And now they are coming for us. We must find another route to exit the building.'

'But there's only one staircase.'

They turned together, startled by the unmistakable sounds of the front door being kicked in.

10

Themba made it look easy, climbing out the bathroom window and inching along the narrow ledge which ran above the concrete panelling, before shimmying down a handily placed drainpipe. Felix tried to follow but ended up losing his grip, and this time there weren't a dozen *Metal Mania* fans waiting to break his fall. After hauling him to his feet, she set off, leaving him with little choice but to hobble after her.

The journey home was just as traumatic. They avoided the railway station, opting instead to jump on a north-bound bus. Felix was a nervous wreck, constantly checking out his fellow passengers and insisting on hiding behind a newspaper when they had to wait twenty minutes for a connection at Garstang. It was after six by the time they returned to Scundale Chase.

'Not a word of what has happened today,' Themba said, at the back door. 'You must go inside and talk to your family. You have been absent for a long time - they may be concerned.'

Chance would be a fine thing.

He wandered into the lounge and was confronted by the awful sight of his brother, sprawled across the settee in his bathrobe, holding forth on his favourite subject - himself. Their mum, Flo, Doreen, and even Mrs Garlick, the old lady from next door, were gathered around hanging on his every word.

'I gotta tell you, ladies, this whole thing has been a game-changer for me,' said Freddie. 'I should have been freaking out down there but it was, like, totally surreal. In the end I just sat back and thought: this is it FoF, dude - stairway to heaven time.'

Felix was distracted by the sound of his mum sniffling.

'But then I'm seeing this flashing light and I'm reaching out towards it,' Freddie continued. 'Suddenly I'm thinking - hey, Freddie... you're young, you're good-looking, and you've still got so much to give to this crazy world of ours! Then I'm hearing this voice in my head saying, "Turn again Dick Whittington! Turn again!" Next up, I'm eyeballing this awesome-looking chick, banging on the car window.'

'It sounds like a classic near-death experience, Freddie,' Flo intervened. 'Some say it's a state of mind brought on by extreme trauma, although others give it a more spiritual significance.'

Felix thought brain damage was the most likely explanation, but Mrs Garlick from next door had her own view.

'It's a miracle!' she exclaimed. 'The good Lord has chosen to spare you, Freddie. We must report this to the Vatican, immediately!'

Freddie looked at her, blankly.

'The vision at the window,' she continued, tears welling in her eyes. 'Would you describe it as a "divine intervention"?'

Freddie looked puzzled for a moment, and then his face cracked into a broad grin. 'Have you seen her, Mrs

G?' he replied, rubbing his hands together. '"Divine" is an understatement - that girl's a total fox!'

His mum leant forward and whispered something in his ear.

'Oh. Sorry,' he mumbled, crossing himself with a half-eaten cheese and pickle sandwich. 'Total respect to the Big Guy upstairs - he was certainly lookin' out for yours truly when the chips were down.'

'Praise the Lord!' Mrs Garlick shrieked.

'Now, where was I? Ah yes - so I'm checking out this babe swimming around the car in her scanties and all I can think is, she must be a mermaid from the Lost City of Atlantis or somesuch. But she can't be, obvs, 'cos she's still wearing her top and most mermaids ain't exactly backwards at coming forwards in that particular department, if you catch my drift. Then she's yankin' on the door handle and–'

Freddie's dramatic monologue was interrupted by a spontaneous round of applause. He sat back in the settee, a satisfied expression on his face.

'Why thank you ladies, it is quite a story.'

'We weren't clapping you, you moron,' Doreen snapped. 'It's this young lady here who's the real hero.' She pointed towards the slim figure waiting at the door. 'Don't stand there like cheese at fourpence, Themba love. Get yourself in here, now!'

'Freddie's been telling us about the rescue,' his mum added. 'We're all *so* grateful. You must stay with us for as long as you like.'

Freddie sprang from the settee. 'Right on! Round these parts, if you save someone's life, it's like this unbreakable bond - a debt that lasts forever. So now my job is to find a really *special* way of saying thank you.'

Themba sidestepped his lunge, leaving him puckering into thin air. 'Please, I am only happy that I was able to help,' she said, shyly. 'Besides, I know that Felix would have rescued his brother had I not been there. He was the brave one.'

Freddie snorted.

'But your offer is extremely generous, Mrs Haythornthwaite,' she continued. 'I would be honoured to remain here with your family for a few days, if it is not too much of an inconvenience.'

After another round of applause Felix's mum began shooing everyone out of the lounge. 'We'll leave you in peace now, Freddie love, but if you need anything just say the word.'

He dived back onto the settee, arming himself with the TV remote. 'Thanks Mum - a mug of tea and some chocolate biscuits would be spot on. And if you could sub me, say, thirty quid? There's this *kung-fu* special on at Rick Shaw's in Slaidforth. I was thinking Themba and me could really use some time together after everything we've been through.'

Felix left them to it and made his way up to his room. Freddie was heading for a fall if he thought he was going to work his charms on Themba, but that wasn't his problem. He kicked off his shoes and lay on the bed, struggling to come to terms with what had happened. He was petrified - in mortal danger - and would have liked nothing better than to curl up into a ball in the corner of his room in the hope that all the bad stuff might magically disappear. But he couldn't do that. Niggling away, somewhere in the cobwebbed recesses of his brain, the journalist within him was telling him there was work to do - that he'd stumbled onto something really big. Taking a deep breath, he closed his eyes, and started scrolling back through the events of the day.

Twenty minutes later, there was one thing that stuck in his head, one thing that kept slapping him around the chops like the tail of a freshly landed mackerel - the mirror message at HB's flat, and one word in particular:

COLINAN..

His eyes strayed towards the Sir Hubert Montague-Dunk *Bugler* article, now pinned to the wall behind his desk.

And then it hit him - Sir Hubert's real name was Colin - *Colin Anderton*! Surely that was the name the scrawl on the mirror would have spelt out if there'd been enough time for the whole message to materialise. Doreen said Anderton had tried all sorts of scams and cons back in the day - distraction, sleight of hand - the kind of stuff Felix had seen magicians do on the telly, countless times. And the old boy had had every chance to make the switch when he'd taken the bag out on his boat. He still couldn't see a connection to the mysterious *Saydoss* word, but it was a start, and if he kept working at it, he was pretty sure things would begin to fall into place.

His train of thought was rudely interrupted by Freddie diving into the room to raid the wardrobe. Wriggling into a pair of jeans, he emptied half a can of Rampant body spray into his T-shirt before dashing out with a gleeful shout of, 'Game on, Bro!'

Felix was about to warn him when his mobile rang. He picked up the call.

'I've been texting you all afternoon. Why haven't you called me back?' Naz said, sounding deadly serious.

Felix checked the alerts on his phone. 'Sorry mate, it must be the signal. I haven't had a message from you, or anyone else for that matter. What's up?'

'It's just that we had this DVD returned at the shop earlier today.'

'Congratulations!'

'Hear me out, will you? It was *The Exorcist*. We've only got the one copy and seeing as Freddie's flat's still in lockdown, I'd already told my dad it would be late coming back.'

'Oh. So who brought it in?' asked Felix, the hairs pricking up on the back of his neck.

'My dad spoke to them but from what he told me, I'm pretty sure it was those guys who tried to kidnap you. One of them had this big scar on his face. Their English was useless, but they were asking after your brother. Don't worry - my dad didn't tell them anything. In the end, they left him this card and said that if he saw Freddie, he should call them because a mutual friend was at death's door and they wanted to let him know.'

'Oh my God, do you think that could be HB?'

'I'm not sure... but this is all getting a bit heavy if you ask me. You really need to tell your brother what's been going on. You need to warn him... Felix...? Are you there?'

Naz was talking to himself. Felix had dropped his phone to the floor and was already hurtling down the stairs. He darted into the lounge then through into the kitchen, shouting all the way, but there was no sign of Freddie or his date for the night. Hearing car doors slamming, he ran out onto the driveway just in time to see a taxi speeding off along Scundale Chase.

Felix called and texted, without any joy. He even phoned Rick Shaw's, but when they found out he wasn't ordering a takeaway, they hung up. And the police? As soon as he told them who was on the line, they offered to send an officer straight away - to arrest him for wasting their time.

He spent the rest of the evening trying to keep his mind occupied, writing up the day's events and failing miserably to find anything on his Colin Anderton web search. Tired and frustrated, he eventually crawled under Freddie's bed and rattled the floorboard loose. Themba had hung onto the 'diamond' he'd given her in the seafront shelter, down on the Prom, and God knows what had become of the one he'd handed to Freddie, but the four remaining fakes were as stunning as the first time he'd set eyes on them.

He pulled out the torn blue rucksack from the bottom of his wardrobe and rolled up the diamonds in the wrap, before heading next door to Themba's room. With the light still off, he dropped the rucksack to the floor and placed the rectangle of material on the dressing table, laying out the four fake stones in a neat line. She was welcome to them as far as he was concerned - he just wanted them out of his life. The battered monochrome image of her grandfather had been stuck to the mirror and he wondered what the tribal chief would have said if he knew the mess his granddaughter had got them all into.

As he turned to head back to the landing, the bedroom light clicked on. Letting out a startled shriek, he knocked the wrap from the dressing table, its contents spilling across the carpet.

'What do you think you're doing?' he yelled at his little sister, who'd appeared from out of nowhere in her light-blue pyjamas, looking as if she'd just woken up.

'I couldn't get to sleep,' she complained. 'Dad's got the TV on way too loud downstairs, and then I heard you crashing around in here. Anyway, this is Themba's room–' She stopped mid-sentence, staring open-mouthed at the diamonds.

'Don't worry, they're not real,' said Felix, scrambling about on the floor as he tried to retrieve them. 'Themba was… err… she was showing me them earlier and ended up leaving them in my room by mistake. I was just putting them back.'

'Wow! They're huge… and really pretty.' Flo picked one up and examined it closely. 'But what's she doing with them?'

His mind went blank. He couldn't tell her what had been going on but he had to come up with something plausible. In a desperate bid to buy himself some time, he opted for a radical change of subject. 'I managed to have that talk with Dad, the other evening,' he began brightly.

'And how did that go?' she asked, sounding surprised.

'Not that well, to be honest. He said everything was fine and it was none of our business.'

Flo looked downcast. 'That would explain why Mum's out at her stupid dance club again tonight, and he's still sleeping on the settee in the lounge.'

'To be fair, we are a bit pushed for space, what with Themba staying.'

Flo rolled her eyes. 'Even you can see what's going on, Felix, so don't treat me like I'm stupid. And stop trying to change the subject! I was asking you about the diamonds. Where did Themba get them from?'

'London,' he began, surprising himself with the authority of his tone. 'She was sight-seeing and ended up visiting the Tower to check out the crown jewels. They sell replicas in the gift shop.'

Flo looked unconvinced. 'I did a project on the crown jewels at school last year. I don't remember seeing anything like this in the collection.'

'Well you wouldn't, would you? These are new-in for the summer season. The Queen likes to mix it up a bit - keep things fresh. She gets a cut from the ticket sales - those corgis don't buy their own dog food.'

'So, where do the original diamonds come from?' Flo asked.

He should have stopped there and then but he was already in way too deep. 'They were found - discovered, you might say - on these remote islands off the coast of Spain.'

'Name?'

'That would be...' His mind went blank. And then the answer splurged from his lips, before he even knew it was happening.

Bundling his sister out onto the landing, he scurried back to the sanctuary of his own bedroom. It had been the narrowest of escapes but he knew, from bitter experience, it was only the start. She'd be back on his case first thing in the morning and wouldn't stop until he'd cracked. He'd have to get his story straight by then or he'd be dead in the water.

He sat behind the desk and stared at his laptop, wondering what to do next. It was nearly midnight but he couldn't turn in until he knew Freddie and Themba had made it home safely. The NKI icon glowed temptingly against the blue of the computer screen and after agonising for a few seconds, he clicked onto the site. Once he'd navigated his way to Hugo Mulholland's email address, he began to tap out a message.

Dear Mr Mulholland, Your friend Jeremy Grindrod at the Lancastrian Bugler said I should work with you on news updates in Frecklesall-on-Sea, here in Lancashire. I'm supposed to be covering UK City of Culture stories but something else has come up which looks like it might be more interesting. I'm just letting you know that I'll be calling you first thing in the morning to give you a full briefing.
Regards

Felix Haythornthwaite
Trainee Reporter (Temporary Work Experience)
Lancastrian Bugler

Moments after pressing the 'send' button, his mobile burst into life. The voice at the other end was well-to-do but friendly.

'Hello, this is Hugo Mulholland from NKI. Might I be talking to the *Lancastrian Bugler's* finest, Mr Felix Haythornthwaite?'

Felix nearly fell off his chair. 'Wow! Yes, that's me.'

'Excellent! I had a hunch a young buck like you might be up at this ungodly hour. Been out clubbing, have we?'

'That was last night, actually, Mr Mulholland.'

The journalist laughed. 'Please, Felix - call me Hugo. Listen, Jerry's briefed me on this City of Culture thing - dull as ditch-water if you ask me. Have to say, I found your message a tad more interesting, though. How about you give me a briefing on what's been going on?'

Twenty minutes later and with the phone still glued to his ear, Felix heard the back door close and the sound of his mum padding up the stairs after her night out at the dance club. Hugo had listened carefully to his story, asking probing questions that focussed on what really mattered. For his part, Felix was relieved to share the crazy events of the past week with someone sensible - someone who didn't think he was barking mad.

'Intriguing,' Hugo remarked, at the end. 'I might be wrong about this, Felix, but it sounds to me like you could be onto something pretty big here.'

'That's just how I'm seeing it! HB's still missing, those Spanish guys are chasing after our Fred, and we've got this Themba woman staying with us. I know she saved his life, but she's really, really scary. To be honest, Hugo, the whole thing's starting to freak me out.'

Mulholland laughed. 'When you're swimming with the sharks, you have to hold your nerve. Flap around and they'll do much more than nibble the dead skin off your toes, if you follow me?'

'I… I suppose so.'

'Good man! Because now's the time to knuckle down and do your job.'

'Couldn't you come up here and help me? Jerry… I mean, Mr Grindrod, said you'd give me whatever support I needed.'

'Here's the thing,' said Hugo. 'First-off - if someone like me pitches up in a dead-end backwater like Frecklesall-on-Sea, it'll set all sorts of hares running and so forth. For my sins, I've established something of a profile in the industry over recent years, which means wherever Hugo Mulholland goes, other lesser-beings tend to follow. So, I know it's a big ask but I need you to fly solo on this particular assignment.'

'I'm doing my best, it's just that—'

'And secondly,' Hugo interrupted him, 'at this precise moment in time, I'm talking to you from the thirty-fifth floor of Trump Tower in downtown Manhattan, New York City. It would take me two or three days minimum to wrap things up here and get back across the pond.'

'Oh.'

'So, here's what I need from you, Felix. Stay close to the girl and try to win her trust. She'll be hanging around for a reason and odds are, it's those diamonds. If the real ones *are* nearby, there's every chance she'll lead you to them.'

'What about Sir Hubert? Is there any way you can help me track him down?'

'You've lost me there.'

'Y'know, Sir Hubert Montague-Dunk,' said Felix. 'The mad admiral I was telling you about. He's the only one who could have done the switch and according to my aunt he's got a track record in this kind of thing.'

'Hmm, I'm not sure I'd be barking up that particular tree,' said Hugo. 'We shouldn't rule anything out at this stage but think it through - how would the old boy have known the diamonds were about to come his way? I mean, is it really likely he'd have a set of replicas stashed on board his rowing boat on the off-chance?'

'But apart from me and Freddie, he's the only person who's been alone with them.'

'Sorry, I'm just not seeing it. My gut says forget this Sir Hubert character and focus on the Themba girl. Stick close to her and report back on whatever she gets up to. If she so much as scratches her nose, I want to know about it. In the meantime, my people will work up the profiles and so forth. I'll let you know as soon as we've got anything concrete. I'm pretty sure we can crack this one if we work together as a team. Are you up for that?'

'Definitely!' replied Felix, his line of thought interrupted by the sound of the back door opening again and voices drifting up from the kitchen. 'Sorry Hugo, I need to go - sounds like Fred and Themba are home.'

'Excellent, but I do have a small favour to ask of you, Felix, if you don't mind. I think it's rather important that we keep this whole thing strictly 'Chatham House'. It'll complicate matters no end if Jerry finds out we're skiing off-piste on this one.'

Felix agreed in an instant, buzzing to be on the inside track. But Hugo had one final warning.

'From what you've told me, I'd hazard that the chaps chasing your brother are from one of the Latin-American neo-mafia cartels. We've been monitoring the activities of one particularly brutal outfit - *Los Quesos Grandes,* they're called. They were set up during the Venezuelan Cheese Wars back in the 50s, although these days they earn most of their money through narcotics, diamond smuggling, extortion and so forth. They're not nice people, Felix - not nice at all. Best steer clear if you can possibly manage it.'

Felix clicked off the bedside lamp and pulled the duvet up over his head. If he closed his eyes and lay very still, he imagined there was a chance he might become invisible. At that precise moment in time, nothing would have suited him better.

11

'Whassup…? Whass going on…?' Felix struggled to prise his eyes open as his bed tilted crazily to one side and a hairy size ten foot landed only inches from his face. He looked up at the terrifying sight of Freddie towering above him.

'*Soz, Bro,*' whispered Freddie. '*Just trying to snag these grundies.*' Standing on the edge of Felix's mattress, he was swatting at the bedroom light pendant which was swinging wildly from the ceiling.

Felix made a grab for his alarm clock. 'It's half-past-four in the morning, Fred. What are you…? Owww! Get *off* me!'

Freddie's foot had slipped over the edge, sending him crashing on top of his brother.

'Keep it down, will you?' the older sibling hissed. Untangling himself, he got up and switched on the light.

It took a few seconds for Felix's eyes to adjust but when they did, he was shocked to see his brother fully dressed and a half-open holdall stuffed with clothes, lying in the middle of the bedroom floor. 'What's going on?' he asked.

Freddie looked up, his lank greasy hair partly concealing the palest of faces, bags hanging heavy under his bloodshot eyes. 'I gotta split, man. My mate Knocker's got this summer gig at Maccy D's, down St

Helen's way. I reckon now's a good time to pay him a visit.'

'Please tell me this isn't to do with those gangsters?' asked Felix, his heart sinking.

Freddie sighed. 'Themba reckons they'd slit my throat soon as look at me. I tell you, Bro - this whole thing's *such* a bad scene. But it's like she said to me last night, "Freddie-babes, you're no use to no one with a knife stuck in your guts. Get out of town, lie low, and when this has blown over, we *will* get it on". She even gave me one of her rings - it's a symbol.' He wafted a hand in his brother's face.

'Why are they after you?'

'I've got something they want, haven't I? Something they'd have to kill me to get their hands on. Word to the wise - ditch them diamonds or you'll be next in the firing line.'

'She's winding you up!' Felix exclaimed. 'They're fakes and she knows it.'

Freddie snorted. 'Answer me this then, Two Brains - why are those bad *hombres* on my case, and why does the hottest babe in the UK - and probably the whole universe - tell me I've got to get out of town before sunrise, even though it's totally breaking her heart to see me go?'

Felix was beginning to lose it. 'I hate to burst your balloon, Fred, but there's something about Themba that doesn't add up. I haven't got to the bottom of it yet but when I do, you'll be first to know. I dumped the rest of the diamonds on her dressing table last night. Do you think I'd hand them over to her on a plate like that if they were genuine? If you've still got your one, you should do the same or… or just chuck it in the bin. They're worthless fakes - it doesn't matter!'

'Yeah, well that's not what she's saying,' Freddie muttered, turning back to his packing.

And then Felix noticed the glint of light reflecting off a shiny metal surface, tucked in amongst Freddie's screwed-up clothing. It took him a moment to work out the source. 'What are you doing with our colander?' he asked. 'Mum will kill you when she finds out.'

Furrows of concern creased his brother's brow. 'That diamond you gave me on the way out of OT's - you remember where I stashed it?'

Felix nodded.

'Well, everything was cool until I whacked that speed bump on Marine Drive. Things went up - sudden-like - then *down*.'

'You mean... you swallowed it?'

Freddie grimaced. 'Yeah, and it got stuck, didn't it? Forget the drowning gig, I almost choked to death before I got anywhere near the water.'

'What's that got to do with Mum's colander?'

Freddie rolled his eyes. 'And they say you're the smart one? Look, I swallowed a diamond worth God knows how much.' He pointed down to his stomach. 'It's in there somewhere and with a bit of luck, it'll be making a guest star appearance sooner or later. Does that help your understanding of the situation?'

'Oh.'

'And here's the thing,' Freddie continued, sounding close to tears. 'There's been no number two action since then, which means it's wedged up in there, log-jamming everything else. Unless I can shift it, I either die of constipation, or... Themba says if those dudes get their hands on me it'd be like having my appendix out all over again, but without the anaesthetic!' He got to his feet and gripped his brother in a manly bear-hug. 'Hey, I know we ain't always been on the same wavelength, what with me being from Mars and you coming from Venus, but I'm gonna miss you, Bro. You take care, and be sure to look out for my chick. She's the one thing that's gonna keep me going when I'm out there on the road.'

And with that, he slung the bag over his shoulder and was gone.

An hour later, Felix caught the sound of footsteps heading down the stairs, followed by the click of the back door. It was too early for his dad to set off for work and there was no way Flo or his mum would be up at that time so, tired as he was, he decided to investigate.

He crept through to the bathroom and peered out of the part-open window. It had rained in the night and the small patio at the back of the house was covered in dirty grey puddles. He watched in silence as Themba, wearing his mum's dressing gown, made her way out to the garden shed. She worked through the keys in her hand until she found the right one for the padlock. Emerging from the shed a couple of minutes later, she locked the flimsy wooden door and looked up.

Ohmygod!

She'd seen him! He ducked down and sat on the edge of the bath, wondering what he was going to say to her. Flushing the toilet for cover, he tried to pull himself together. All sorts of implausible excuses popped into his head but he knew she'd never buy them.

And then he started to get annoyed.

The more he thought about it, the more he realised that this was her problem, not his. She was the one who was out of line, the one with the explaining to do.

137

Steeling himself for the task ahead, he made his way downstairs, finding her alone at the kitchen table.

Ignoring the dirty look she gave him, he dived straight in. 'What were you doing in our shed just now, Themba?'

'Why should that concern you?' she replied, frostily. 'And why were you spying on me?'

'I was on the toilet when I heard the back door open, so–'

'For your information, I was finding it difficult to sleep and decided to check on my bicycle. I have already told you how important it is to me.'

'Actually, Themba, I think you'll find…' Felix's ownership claim was cut short as she passed him Freddie's hastily scrawled farewell note.

'I found this on the kitchen table,' she said. 'It is for the best. It is no longer safe for him to remain here.'

'He's terrified - why didn't you tell him those diamonds are fakes?'

'It is easier for all of us if he goes,' she replied. 'I instructed him to post a Facebook message to let his friends know he has taken an overseas holiday. It should help throw them off the trail.'

So many weird things had happened, her comments barely registered as unusual.

'I know they saw him flashing those earrings at OT's but I still don't understand why they're not chasing me as well,' said Felix. 'If they really are holding HB captive, he'll have told them everything he knows by now.'

'This has been a surprise to me, also,' she replied. 'But now I believe it to be a case of mistaken identity.'

'What do you mean?'

'I have read some of the text messages this HB has sent you. He only ever refers to you as "Haythornthwaite". Why is this?'

Felix laughed. 'I don't think he even knew my first name. I told him loads of times but he either forgot or was too far up himself to use it.'

'Be grateful for his ignorance,' said Themba. 'It means all he can tell his captors is your surname, and that you live somewhere in the vicinity of Frecklesall-on-Sea. We know their English is poor which makes it more difficult for them to investigate this properly. I am thinking perhaps they spotted the name on the posters for your brother's musical show, when they first arrived. "DeeJay FoF Haythornthwaite" could be either one of you. And any uncertainty they might have had would have disappeared when they saw your brother on stage, flaunting the diamond earrings.'

'But if they check out our Facebook profiles with HB, they're bound to realise their mistake. There are loads of photographs of us on there.'

'I have considered this, also,' she said, frizzing out her hair and pulling a stupid face. 'The images posted on Facebook look nothing like you.'

She was right, of course - he was virtually unrecognisable after the 'ultra-bosh' haircut, endured for the *Bugler* job.

'And your brother's profile pictures,' she added, 'consist entirely of elderly and infirm white men holding electric guitars.'

Freddie had taken down his own mugshots a couple of weeks earlier on the basis that photos of veteran axe heroes like Clapton, Keith Richards and Slash, would go down well with his old-school fans. Felix had thought it was a really stupid idea at the time but having seen the average age of the Metal Maniacs at the OT's gig, now understood where he'd been coming from.

'And now, when they check his timeline, they will believe he has left Frecklesall to go away on holiday,' she continued. 'With luck, they will pursue him, giving us the opportunity to locate the real diamonds.'

'Actually, I might have some news on that front,' said Felix. 'You remember you asked me whether anyone else might have had the chance to do the switch after I picked up your bag?'

He had her complete attention now.

'That Sunday after we first met,' he continued, 'I was following up a story for the *Bugler* on Frecklesall beach. There was this old guy setting off to row across the Atlantic. It was some kind of mad tribute to the Queen.'

Once Themba had got over her disbelief that anyone could even think about doing something so stupid, she listened carefully, quizzing him on changes in the bag's appearance after he'd retrieved it from *The Diamond Queen,* and in particular, about Colin Anderton's shady past. Felix told her what he knew, although he didn't mention the mirror message in HB's flat. He had no desire to get beaten up again, guessing she wouldn't be too pleased to discover he'd been withholding crucial information. The odd thing was that while Hugo Mulholland had dismissed his Colin Anderton theory, Themba seemed quite taken with it.

'We must find this man, now,' she declared.

'Yeah right!' Felix snorted. 'I mean, seeing as he's out in the middle of the ocean somewhere and has probably drowned already, that shouldn't be too tricky!'

'So, you have exhausted all possibilities? You have searched the internet, reviewed the postings of your contacts, checked with your coastguard service?'

'Well, err…'

She sighed. 'Then I am afraid we must wait here until they find us, and pray the end is swift.'

Felix was aghast. 'I haven't had a chance to get onto it yet, Themba, but I will, I promise!' Their conversation was interrupted by the sound of footsteps on the stairs. 'That'll be Flo,' he said. 'She caught me putting the fakes back in your room last night. She gave me a real grilling.'

'What did you tell her?'

He heard his sister jump down the last couple of steps into the hallway, before detouring via the front door to check for post. 'They're on display with the crown jewels,' he said quietly. 'You picked up some replicas from the souvenir shop when you were visiting the Tower of London.'

Themba's face was a picture.

'Oh… and I had to come up with a name for them,' he added. 'You know what she's like…' His words faded away as the kitchen door opened. 'Morning!' he greeted his sister.

Flo stood there in her pyjamas, glowering at him. 'I've spent the last hour searching the web,' she said. 'There's absolutely no record of any *Saydoss* islands off the coast of Spain, or anywhere else for that matter. And as for a set of diamonds of the same name…'

Before she could get into her stride, Themba handed her Freddie's note and the eleven-year-old scurried off upstairs to wake her mum with the news of her eldest brother's surprise holiday.

Themba rounded on him the moment his sister was out of earshot. 'Of all the names you had to choose. I cannot believe your stupidity!'

'It was all I could think of,' he replied. 'Anyway, it doesn't mean anything, does it?'

'It means something to *them*, and by mentioning it to other members of your family, you place their lives in danger as well.'

He slunk back to his bedroom. Settling down at his laptop, he opened his web browser and started the search for Sir Hubert. It was going to be a very long day.

Four hours later his brain was turning to blancmange, so when Bernie called suggesting they meet up on the Prom, he jumped at the chance. He felt a bit guilty about leaving Themba, given the promise he'd made Hugo to stick by her side, but she'd stayed in her bedroom all morning and was showing no signs of coming out. Anyway, he thought, there was still a reporting job to be done for the *Bugler*. With cultural events planned every day in the run up to that Friday's live TV finale, he had to make sure all the bases were covered.

Pulling on some old jeans, he grabbed a T-shirt from the dirty washing basket and checked himself out in the mirror. He looked a mess but it was only Bernie and his friend had seen much worse over the years.

He crept down the stairs and out through the back door, picking up his bike from the shed. As soon as he jumped on board he realised that someone had been messing around with the saddle. It had only been dropped a few centimetres but it felt like his knees were up around his neck. Cursing his dad, who'd borrowed it to get to work the day before, he climbed off and flicked the quick-release lever, heaving it back up to its usual height.

He cycled into town and made his way to the seafront, where a small crowd was huddled against the railings, looking down over a large, moth-eaten gazebo, pitched on the beach. A battered sign, propped up on the sand, confirmed what all the fuss was about:

Lanky Cowboys

The North's Premier Wild-West Appreciation Society

A council man was wandering around, doling out purple Got it All! baseball caps. Felix grabbed one but thought better of putting it on.

'Oof!'

A punch to the kidneys heralded Bernie's arrival. Felix turned to greet his friend and was alarmed to see some familiar faces.

'Surprise!' Bernie yelled.

Zoe and Neesha eyed him warily, while Naz, who was sporting one of the freebie caps, looked suitably embarrassed. But the one person he really wanted to avoid was making a beeline for him. Unlike her friends, who were in their scruffs, Dannii looked like she was heading off on a night out. He hardly recognised her at first - the eye-popping white shorts, black, knee-length socks and figure-hugging crop top were definitely not the outfit of someone who'd dived into the first clothes they'd found on their bedroom floor. And her hair was different - deep auburn, it had been back-combed and piled high into a 1960s beehive. She looked amazing and

Felix kicked himself, yet again, for making such a mess of their first time together.

'Felix, babes!' she shrieked, her jaw working away on the ever-present blob of gum. 'Ohmygod that was like, totally awesome the other night - Un. Be. *Leevable*! I was telling my sister and she's like, "How many shots had you necked, Dannii, babes?" and I'm like, "Portia babes, you gotta meet this guy, he's totally *loco*! First up he's bustin' these crazy moves and then he only goes and does one off the top balcony, doesn't he?" and she's like, "No way - he's a top journo on the *Bugler, and* a pop star?".'

Before he could get a word in, she'd lunged at him. There was an awkward near miss on the head-butt front but he then experienced his first ever luvvie air-kiss ('Mmwah, Mmwah!'), both cheeks as well.

Bernie winked at him.

'It's really nice to see you too, Dannii,' Felix mumbled. 'Sorry I'm such a mess.'

'Actually, I'm loving the vintage boho vibe,' she said earnestly.

He looked confused.

'Been thinking about you a lot, babes,' she added.

It was beyond weird - he'd written off his chances but now, to quote his big brother, it looked very much like it was 'game on'.

'I'm so sorry about how things ended the other night, Dannii,' he said. 'I don't know what came over me.'

She smiled. 'That's what I like about you, Felix, babes. You're out there on the edge, just like your Freddie.'

He decided to go with it. 'Yeah, he is a bit mental, isn't he? He only went and woke me up in the middle of the night to tell me he was off on his holidays - St Helens, of all places! How stupid is that?'

'Is that in the south of France too?' she asked. 'Because according to Facebook he's gone to this arty-farty film festival in a place called *Cans*.'

'Oh… yeah. St Helens is right next door.'

The sounds of geriatric Wild West enthusiasts whooping and hollering, drifted up from the beach, and they wandered across to see what was happening. The crowd had spread out, pressing up against the seafront railings to check out the action. Dannii quickly found a gap that offered the perfect view but it was only when they climbed up to sit on the top rail that they realised why the space had been left. A pungent whiff wafted up from the old tidal boating pond, a few metres below. A concrete-bound semi-circle crammed against the sea wall, kids used to sail their model boats in it, back in the day. That was then, of course - with the tide rarely coming in high enough to give it a proper swill out, its stagnant waters were now a magnet for rubbish blowing off the Prom, the oily sheen of beige scum that glistened on its surface fuelling rumours of a direct sewer connection from the nearby Passage of the Sultan curry house. Throw in a skip-load of stinky brown seaweed and a rotting seagull carcass or two, and you've got the full picture.

The Wild West show was a pathetic stand-off between a gaggle of elderly men in giant ten-gallon hats, leather waistcoats and false moustaches, and a bunch of similarly decrepit Native American impersonators, clutching bows and plastic tomahawks, clad in little more than oversized nappies. When the shooting started, things went from bad to worse.

'Hold fire 'til you see the whites of their eyes!' a gnarled old cowboy yelled from the midst of the fray, as he raised his gun to take aim.

'Bang!'

Sadly, it wasn't the ear-damaging 'Boom!' of a Colt '45 or the sharp 'Crack!' of a Smith & Wesson Schofield. No. The sound effect came straight from the pensioner's lips. To be fair, he put as much welly into it as he could muster but somehow it didn't quite do the job.

'What's going on?' Felix asked the council guy, who'd been skulking around just behind them.

'We had some complaints about the noise so we had to ask the guys to tone it down,' he replied. 'Still a cracking show, though, isn't it?'

Felix doubted whether even the use of live ammunition would have spiced things up enough to make it watchable, and was about to say as much when Dannii edged along the rail to snuggle up close.

'Anyway Felix,' she said, 'now I've got you all to myself, there's something important I want to say.'

He found himself drawn to the exotic whiff of her hairspray.

'This boy-band thing,' she continued. 'My sister Portia's like, "Dannii babes, you're such a *stoopid* mare when you're on one".'

'It's really not a problem,' he said, over the half-hearted 'Bangs' drifting up from the beach. 'I'm just glad we're OK.'

She kissed him on the cheek.

Down on the sand, the Native American chief had squared up to the head cowboy for a fist-fight on the rim of the boating pond. Felix spotted the photographer from the *Journal*, lining up a shot - those guys didn't miss a thing. A dig in the ribs brought him back to reality.

'Are you listening to me, Felix babes?'

He smiled. 'Sorry, Dannii... err... *babes.*'

'I could of pasted Bernie when he told me ToyBoyz2 split last year. You must be gutted! I think he's a bit jealous, actually, what with him having a mingin' job in IT and you being so successful with your newspaper career and everything.'

He looked at her, blankly.

She stifled a giggle. 'You're so naughty! You said you worked at the *Bugler* but you kept the Fashion Editor bit quiet, didn't you?'

The spell was broken in an instant. 'What? Bernie told you I'm the *Bugler's* Fashion Editor? But that's Giuliano Fiorentino!' (Actually, it was Dan Pickles, with a bit of help from the Next Catalogue, Darlene from tele-sales, and a job-lot of syndicated articles bought in from an agency based just outside Middlesbrough - but that was another story).

'He told me how it works,' she said. 'That's just the name you use in the paper. He said you'd be a bit shy about it, seeing as you're not actually Italian - although I bet you could be if you wanted to. Portia reckons she saw you out in Preston yesterday with this supermodel. Bernie says she's visiting from Milan! It'd be fab to meet her. I bet the girls try all sorts to persuade you to give them the *Bugler Belle* spot. My mum sent my photo in a couple of weeks back but I guess you haven't seen it yet - or maybe you have and you don't think I'm pretty enough?'

Felix started flapping. 'Yes... that is, no. I mean, you're absolutely gorgeous Dannii.'

Sensing movement to their side, they turned to see an elderly figure in a white, broad-brimmed hat, hobbling along the Prom towards them. The eyes of the crowd were drawn to the battle-weary cowboy as he edged Dannii along the railings, with a courteous, 'Excuse me, li'l missy, this old-timer's gotta right some wrongs before he hangs up his spurs one last time.' Hoiking up his trousers, the old boy drew an awesome-looking six-shooter from its holster.

'Say your prayers, Wind-Breaker!' he yelled, pointing the gun at the sagging Native American Chief, who was still trading half-hearted blows with his cowboy counterpart on the beach, below.

The pensioner in the oversized nappy and bedraggled feather head-dress, pulled back from the fray. Climbing up onto the edge of the boating pond, scrawny white arms outstretched, his face was a picture of defiance.

'Wind-Breaker, he say - better to die on feet, than to live on knees!'

To this day, it's unclear whether 'Calamity' Curtis, as the *Journal* later named him, made an honest mistake in the heat of battle, or meant it as a noisy protest against the council's firearms ban. Either way, when the pensioner squeezed the trigger, with a shout of, 'This one's for mah Pappy!' an ear-splitting 'BOOM!' blasted from the barrel of his gun.

There was an audible gasp from the audience, followed by a moment of stunned silence.

Wind-Breaker looked up accusingly at the cowboy. 'Flippin' 'erry, Curtis! What were that all about, then?' he shouted, before belatedly reverting to character and crumpling to the sand, clutching at his chest.

The plotline required that Curtis show no mercy, and he took aim once more.

BOOM!

There were shrieks and shouts as people dived for cover, and in the midst of the chaos, two burly men burst forward from the crowd. Before Curtis could protest his innocence, the first guy had grappled him to the floor and locked his arms behind his back, while his sidekick made a grab for Felix. Still perched on the top rail, Felix tried to fend him off but only succeeded in shunting sideways into Dannii.

His resistance crumbled in a matter of seconds and, yelling for all he was worth, he crunched painfully onto the pavement. Flat on his back, pinned down by his assailant, he was left gasping for breath. Moments later, he heard a shrill scream and was able to lift his head just enough to catch the blur of a cheeky pair of white shorts as they disappeared over the railings.

The devastating 'SPLUDGE!' that followed, confirmed his worst fears.

12

Felix's voice was ragged as he yelled down the transatlantic phone line, late that evening. 'They jumped me, then they just kind of… disappeared. It was the same pair who rescued me at Freddie's flat. Tony and Eric - they work for the Gas Board. I'm pretty sure I saw them in a punch-up outside OT's the other night, as well!'

Hugo Mulholland's suave tones did little to calm the situation. 'I must say, it all sounds rather odd, Felix. Have you run the checks with the gas company to see whether they had any operatives in the area at the time?'

'No, but…'

'And the police?' asked Hugo. 'Any pointers there?'

'Like I said, as soon as they found out the gun was firing blanks, they weren't interested.'

'I'm not doubting your story, but are you absolutely certain your recollection of events is accurate?'

'I am, I swear. My mates were there, and my girlfriend as well. Correction, that's my *ex*-girlfriend, now. She got knocked off the railings and would have done herself a real nasty if she hadn't landed in the old boating pond.'

'Well that's something to be grateful for, at least.'

'You obviously haven't seen the old boating pond…' Felix winced at the memory of his telephone conversation with Dannii's dad, who'd explained in no uncertain terms that his daughter didn't want to speak to him - not now, not ever - and if Felix tried to contact her again, he'd come round to 21 Scundale Chase to settle the matter in person.

'Look, you asked for my opinion, so here it is,' said the NKI man. 'You're struggling to verify what happened through credible, independent witnesses, and with all due respect, you do seem somewhat emotionally involved. So for me, the bottom line is this - no one got hurt, no one got killed, which in my book means this just hasn't got the legs.'

Felix nearly exploded. 'You what? I got mugged, my girlfriend ended up in the boating pond *and* she's just dumped me. She's a model, Hugo - they don't exactly grow on trees around here!'

'Word to the wise, Felix - it never pays to mix business with pleasure. Send in your copy to the *Bugler* if you must, but I won't be backing it. The truth is, we've got much bigger fish to fry. A confused pensioner firing off a couple of blanks in a Wild West show is not going to bring us any closer to finding those diamonds.'

'That's ridiculous, I mean–'

'Listen to me - if you're going to hack it in this business, you need dedication, focus, and balls of steel. Pull yourself together - go and stand under a cold shower if that helps - then get back out there and do your job.'

Felix didn't much like the message but he knew deep down that Hugo was right. It was over with Dannii, which meant it was time to put his career first. The shadowing role was easy enough. Since his brother had left town, he and Themba had spent more and more time together - it was just a case of taking things that little bit more seriously. So he made sure he was up and dressed before she came down for breakfast each morning, then he stuck to her like glue. When he got the chance, he was checking the web for news of Sir Hubert and late each night, when everyone else was asleep, he'd email his report through to Hugo. More often than not he'd receive an instant call back, the NKI correspondent probing constantly on the fine detail of what Themba had been up to.

In truth, things had cooled down considerably. Frecklesall had been invaded by gangs of talentless buskers, plying their trade on every street corner, but on the upside, there was a complete absence of anyone looking even vaguely Latin American. Meanwhile, Themba had eased comfortably into her role as honoured guest. She was still giving Felix grief by the bucket load, but her relationship with the rest of the family could not have been more cordial. She chatted away with his dad and patiently fielded Flo's endless questions about life in Lesotho. She even stayed up drinking into the late night on Doreen's weekly visit, the two of them getting on like a house on fire.

Like Hugo, Themba maintained that the incident on the Prom was of no consequence, but oddly, it seemed to have an immediate impact on her behaviour. Felix suggested they stroll through town to visit Doreen on the Monday afternoon but she backed out at the last minute. Later that evening, he couldn't tempt her with the delights of the Got it All! cage fighting exhibition over at the Fishfoot Lane community centre. She even turned down the opportunity to check out the Hebden Bridge Tribal Belly Dance Collective, who were performing live on the Prom the next day.

And while the mind-numbing fog of normality was returning to the streets of Frecklesall, Freddie kept up a rolling Facebook blog on his last-minute break in

Cannes, down on the French Riviera - banging on about nights out with gorgeous Hollywood starlets and vintage Champagne being quaffed by the gallon. Felix knew it was total fiction, but reading about his big brother even pretending to have a good time was beginning to get him down. Stuck indoors with nothing to do, he tried to maintain his focus. But the more he moped around the house, the worse it got. Dannii was never far from his thoughts and he began agonising over whether to call her. And then his dad turned up with a copy of that week's *Journal*.

'She always wanted her picture in the paper,' said Bernie, when he phoned later that evening, 'but if I was you, I'd keep a low profile for a few days.'

The screaming headline above the *Journal's* double-page spread, said it all:

Local Model's Hot Pants Plunge!

The photographs caught the terrible sequence of events perfectly, and the look on Dannii's face as she was hauled from the sludge by a pair of wrinkly, nappy-clad septuagenarians, was one that would haunt him forever.

Late that Wednesday afternoon, with Themba having spent most of the day in her room, he drifted into the lounge to catch up on some daytime TV. It was dark in there, the curtains closed, but he was not alone. The raucous sounds of unbridled snoring confirmed an unwelcome presence on the settee. Felix's arrival triggered a sudden, spluttering halt in proceedings.

Wearing a string vest tucked into a fulsome pair of Y-fronts, his dad emerged, puffy-faced, from beneath a quilt.

'Come on, Dad,' said Felix. 'I want to watch some telly.'

'Oh… sorry, Son.' His dad's voice sounded dry and croaky. 'I did an "early" this morning down at Mart's - I must've dropped off.'

Keen to improve the air quality, Felix drew back the curtains and opened a window. 'Couldn't you just go up to your bedroom?' he asked.

'It's more your mother's room, these days, to be fair,' replied his dad, ruefully. 'Anyway, the settee's comfy enough, and sleeping down here means I can watch the box whenever I want.'

Felix grabbed the remote and switched on the TV. 'By the way, Dad, next time you borrow my bike, put the saddle back to the right height, will you? I nearly did myself in, setting off the other morning.'

'Never touched it, Son. In fact, that's why I stopped using it. I could barely reach the pedals.'

'As if! I know what you're like - you'll have forgotten you did it.'

A few weeks earlier he wouldn't have dreamt of talking to his father like that, but he didn't care now - or maybe he did care, and that's why the whole thing was so frustrating. His mum was out until all hours, dancing the night away, while her husband slouched around at home in his trollies, staring open-mouthed at the television. Felix was beginning to think his sister might be right about their parents' marriage, after all.

They sat together watching some adverts, and then his dad broke the silence.

'What you were saying the other night, Son - when we were down at the police station…'

Felix's ears pricked up.

'Me and your mum are both busy people, which means we don't get the chance to spend that much time together,' his dad continued. 'But after talking it through with Themba, I've come up with a plan.'

Felix looked across at the flabby, unshaven figure, lounging on the settee in his pants, and rolled his eyes.

'Lovely girl, Themba, don't you think?' his dad said. 'She's over here, thousands of miles from home, yet she still manages to stay in touch with her family. I only hope you'll be as considerate when you head off to uni. It's funny, but she has this amazing insight - always coming out with these wise words. It can be quite inspirational at times.'

Felix groaned. 'What's she said now?'

His dad pulled out a crumpled scrap of paper from under a cushion. 'She shared this old African proverb with me this morning and it really got me thinking.' He balanced a pair of glasses on the end of his nose and started reading. '"A happily married couple are like a pair of hippopotamus buttocks. Although there may be constant friction between them, somehow, they will always find a way to rub along together in harmony".'

'Wow. That's… interesting.'

'My thoughts exactly! So I've booked a table at *Le Rognon Flambé* in Preston for tomorrow night and me and your mum are going to have a nice meal and a proper heart-to-heart. The truth is, the two of us have rubbed along quite nicely for more years than I care to remember. I have to admit, there's been a bit of chafing recently–'

'That's great, Dad,' Felix interrupted him, keen not to hear any more.

The lounge door opened and his dad dived across the settee, grabbing for his dressing gown as Themba walked in.

'No... come in Themba, love,' he said, doing his best to cover himself up. 'Nothing you haven't seen before... I mean, what with all those brothers you've got back home. You can squeeze in next to me - there's plenty of space if I shuffle up a bit.'

She made for the armchair on the opposite side of the room, as far away from him as possible.

'I was just telling Felix about our little chat,' he continued. 'I've booked this top restaurant in Preston and Christine's actually free for once, so it's all systems go! And before you say anything, Son, I know I need to smarten myself up a bit. Our Freddie gave me some style tips before he cleared off on his holidays. You won't recognise me tomorrow evening!'

They settled in to watch the six o'clock news, which was as dull as ever. Felix was on his way to the kitchen to get a snack when something on the screen caught his eye.

'And finally...' announced the newsreader, arching an eyebrow, 'for most of us a quiet game of bowls is about as exciting as life gets when we head into our twilight years. But that is most certainly *not* the case for eccentric seventy-eight-year-old Lancastrian, Colin Anderton, who has a radically different take on retirement! A week ago, Colin - in the form of his *alter ego*, Rear Admiral Sir Hubert Montague-Dunk (Retired) - set sail from the Lancashire resort of Frecklesall-on-Sea, on a single-handed adventure to row across the

Atlantic, as part of an extraordinary personal tribute to Her Majesty The Queen.'

'Bloody hell, it's *him*!' screamed Felix.

'With little in the way of communications since then, friends and family were beginning to fear the worst, but against all the odds, Lancashire's favourite nautical pensioner has arrived safe and well... on the Isle of Man! And we're going live now to our north of England correspondent, Roger Mutton, for an update us on this remarkable story - Roger.'

The picture cut to a windswept reporter, standing on a grey, pebble-strewn beach. 'Remarkable indeed, Derek. And I'm joined here in the charming seaside resort of Old Laxey, on the east coast of the island, by the man himself - Rear Admiral Sir Hubert Montague-Dunk (Retired), together with his ocean-going rowing boat, *The Diamond Queen*. Tell me Sir Hubert, how did you cope out there, alone on the high seas?'

The camera panned across to the craggy-faced pensioner, who was wearing full naval regalia. 'Like all of us who've had the honour to serve, I am fortunate to be blessed with something called British pluck,' he replied, proudly. 'A few navigational challenges here and there, but otherwise it was a fair wind and plain sailing!'

Felix dived onto the floor in front of the TV, straining his eyes to check out *The Diamond Queen*, which was beached on the pebbles in the background.

'Hey! You're blocking my view,' shouted his dad.

Felix waved him away. 'It's the guy I did that *Bugler* article on. I need to check out his boat. It's really important!'

'That's no reason to–'

'Please!' Themba's voice cut across the squabble. 'I would like to watch this piece.'

'And in spite of everything, you intend to press on?' the reporter asked.

'Mission objective remains unchanged,' replied Sir Hubert. 'Restocking, courtesy of H.M. Quartermaster services, scheduled relaunch at high tide tomorrow - that's fifteen-hundred hours, sharp.' He gave the reporter a smart salute. 'And now sir, if you would excuse me, I have a vessel to prepare.'

There are times in every big story when even the best investigative journalist has to rely on gut instinct. Make the right call and the obstacles that have held you back for so long, suddenly fall away - get it wrong and you're staring down both barrels of a bottomless pit full of hungry crocodiles. With one or two notable exceptions, Felix's life had always been governed by an underwhelming sense that things seemed to happen to him, rather than the other way around. But as he sat in the empty carriage of the 06.55 Trains4U service from Slaidforth Sands to Lancaster, he realised that for once in his life he'd taken control, and it felt pretty good!

After watching Sir Hubert on the news, the evening before, he'd known exactly what he needed to do. Themba had backed him all the way, sorting out the train and ferry times - even paying for his ticket to the Isle of Man. She wasn't about to come with him, though - too conspicuous, she'd said. It was a relief actually, especially as he'd forgotten to set his alarm and ended up missing the early morning bus out of town. The frantic bike ride to Slaidforth station was the last thing he'd needed but it was the only way he could be sure of making the connection.

The previous night's call with Hugo had been just as uncomfortable. The investigative journalist told him he had to stay put, insisting that the NewsKwest team had picked up intelligence confirming the Venezuelans' plans to head back to Frecklesall in the next few days. When Felix told him he was going anyway, Hugo got shirty, threatening to report him to the *Bugler's* editor if he abandoned his posting at Themba's side. Felix had agreed in the end, just to shut him up, but he'd already printed his ferry ticket and nothing was going to stop him from using it. And anyway, in the unlikely event that he had got it wrong, he was pretty sure he could make it back to the mainland before the NKI man was any the wiser.

It was a work assignment, of sorts, so Felix opted for the suit, checking and rechecking his jacket pocket to make sure the *Bugler* press pass was where he'd left it when he'd smuggled it out of work the week before.

After his train arrived at Lancaster station, he transferred onto the connecting service. Twenty minutes later, the ping of the guard's signal prompted an unhealthy rattle from the ancient diesel engine as the Pacer lurched away from the platform. They lumbered alongside the River Lune, descending through the drab industrial estates of Morecambe's nether regions to arrive, twenty minutes later, at Heysham Ferry Port.

The desolate muddle of lorry parks and container depots, combined with the view across the bay to the bleak concrete slab of the nuclear power station, made Frecklesall seem almost charming. Armed with his ticket, Felix joined the queue.

'Move along, please, ladies and gentlemen!' the policeman on the security desk shouted over the heads of the passengers.

Felix was stuck behind a couple of Dutch bikers who clumped along in their boots and leathers, looking bedraggled and hungover. A dodgy pair, he thought - exactly the kind of characters they'd be likely to pull in for questioning. His mum always said it paid to dress smartly and as he watched the constable preparing to make an interception, he began to understand why.

'Excuse me, would you come this way, please?' the policeman asked, his tone polite, although he clearly meant business.

The Dutch guys didn't react.

The request was repeated, with more insistence this time. 'Sir, I need you to come with me, now!'

Felix chuckled to himself - there was no way those two were getting on the ferry!

The hand clamped firmly onto his shoulder, suggested otherwise.

'What's going on?' he asked.

'Felix Haythornthwaite?' The enquiry was made by a solid-looking officer with a shaved head, a no-nonsense expression and thick black eyebrows that joined in the middle.

'Oh... Yes, that's me.'

'We need to talk to you, lad. Would you follow me through to the security suite, please?'

There was a depressing hopelessness about his new surroundings - antiseptic white walls and grey vinyl flooring, narrow window slits set above eye level, obscured with thick security mesh. Felix was in police custody and no one, least of all Police Constable Nigel Scoggins, seemed interested in telling him why.

'Please, officer,' he begged. 'I've got an important appointment on the island. If I don't catch this ferry, I'm going to miss it.'

'I'll be with you any moment now, sir,' said Scoggins, as he disappeared out of the room.

'Oh come *on*!' Felix yelled after him. 'It's the third time you've said that!'

Normally, he would have been petrified, worrying what his mum was going to say when she found out what had happened, but he had other, more pressing concerns. It was nearly half-past-eight and time was tight.

Twenty-five minutes later, the policeman sauntered in. Felix rounded on him before he'd even had the chance to sit down.

'This is ridiculous! I've been waiting here for ages and I've still got no idea why I'm being held.'

Scoggins sighed as he flicked through the sheets on his clipboard. 'We'll get to that in a minute, lad.' He spoke slowly and deliberately. 'I'm just after running through a few security questions with you first. Can we start with the reason for your visit to the island today?'

Felix waved his press pass in the policeman's face. 'I'm a journalist with the *Lancastrian Bugler* and I've got to interview a lead about a really big story. If I don't catch this ferry, I'll miss my appointment, which would mean big trouble for you. My editor has friends in very high places.'

'Really?' said Scoggins, 'because according to my information you were on a part-time work experience placement at the *Bugler* until a couple of weeks back, which was when they let you go.'

'Oh...' It took him a few seconds to regain his composure. 'I'm *embedded*, you see - it's like being undercover. They'd never admit to having me on their books.'

The policeman looked unimpressed.

'You can't just keep me here,' Felix blustered. 'I know my rights! You've got to have a reason.'

PC Scoggins snapped a black and white faxed photograph from his clipboard and slid it across the table. It was a grainy image - the hair unrecognisable, the pout distracting - but Felix knew all too well who it was.

'Last Sunday,' said the policeman, 'down on Frecklesall Prom. They're treating the incident as a possible assault. You can't leave the mainland with this hanging over you, especially when the victim is a defenceless, fifteen-year-old girl.'

Felix nearly fell off his chair. '*Fifteen*? Dannii's never fifteen - nineteen or twenty, at least!'

One end of the policeman's mono-brow twitched upwards. 'Perhaps not the best line of defence if you were after defending yourself in a court of law, if you don't mind me saying?'

Felix pleaded, he cajoled, he even tried to turn on the charm, but it was like talking to a brick wall. In the end, all he could do was sit there, trying not to scream in frustration. The minutes clicked by on the ancient digital wall-clock and he let out a wail at the blast of the foghorn marking HMS *Ben-My-Chrees'* departure. Scoggins left him to it, popping back from time to time but refusing to answer any more questions.

More than an hour later, he was led out to the deserted embarkation foyer.

'Train's leaving for Lancaster in fifteen minutes,' the constable announced. 'Take my advice, lad - get yourself home and keep your head down.'

'It was an accident - I swear! There were these two guys—'

'Actually, I wouldn't be fretting too much about that,' Scoggins interrupted him. 'I made some enquiries with a couple of the lads back at Frecklesall nick and they've assured me they won't be pressing charges.'

'So why did you hold me then? The ferry's gone and my big story's sailed off with it!'

Scoggins sucked the air in between his teeth. 'That *is* a pity, isn't it?' He looked down at his clipboard. 'Sorry, but it's standard protocol in this kind of situation.'

'And what kind of "situation" would that be, when it's at home?' Felix asked, pointedly.

The policeman patted him on the shoulder. 'Best get for going, lad. If you miss this one, you'll have a good two-hour wait.'

Felix caught the train but missed his connection at Lancaster and when the next service to Slaidforth was cancelled, he sensed the gods had not exactly been smiling on his venture. By the time he was cycling past the lido on his way home, it was mid-afternoon. And then he got caught in a torrential downpour which forced him to seek emergency shelter in the Hussein's shop.

His bedraggled appearance caused great hilarity on the part of Naz and his brother, but after changing from his sodden suit into a pair of his friend's old trackie bottoms and a T-shirt, and slurping his way through a mug of tea, he began to feel half-human again.

Naz listened to his story in disbelief, even phoning Bernie to get the inside track on Dannii. There was nothing in it, of course - Zoe had told Bernie that while Dannii's dad was still livid about what had happened, the boating pond incident hadn't been reported to the police, or anyone else for that matter.

'It's outrageous!' exclaimed Naz. 'And he didn't give any other reason for holding you?'

'"Standard protocol",' Felix said, 'although who the hell knows what that means? There was this one other thing that struck me as being a bit odd, though.'

'Please tell me it wasn't another severed finger?'

'No - nothing like that. It was this printout I spotted on the guy's clipboard, just as I was leaving. The top sheet had come through on a fax. It was a bit smudged, so I couldn't make out much more than the logo.'

'And?'

'When I got closer, I could see this funny little crest of arms and above that, in capitals, it said something like, "Security Service".'

Naz shrugged. 'What's the big deal? The police would be into that kind of stuff, wouldn't they?'

'The big deal,' Felix replied, 'is that immediately below that, I'm pretty sure it said "Mi5".'

13

Once Naz had stopped hyperventilating, they tried to work through the possibilities. Early excitement at the prospect of James Bond parachuting into town was dampened by a web search which revealed that Special Agent 007 worked for Mi6, the UK's international security agency, and that Mi5's scope was limited to the domestic front. Try as they might, they couldn't think why Mi5 would be the slightest bit interested in anything that was going on in Frecklesall, let alone Felix's Isle of Man trip. In the end, they gave it up as a bad job and dropped onto an Xbox session to clear their heads.

Saj joined in, gleefully killing them on every game they played, and an hour later Felix decided to head home. His suit had been hung up to dry but when he checked, it was still soaking. It would have made sense to leave it where it was and pick it up the next day but there was no way he was cycling back in the gear Naz had lent him.

'Do you know how this tumble dryer works?' Felix asked, as the pair stood together in the kitchen.

'Yeah - you just shove the clothes in and turn the dial,' replied Naz.

'Right then...' Felix peeled his suit from the hanger and started stuffing it into the machine.

'Hold on! You have to check the pockets first. If you've got coins or keys in there, it can damage the drum. A tissue's bad as well - they end up disintegrating and going all over the place.' Naz groaned as he pulled the jacket from the dryer and started fishing soggy shreds of paper from its pockets. 'Eughh! This is disgusting - you can finish it off.'

The suit was giving off a stale pong and Felix grimaced as his fingers touched something cold and mushy, tucked away in an inside pocket. Gingerly, he extracted the offending article. It was a business card:

Harry-Karry (London) Ltd
Don't kill yourself making that delivery
Let us do it for you!
Call Harry on 08793 789077

He was about to dump it in the bin when the penny dropped. This was the card that had slipped from Themba's wallet when he and HB had first discovered the diamonds at Bugler House. It was Harry Carey's card. Harry, the villain who'd been blackmailing Themba - the man whose core business was violence, intimidation and the sale of Class A drugs to the south London underworld... and more importantly, the nut-job with the direct connection to the Venezuelan gang. After cramming the jacket back into the dryer, Felix got out his mobile and started keying in the number.

Naz tried to snatch the phone from him. 'You can't call him - it's not safe. The guy's a psycho!'

'It's all we've got, Naz,' Felix said, fending him off. 'Harry's our only lead. Anyway, he's hundreds of miles away - he'll never be able to track the call.'

'You say that, but he could be here in Frecklesall right now, looking for the diamonds. And what about that tracing app you said Themba has on her phone? Harry might have the same piece of kit. He could be knocking on our door two minutes after you call him. For pity's sake, don't do it!'

Felix's stomach was in knots but he knew he had to stick with it. 'Sorry mate, you're just going to have to trust me on this one.'

Naz made another attempt to grab the mobile but their inept wrestling match was interrupted by a voice coming through on the handset.

''Arry-Karry couriers at your service. And what can I do you for, this fine evening?'

Felix pointed a warning finger at his friend and switched the phone to 'speaker'. It took a second for him to tune into the broad London accent, but even then he couldn't shake the impression that Harry sounded remarkably friendly for someone whose job majored on murder, drug dealing, and inflicting pain on others.

'Hi, this is Nigel… err… Nigel Scoggins,' Felix replied in the poshest accent he could muster, desperately trying to hide the wobble in his voice. 'May I speak with Harry Carey, please?'

'You are currently enjoying that particular pleasure, my son,' Harry replied, brightly. 'Where you from then, Nigel?'

'Err… Heysham.'

'Is that norf of the river? Look, we're a bit stretched at the moment but I could probably do a bike for you in a couple of hours.'

'Actually, I'm not looking for a courier, Harry,' said Felix, 'but I *was* hoping you might be able to help me out with some information. It's… it's a personal matter.'

'Go on then, mate, I'm all ears.'

'You see, I'm trying to track down this girl I met the other night. She's in her early twenties - tall, slim, and black - from Lesotho, near South Africa, I think. She's an absolute stunner, Harry, and I've simply got to see her again. Trouble is, I don't know how to get in touch. She left me with one of your cards and I was hoping you could point me in the right direction.'

Harry chuckled. 'Actually, I fink I know who you might be talking about. The young lady in question worked for me for a few months, although to be honest, I ain't seen her in a while.'

'Do you have any idea where she is now?'

'No, I don't. And I know she seems like a lovely girl, Nige, but looks can be deceiving, can't they?'

'What do you mean?'

There was a long pause. '... I shouldn't really be doing this, what with the data protection an' that, but you seem like a straight-up kind of geezer, so... The long and the short of it, is that Kefie Ngwane is big trouble. If you want my advice, you should steer well clear.'

'*Kefie*?' Felix repeated the name, trying to get his head around what he was hearing. 'But she told me she was called Themba - Themba Kigelle.'

'Why don't that surprise me?' Harry said, laughing. 'I always knew there was somefing funny going on there but I never quite worked out what it was. Anyway, Kefie was one of the top earners on my books - reliable, hardworking and popular with the customers, too. Then, a couple of weeks back, she goes and does a runner. Next fing I know, the Bill's come around 'ere, knockin' on my door. Speaking personal, like, I don't think she done it, though - not for one minute.'

'What? What did she do?'

'Well, this African geezer phoned in a pick-up. He wanted her to do the job - most insistent about that. So I called her up with the details and that's the last I ever 'eard from her. The police found the guy's body in his hotel room. Poor sod was stabbed, then had his neck broken, apparently.'

'He was murdered? Ohmygod, that's terrible! So what was in the package she was supposed to collect?'

Harry snorted. 'Tell you what Nige - why not ask her yourself, next time you're smooching up close?'

Felix's head was spinning. 'Actually, I think she mentioned something about this when we were together, Harry. She told me she'd done the pick-up and brought the package back to you. She said *you* were the one who'd sent her up north to Scotland to deliver it to these South American gangsters.'

Harry guffawed. 'I dunno what sort of cock an' bull she's been feeding you, mate, but the furthest norf we go is Watford, and the only South American gangster I know is that Diego Maradonna. Hand of God? You're having a larf! Listen, if you know anyfing about this you should call the Old Bill. I reckon they could use all the help they can get.'

'Oh, right. Listen, I'm sorry, Harry, this has come as a bit of a shock. Is there anything else you can tell me about her - anything at all?'

'Well, there was this one fing. Y'see, the geezer who phoned in the pick-up said to mention this word to her and she'd know what it was all about.'

'What was it - what was the word?'

'I told the police, so I don't suppose it matters too much if I tell you. He had this accent, so I might not have got it right - but it sounded somefing like... *Seetoo.*'

'*Seetoo?* What does that mean?' Felix asked.

Harry laughed. 'You tell me, mate!'

'Harry - did she ever mention someone called Colin - Colin Anderton?'

But Harry had hung up.

The two friends sat staring at each other, the silence eventually broken by the sound of banging on the back door. Naz dived behind the settee, convinced Harry had traced the call and was paying them a visit. He only began to calm down when Saj trotted in asking for money to pay the milkman.

'*Seetoo,*' muttered Felix. 'It's got to mean something, hasn't it? And Harry didn't exactly sound like the crazed killer Themba told me about, did he? And he called her Kefie - Kefie Ngwane. She must be using a false name!'

'That's not the point, Felix,' Naz said, his voice full of concern.

Felix was pacing up and down now. '*Seetoo... Saydoss* - there's got to be some kind of link with Colin Anderton.'

His friend shook him by the shoulder. 'For God's sake, will you wake up? Themba's up at your house with your mum and dad, and your sister, isn't she?'

'Yeah, and when I catch up with her she's going to be in big trouble!'

'Don't you get what I'm saying?' Naz was screaming in his face now. 'Harry just told us that Themba's wanted by the police for *murder*. You need to go home, right now! You need to warn them!'

He'd phoned all the numbers he had - even the landline - but no one was answering. They'd probably already been killed, he thought, as he pedalled flat-out around the Big Lamp roundabout, barely noticing the bottoms of his newly shrunken suit trousers flapping mid-way up his calves. After sprinting the length of Scundale Chase, he dumped the bike in the driveway and burst into the kitchen, all but falling to his knees in relief at the sight of his little sister, who was sitting at the table.

'Flo! Thank goodness you're OK!'

Her eyes were red from crying. 'I texted you hours ago - where have you been?'

He pulled up a chair. 'Sorry, there's a fault on my phone. I haven't had any messages for days now. Anyway, when I rang before, there was no answer.'

'I couldn't pick up with this going on, could I?' she said, angrily. 'I told you it was happening but you wouldn't believe me.'

'What are you on about?'

Big fat tears started rolling down her cheeks. 'Mum and Dad have split up.'

'But I spoke to Dad yesterday and he said everything was fine. He was taking Mum out for this slap-up meal. He'd even picked up a few style tips from our Fred.'

'Don't talk to me about *him.*'

Felix looked at her, uncertainly.

'You'll see,' she said, getting up from the table. 'Dad's in the lounge. Oh, and in case you were wondering, Themba left this afternoon.'

It took a few seconds for the news to sink in. 'Why? Where's she gone?'

'How should I know? I ran an errand for her down to the post office and when I got back, I found her in your room messing with your laptop. I asked her what she was doing and she got really nowty with me. Next thing, she'd packed up her stuff and walked out. She didn't even say goodbye.'

Flo stomped off, leaving Felix to wander through into the lounge.

The curtains were drawn, the room lit only by the low flicker of the TV, which was showing a ladies' underwear 'special' on the home shopping channel.

'Take a look at me now!' announced the puce-faced woman on the screen, who had somehow shoe-horned herself into a heavily elasticated, skin-tone, neck to knee all-in-one. 'With this Body Grip 2001 Ultra-Control technical undergarment, I'm slim, pert and ready for fun! I can fit into clothes I haven't worn for years, and feeling as great as this, I'm literally brimming with confidence. Ladies, this product is a total game-changer, and at a specially discounted price of only £59.99 the Body Grip 2001 is our best-buy bargain of the week. Phone lines are open now, but be quick - these are selling fast!'

Felix stood by the door, open-mouthed.

'Do you think they do them for men?' asked the dismembered voice from the depths of the settee.

'I'm not really sure,' Felix replied, clicking the light on to a dimmed setting.

His dad was looking unusually dapper in a light-blue shirt and a pair of navy trousers, but that wasn't what caught Felix's eye.

'That's our tea cosy, Dad - what's it doing on your head?' he asked.

Ignoring the question, his dad gestured towards the TV. 'Only, I had thought about trying to get into shape, but with this kind of kit on the market, there's not much point, is there?'

Felix sidestepped the tea cosy issue and cut straight to the chase. 'Flo said things didn't work out with Mum this evening. What happened?'

His dad grunted. 'Salsatastic have just been told they're topping the bill at Saturday's culture final. Obviously, your mum's really excited at the news, but it means she's got to spend more time at the club to nail their showcase routine. Staying here is too much of a distraction, apparently, so she's stopping at Norma's for a while.'

'Weren't you supposed to be sorting things out with her at the restaurant?'

His dad slumped back into the settee. 'We didn't quite get that far, Son.'

Felix looked at him, incredulously.

'Your mum came home early to do Florence's tea, so I nipped upstairs to get ready,' his dad began in a downbeat tone. 'I had a shave and opted for a quick shower - it's been a few days, to be fair. I was giving my hair the once-over when I remembered that special conditioner Freddie was raving about, so I thought I'd try it out.'

Suddenly, Felix didn't like the sound of where this was going.

'I didn't have my glasses on me,' his dad continued,' so I couldn't read the instructions on the bottle - which was a pity.'

'Why's that?'

His dad pulled the tea cosy from the top of his head, like a waiter in a swanky restaurant lifting the domed silver cloche from the plate to reveal the main course.

Felix gasped. One side of his father's scalp was billiard-ball smooth, the other had tufts of hair sticking out in between acres of lilywhite baldness. He looked like a badly plucked turkey.

'*Svelte*,' his dad spat the name out. 'Turns out it's not hair conditioner after all. Turns out it's the stuff your mum rubs on her legs to get rid of the stubble. Freddie does like his practical jokes but *she* didn't see the funny side. As soon as she saw the state I was in, it was all off.'

Felix felt terrible. He'd forgotten about the Svelte set-up and now his parents were getting divorced as a result.

'I'm so sorry, Dad.'

'It's not your doing, Son.' His dad grimaced as he slipped the tea cosy back into place. 'Believe you me, after I've finished with your brother, he won't be laughing for a long, long time.'

'Couldn't Themba have talked Mum round?'

'You know she's left, don't you? She was up in her bedroom and Flo popped in to see her. I don't know what went on but it all ended in a massive row. Next thing, the back door's slamming and she's cleared off.'

'Where's she gone?'

'Haven't a clue,' replied his dad, turning his attention back to the TV. 'Hey, the power tools slot is coming up now so you can either zip it and watch it with me, or get off to your room. You look like you could use some kip.'

Felix headed upstairs and lay on his bed, trying to think calm thoughts. On the up-side, his family had not been murdered, but somehow that joyous news had been overshadowed by the jarring reality of his parents' split. It was no wonder Flo was so angry with him. And then another, more immediate problem hit home - he was going to have to explain Themba's disappearance to Hugo. The NKI man would do his nut!

After agonizing for a good ten minutes, he decided to swerve the grief that was coming his way by sending Hugo an email. He realised something was wrong the moment he opened up his laptop. It was bad enough that

Themba had checked out all the websites he'd been on over the past few days, but the appearance of the NewsKwest folder at the top of his 'recently visited' list, set his nerves jangling. He scrolled through the files containing his updates to Hugo, discovering that every single one had been accessed earlier that afternoon.

Clicking the NKI icon on his desktop, he sat back and waited. And then a message popped onto the screen.

Sorry - Website Unavailable

He tried again, without success, and emails to Hugo's work address came bouncing back with an 'undeliverable' message. He only had a few quid left on his phone card, which wasn't going to buy much time on a transatlantic connection, but he had no choice. He punched in the number and was greeted by a continuous tone, followed by a computer-generated message:

'I'm sorry, this number is not recognised.'

Suddenly he felt very alone. He was about to switch off the computer when he spotted a new email. It was from Themba. Heart pounding, he opened it up:

Felix, It is time for me to leave. Matters are finally drawing to a close, but I urge you to be vigilant as the next few days may bring danger to us all. Do not believe everything they tell you. As a journalist, I know you will discover the truth.

I wish you every good fortune.

Themba

He saved the message, hoping it would make more sense once he was thinking straight. And then he noticed an email news alert from the Frecklesall: It's Got it All! Bid Team. While he wouldn't normally have bothered, there was something about it that caught his eye:

Frecklesall: It's Got it All! Newsflash:

Local DJ to Host Saturday's Culture Spectacular

Frecklesall FM's top DJ, 'Full-on-Freddie' Haythornthwaite, is to host Saturday night's prestigious Capital of Culture broadcast, live from the town hall, following the last-minute withdrawal of Bernard Henman, presenter of It's Grand Up North's weekly poultry programme, *Professional Fowl.*

DeeJay FoF's legendary *Metal Mania* radio show has been attracting record audiences and his recent sell-out gig at OT's is still the talk of the town. Got it All! Chief, Councillor Ron Snodgrass, believes the youngster can give Frecklesall's bid the boost it needs. 'We were gutted when we heard Howard had pulled out and, naturally, we wish him all the best with the forthcoming court case,' he said. 'However, in DeeJay FoF we've secured a more than able replacement. It's a big responsibility on young shoulders, but you know what they say: "Cometh the hour, cometh the FoF!".'

Cutting short his appearance at the Cannes Film Festival in the south of France, Frecklesall's rising star described the news as, 'Mind-blowing, like, totally awesome.'

It was a joke, it had to be. There was no way Freddie would come back for a gig like this after everything that had happened, and anyway, who would be stupid enough to ask him to do it? But the item had one more sting in its tail. Immediately below the article was a tiny 'Jpg' icon, beside a cheery caption:

Bling-Tastic 'FoF' Celebrates with younger brother Felix!!

Felix clicked on the file, his stomach lurching as the pixels organised themselves on screen. A grinning Freddie was pictured behind the sound deck at OT's but for once it wasn't the gigantic pair of diamonds hanging from his brother's earlobes that grabbed Felix's attention. Another figure was standing beside the DJ - ruffled, spiky hair, lilywhite complexion, a haunted expression on his face, and to top it all, that excruciating Born to Boogie! Hawaiian shirt.

He stared at the image in dismay. Themba's plan had worked brilliantly - the *Quesos Grandes* gang had disappeared on a wild goose chase to the south of France, and Frecklesall had returned to something vaguely resembling normality. But with the shock announcement of Freddie's next on-stage engagement and this picture doing the rounds, all of that was set to change. Only now, it wasn't just the *Metal Mania* DJ who'd be in the firing line.

14

The next day, Felix cycled into Frecklesall, locking his bike to the racks beside the town hall before ambling across to the Full Monty for a late lunch appointment. They say a problem shared is a problem halved but in his experience, talking things through with Naz almost always stood this simple formula on its head. After twenty minutes, anxiety levels were going through the roof.

'You shouldn't even be here,' Naz said, leaning forward across the table. 'If those gangsters really are coming back, you need to get out of town, and fast.'

Felix looked at his friend, incredulously. 'I can't just clear off, can I? Freddie's an accident waiting to happen, and you know what our Flo's like - she's already had one lucky escape after she had a go at Themba.'

'You don't think she'd have hurt her, do you?'

Felix shook his head. 'I can't see it... but she got into a right strop when she was caught out with my laptop. Flo reckons that's why she left - well, that and she'd obviously worked out what I'd been up to with Hugo. Apparently, she did her nut a second time when she discovered I'd taken the bike with me on the Isle of Man trip. What a cheek! There's no way she's getting that back - not after everything she's put me through.'

Wally Nockles sidled up to their table, sweat dripping from the end of his nose, a grubby tea towel draped over a shoulder. 'Big break for your Freddie, hosting this culture gig, Felix,' he said. 'You must be chuffed for him.'

Felix forced a smile. No one could possibly have missed the Got it All! flyers, featuring the press release shot, that had appeared overnight on just about every blank wall and the many vacant shop fronts across the town centre.

'And those diamonds are crackin'!' continued the café owner. 'It's a pity he didn't have them on him when he were in earlier this morning.'

'You what?' Felix spluttered. 'Our Freddie's back in town, already?'

'Certainly is... Hey, what's with that colander he's carting around?'

'I couldn't say, Wally. It's probably some kind of fashion accessory. He didn't mention where he was staying, did he?'

'Sorry lad, you know me - never one to pry...' Wally's attention was diverted by the ping of the bell as the café door opened.

Two girls walked in. Neesha acknowledged Naz's wave but the moment Dannii spotted Felix, she dragged her friend back outside.

Naz only just managed to stop him from giving chase. 'Let it lie, Felix, you'll only make things worse.'

'But it's so unfair,' he moaned. 'I just want the chance to say sorry, and explain what really happened.'

'Perhaps Bernie can talk to her. She seems to listen to him. They all do, for some reason.'

'He's the one who dropped me in it, in the first place. There was the boy band thing, then all that stuff about

179

me being *Bugler* Fashion Editor. If he'd kept his mouth shut, none of this would have happened.'

Naz chuckled. 'Maybe, but then she wouldn't even have given you the time of day. At least Bernie gave you a shot, even if you did totally blow it.'

'Thanks mate, you're making me feel a whole lot better about myself. Talking of Bernie, where is the little squirt? I could do with someone to kick up the backside, the way I'm feeling right now.'

'He sent us a text, earlier. Didn't you get it?'

Felix groaned - the fault on his phone was totally killing his already pathetic social life.

'He said he was going shopping in Preston with Zoe,' Naz continued. 'There's some kind of dance festival on in Frecklesall today which he reckons is going to be really lame. He said we should steer well clear.'

'Don't exactly have his options, though, do we?' said Felix, glumly. 'How does he do it, Naz? I mean, how does someone like Bernie end up with a girl as fit as Zoe?'

'I don't know, but that's not really important right now, is it?'

Felix gave him a puzzled look.

Naz rolled his eyes. 'You've got a pack of Venezuelan gangsters on your tail, you've been sharing your house with a woman who's wanted for murder - I'll tell you what, why don't we throw in some Mi5 agents and a fistful of fake diamonds, just to keep it interesting? Isn't it about time you stopped moping around and actually started *doing* something, for once! From where I'm sitting, the one person who's even deeper into this mess than you are, is your brother. If he really *is* back in town, you've got to warn him!'

They spent a frantic few minutes running through the lengthy list of Freddie's ex-girlfriends, his usual sanctuary when the going got tough, but it was as they were getting up to leave the Monty that Felix finally cracked it.

'Pig and Whistle!' he yelled. 'It's three o'clock on a Friday afternoon - where else would he be?'

Naz looked at him in disbelief. 'But surely he'd have the sense to lie low?'

'You're joking, aren't you? He'll be holed up in the public bar, boring his mates senseless about tomorrow night's gig. Come on, let's get over there!'

It was a sunny day and the unusually pleasant weather had enticed a smattering of day trippers out onto the seafront. Dodging a wayward mime artist pretending to be trapped in a box, the pair darted up the Prom before switching to the back streets, ducking behind wheelie-bins and hiding in front gardens whenever they saw anyone coming. A few minutes later, they were crouching behind the yard wall of a terraced house, checking out the boisterous crowd gathered on the Pig & Whistle's cobbled forecourt beneath a Got it All! Beer Festival banner.

Naz turned to his friend. 'Careful, Felix - it might be a trap.'

His words were drowned out by loud cheers, followed by the wonky tones of a melodeon squeeze-box. Peering tentatively over the wall, they spotted what looked like a synchronised hanky-waving display - flailing arms wheeling back and forth above the heads of the crowd.

Felix grimaced as he caught the sounds of jangling bells and the hefty 'Thwack!' of willow against willow. 'Morrisers,' he said. 'Looks like a fair few of 'em as well.'

Naz sighed. 'It'll be that thing Bernie warned us about.'

Seconds later the pair were scuttling across the road to join the throng.

The crowd was raucous, smelly and a bit drunk, a description equally applicable to many of the dancers - a ragtag collective of ageing hippies, real-ale beardos and a handful of youngsters who should have known better. Dressed in grubby white shirts, purple waistcoats and white, knee-length breeches, with jingly bells strapped to their calves and crumpled straw hats on their heads, they lumbered across the cobbles swinging their arms high into the air, pausing occasionally to whack each other with big wooden sticks. The forecourt was packed and after elbowing their way through the crowd, Naz and Felix eventually found themselves teetering on the brink of the action.

The Morrisers clattered back and forth, knees lifting high in a flurry of flailing ribbons, while some of the dancers stood around the edge of the circle, clapping along to the music. The crowd were lapping it up, yelling abuse and encouragement in equal measure.

Naz pointed across the cobbles, shouting to make himself heard over the din. 'That Morris girl, over there on the other side - she looks just like Zoe!'

'Don't be daft,' said Felix, 'she's in Preston, with Bernie.'

Naz cupped a hand to his ear. 'Sorry, what did you say, mate?'

'I said, SHE'S IN PRESTON, WITH BERNIE!'

The diminutive Morriser standing immediately in front of them, span around, and the three of them stared at each other, open-mouthed.

'It's not how it looks!' Bernie shrieked from beneath his grubby straw hat. 'I'm only in it for the girls and the ale! How else is someone like me going to cop off with a lass like Zoe, or… or get served in a boozer?'

It was Felix who found his voice first. 'Ohmygod, Bernie, you're a *Morris dancer*! This is priceless!'

The rest of the group had jumped back into the middle of the circle for some hanky action but Bernie stayed put. 'Don't be like that,' he pleaded. 'You should join us. The side's stuffed full of girls - there's so much talent around, even a dork like you couldn't fail to score.'

Felix was having none of it. 'You look so cute in your little outfit, Bernie. I can't wait to tell everyone. We should post some photos on Facebook… Oof!' He reeled as an elbow jabbed into his ribs. 'Bloody hell Naz, what did you do that for?'

Naz's eyes were staring, his mouth opening and closing like a startled goldfish, but no words were coming out.

'What is it?' asked Felix. 'What's the matter?'

Naz pointed past the clacking sticks and wafting hankies at a rumpus in the crowd opposite. 'It's… it's *them*,' he mumbled. 'They're coming for us…'

There was no missing the scar-faced gangster and his gold-toothed mate, who were bulldozing their way through the assembled masses towards them.

'Friends of yours?' asked Bernie.

Now it was Felix's turn to look petrified.

'Here's the thing,' continued Bernie. 'Me and the guys would normally be only too happy to help out a mate in a tight spot - it's just that, well, we've been kind of struggling with the negativity you've been putting our way, recently.'

'I'm begging you, Bernie,' Felix said, his eyes still locked on the Venezuelan duo. 'I think what you're doing here is really cool. I won't tell anyone - in fact, I might even sign up myself. If you and your mates could just hold them off, even if it's only for a few minutes… *Please*!'

After a quick bump of fists to seal the deal, Bernie span around, yelling instructions at the bearded melodeon player. 'Darryl - let's spice things up a bit. How about a dose of the *Black Joker*?'

The sound of the melodeon kicking into a new and much jauntier rhythm, instantly energised the dancers, who sprang into action, waving their sticks over their heads just as the gangsters barged into the circle.

'Get yourself out of here, Naz!' Felix yelled above the jeers of the crowd. 'I'm heading in to find Fred. If you haven't heard from me in fifteen minutes, call the police.'

Naz didn't need asking twice and he darted away, leaving Felix battling towards the Pig's front door.

Everything would have been fine for the Venezuelans if they'd stayed put, but the sight of Felix making his escape was clearly too much for them to bear. As they tried to press forward, they were rebuffed by some well-aimed clouts and in no time, things had escalated into a good old-fashioned punch-up.

Elbows out, Felix eventually shunted his way into the Pig and Whistle's public bar. There was a group of pensioners huddled around a game of dominoes in the corner, the only other customers standing on the bench seats, peering through the windows to try to get a view of the action outside. A scruffy-looking man in his mid-thirties, with long greasy hair and a squint, stood behind an array of beer taps.

'What d'you want?' he asked gruffly.

'My brother,' replied Felix, breathlessly, 'Freddie Haythornthwaite - have you seen him?'

'Barred!' came the blunt response. 'And if you're his brother, you're barred too.'

'Why? What's he done?'

The pub landlord folded his arms across his chest. 'If that no-mark thinks he can sup in here for nowt and then go and do *that* in our toilets, he's got another thing coming!'

The exchange was interrupted by yells and shrieks from outside.

'Ay up, these Mexicans look like they can handle themselves!' shouted an elderly man from on top of one of the benches. 'Better batten down the hatches, Davey boy, trouble's brewing!'

Davey barked a few words into a two-way radio before pulling out a large baseball bat from beneath the bar. 'Clear off!' he said, waving the bat in Felix's face.

'But... but they're after me as well,' Felix pleaded.

'Unbelievable! You have the brass-neck to walk into my pub with a pair of head-the-balls on your tail, and then complain when I kick you out? I'll tell you what, lad - next time we'll organise a ruck round at your house, so it's your living room that gets trashed. How would that suit?'

'They'll be in here any second!' someone shouted from up at the window. 'Big Eric's having a pop but I don't fancy his chances... Oof! That must have hurt.'

'You don't understand!' screamed Felix. 'They're hitmen from Venezuela. They're going to kill me.'

'Not if I do it first, they won't,' Davey replied, jabbing at him with the end of the bat. 'Now do one before I start using this thing for real!'

Felix was forced back to the door, knowing that the moment he stepped over the threshold it would all be over. And then a familiar voice from the corner table came to his rescue.

'Leave the lad be, Davey, you can see he's in trouble.'

He'd never been so relieved to hear his great aunt's dulcet tones.

The barman hesitated. 'But I could lose my licence because of this, Doreen - not to mention the damage that'll be caused.'

She stood up from her dominoes match, wagging an arthritic finger at him. 'I've been drinking in here from before you were a twinkle in your dad's eye, Davey lad, and he'd be turning in his grave if he could see what you're up to now. Kicking out one of our own in his hour of need? You should be ashamed of yourself!'

'Oh right. Sorry,' mumbled the barman.

'Use your brain for once, you dopey bugger. The police'll be here any minute, so lock up and take the lad through to the back.'

Davey pushed past Felix and slammed the main door shut, sliding two heavy-duty bolts into place. Seconds later the whole pub shook as a boot slammed into the door's steel panelling. Everyone heard the shouts from outside.

'*Abre*! *Abre la puerta*! *Ahora*!'

The drinkers picked up chairs and anything else they could find to defend themselves, while Davey led Felix through some gloomy living quarters and out into a tiny back yard stacked high with metal beer barrels. Doreen was already there, standing beside her mobility scooter. She peered around the yard gate into the pub's car park.

'Get yourself on the scooter and clear off out of here,' she said.

'What if they see me?' Felix asked nervously.

'Shut up and get going before I change my mind.'

He climbed up onto the seat knowing there was little point in arguing. 'What will you do, Doreen? I can't just leave you here.'

She pulled the rectangular plastic rain cover over his head. 'Don't worry about me, lad. I'll see you at the Paddock in half an hour - there's something important I need to talk to you about.'

She eased the gate open and Felix trundled away at a steady five miles per hour, praying that his great aunt had charged the battery.

'She's wanted for murder *and* she's a compulsive liar,' Felix said, twitching the lounge curtains to check the weed-ridden front garden for intruders. 'I don't know where she is, and to be honest I really don't care.'

His great aunt was having none of it. 'You've got her all wrong, lad. Anyway, this is family, which means you can't just walk away like it doesn't matter.'

He glanced around the tatty, down-at-heel, 1970s-time capsule that was his great aunt's lounge - an explosion of brown and beige with newspapers scattered about the threadbare carpet and stuffing poking from the tears in the settee's upholstery. Doreen was looking older these days and he could have sworn she'd shrunk since he'd last spent time with her, but he knew all too well how deceptive her appearance could be.

'I tried my best to be nice to her,' he said. 'All I've had back is a load of grief. We're well rid if you ask me.'

His great aunt laughed. 'That's nonsense. After she left your house, yesterday, she came straight over here. We were up talking for most of last night. She told me what's been going on.'

'She's not still here, is she?' he asked, half-expecting Themba to pop up from behind the settee.

Doreen dismissed the question with a wave of her hand. 'Those diamonds - the real ones - have been in her family for generations. They're like an heirloom and losing them is killing her grandfather. Now she's got them back, all she wants to do is get them home safely.'

Felix rolled his eyes. 'Here we go again! She's got a different story for every day of the week. No one's actually seen these *real* diamonds, have they? We don't even know if they exist.'

'Which would explain why those Venezuelan thugs are chasing you and your brother from pillar to post! Themba's an honest girl, Felix - you can't blame her for spinning you a yarn given some of the stunts you've been pulling. Going behind her back to that news agency? It's a disgrace!'

'The *Bugler* editor set that up - what was I supposed to do? Anyway, if you're her new best friend and she really has got the diamonds, did she happen to mention where they are?'

'They're probably on their way out of the country by now, Doreen replied. 'I don't know any more than that, and I don't want to. It's none of our business.'

'It *is* our business, *actually*!' said Felix. 'She's dragged all of us into this. We're in the firing line and now she's just... disappeared! If I could get my hands on her I'd... I'd...'

'You'd run a mile, that's what you'd do.' Doreen reached over and handed him the padded envelope resting on the arm of her easy chair. 'She asked me to give you this.'

Ripping it open, he pulled out a cheap pay-as-you-go mobile, still in its wrapper. 'Great!' he exclaimed. 'Just what I always wanted!'

'That's right lad, it is. It's called a "burner" phone, which means it's new and untraceable. And before you make some snidey comment about already having a mobile, Themba said to tell you that your phone's been compromised - which means you shouldn't be using it.'

'*Compromised*? What's that supposed to mean?'

She sat down next to him on the settee. 'You haven't had any text messages for a while, have you?'

Felix pulled out his own phone and studied the screen. 'It's not been right since the explosion at Fred's flat. But how would you know about that?'

'Themba showed me on that fancy telephone of hers. You're not exactly Mr Popular, Felix, but you have had *some* texts over the past week. She's been intercepting them, and all the voice messages from HB's number. If she's been doing it there's every chance others have, as well.'

'What? That's outrageous! There are laws against phone tapping, you know!'

Doreen was struggling to keep her temper. 'Shut up and listen to me for once, you big soft lad. This isn't about you, it's about your boss - HB.'

'What's he got to do with anything?'

'He's still missing, isn't he? Themba says they're holding him hostage.'

Felix laughed. 'Assuming that's true, which I very much doubt, then it's her problem.'

Doreen shook her head. 'She's a good girl. She's got what she came for and now she wants to do the right thing - to help HB.'

'Bravo!' Felix clapped his hands, mockingly. Give that woman a medal!'

'Listen, if she hadn't hacked into your phone, you'd be the one in the firing line, right now. We both know how that would have ended, don't we?'

'I can look after myself.'

'Give over!' Doreen exclaimed, laughing out loud. 'Enough of the larking around, lad, it's not good for my heart. Themba picked up a text while she was here and next thing, she was up and out the door like greased lightning. I offered to help, but we all know I'm too old to be of use to anyone these days. Don't ask me why but despite everything that's gone on, she seems to trust you. So I volunteered you as her emergency back-up. There's a strong signal on that new phone and she's going to message you if she needs a hand. God help her if it comes to that, but beggars can't be choosers. If she does get in touch, she said you have to follow her instructions to the letter - none of the usual mucking about.'

'No way am I getting into this, Doreen!' he yelled. 'I'm glad she's got the diamonds back, but she should call the police if she's worried about HB.'

His aunt fixed him with her steely gaze. 'This is *personal* Felix. And after what she did for our Freddie, it's *family*. Nothing is more important.'

Felix looked at her, aghast.

'I don't want you taking any risks and getting yourself hurt or owt like that, but I promised her you'd help,' she continued. 'So, if it makes you feel better, you're doing this for me, not her. Now, put your head between your knees and breath into a paper bag - or whatever it is you do when things get a bit much - while I make us a brew. Once you've heard me out, you'll think differently.'

Doreen shuffled through to the kitchen while Felix fumed in silence on the settee. His great aunt was mid-way through pouring the tea when the landline rang. She picked up the call on the kitchen extension and Felix eavesdropped on her side of the conversation.

'Hello Brian…You sound a bit… Well, yes, if it's urgent - bring her over. You know I'm always happy to look after Florence… Our Felix? No, I haven't seen him in days - what's he been up to now?'

His aunt hung up and appeared at the doorway looking even more dishevelled than usual. 'You've got to go,' she said. 'You need to get weaving, right now.'

'Why? What's happened?'

'Nothing - well, nothing yet. And if anyone asks, you were never here. Get yourself home, quick as quick, but keep away from the main roads, just in case.'

'What's going on, Doreen?'

'Put that new phone in your pocket, keep it charged up and *do not* forget what I told you.'

He got as far as the garden gate and looked back, convinced more than ever that his great aunt had lost her marbles. There she was at the lounge window, shooing him away with a dirty tea towel.

It was normally a fifteen-minute walk home from Doreen's but sticking to the back streets was going to add another ten. Felix was still furious about having his messages intercepted but the more he thought about it, the more he was kicking himself for not spotting it earlier. Themba had cleaned out his laptop and now, that

191

time at the Full Monty when he'd caught her taking his mobile apart, made a lot more sense.

Heading along the footpath, he barely gave the man walking towards him a second thought. Late thirties, well-built and with tattoos on his muscular arms, alarm bells only started ringing when the guy stepped in front of him, blocking his way.

'Haythornthwaite?' the man barked, and before Felix could respond, his face had cracked into a cold, hard smile. 'It is you, isn't it? You're Felix Haythornthwaite - the joker who's been messing with my daughter.'

Felix's voice sounded as wobbly as his legs felt. 'You must be Dannii's dad. Pleased to meet you, sir. I... I can explain everything. It's all been a terrible misunderstanding.'

'I'll give you a "misunderstanding"!' The man lunged at him.

Felix sprinted away as fast as his size elevens would carry him. Careering around the corner, he shimmied between some parked cars before charging blindly into the middle of Bogs Lane, one of the busy routes out of town. He barely registered the squeal of tyres as the high-powered BMW slammed on its brakes. In the next instant, a door flew open and powerful hands were hauling him into the back of the car.

15

He'd been in 'solitary' for what seemed like an eternity, sleep deprivation transporting him into a twilight zone of tortured paranoia. The brutal interrogation techniques of his captors had pushed him to the edge… and beyond. He'd pleaded with them to stop, come *this close* to cracking but somehow, against all the odds, he'd managed to hold it together.

The lack of food had left him gaunt but still strikingly handsome. *Let's see who blinks first,* he thought, allowing himself the luxury of a grim smile. As if on cue, the cell door opened and a tall, curvaceous blonde with the looks of a supermodel, walked in. Distracted by her striking appearance and the heady scent of Chanel, he barely noticed her white medical coat and the stethoscope slung around her neck. It was only as she got closer that he spotted the syringe concealed in her hand.

She hesitated, momentarily taken aback by the rippling contours of his manly torso, now clearly visible through the sweat-soaked Frecklesall: It's Got it All! T-shirt.

'Good afternoon, Mr Haythornthwaite, my name is *Ursula*,' she spoke in a low, sultry Russian accent, her eyes smouldering. 'I was warned about your good looks, but it seems I was misled.' She reached out to stroke his stubble encrusted cheek. 'You are so much more *beautiful* in the flesh, which in many ways, makes my task all the more pleasurable.' She pushed the glinting metal syringe up close to his face. 'This is sodium pentothal - they call it the truth serum. The after-effects are unpleasant, but...'

'I hope you're not trying to get on the internet,' said Mi5 Intelligence Officer, Vikki DeBrett, as she walked into his bedroom carrying a tray piled high with food. 'You do understand why we've had to disable the Wi-Fi and secure your phone, don't you?'

'Don't worry - I know the rules,' replied Felix, slamming the laptop shut. 'I was just checking out some files on the hard drive.' The opening paragraphs of his true-life memoir, beginning with his dramatic capture by ruthless government agents, would have to wait - there was a Pot Noodle on that tray and it had his name on it.

In her late-twenties, Vikki was tall, slim and attractive, and she'd been really nice to him since they'd got home. The Mi5 anti-stab vest wasn't the most flattering of outfits, and she definitely had a bit of the uptight 'head girl' vibe going on, but all things considered, Felix could think of worse ways to spend a Friday evening.

'My boss is here now,' she said. 'He's asked if you'd come down for a chat, once you've eaten.'

'No problem,' he replied, 'although there's nothing I can tell him that I haven't already been through with you.'

This was not entirely true. Certain facts had been withheld - particularly those relating to the earlier involvement of his great aunt and, of course, the 'burner' phone she'd given him on Themba's behalf.

Heading down the stairs, fifteen minutes later, Felix could hear his dad droning on in the lounge.

'…When something like this kicks off, it's great to know you guys are primed and ready to rumble. My eldest lad's flat blew up, only last week. Gas explosion they're saying, but word on the street is, *Al Qaeda* were involved–' He stopped abruptly as Felix entered the room. 'Oh, hello Son, I was just telling these gentlemen…'

Felix didn't hear any more - he was staring, open-mouthed at the two lummoxes standing to attention on either side of the bay window. 'It's… it's *you,*' he eventually croaked.

'Ollie and Rupert to their pals!' announced his dad, the tea cosy that had hidden his baldness, now replaced with a navy-blue and white Preston North End bobble hat. 'I tell you, son, we're in safe hands with chaps like these looking out for us.'

'I've met you before,' said Felix, barely able to believe his eyes. 'You're Tony and Eric, the gas men.'

The Mi5 officers exchanged awkward glances.

Felix's dad looked confused but carried on, regardless. 'Oh… right. Well, allow me to introduce Mr Trenton Fotherbridge, Mi5's Director of UK Field Operations and Homeland Security, no less!'

He'd completely missed the chubby, goblin-like character, ensconced in the armchair in the corner of the room. The prominent eyebrows and jowled chops, combined with the made-to-measure pin-striped suit and old school tie, reflected a lifetime of privilege.

'Delighted to make your acquaintance at last, Felix. A pleasure and so forth.' The Mi5 chief's voice was deep and suave… and uncannily familiar.

Felix's world suddenly began to unravel.

*

'Intelligence work can be a messy business at times,' Fotherbridge mused, leaning back in his chair, hands behind his head. 'You may think it's all James Bond - fast cars and faster ladies - but the truth is far less glamorous. I can appreciate your disappointment–'

'*Disappointment?*' shrieked Felix. 'That's the understatement of the year, Trenton - or should I call you *Hugo*? Do you have any idea what you've done to me? Teaming up with NewsKwest International was the one thing that kept me going through this nightmare, and now you're telling me it was all a sham! I thought I was working with a top international news agency, when all along it was you, sitting in a broom cupboard in your trollies, like some pervy internet stalker!'

The Mi5 chief offered him a patronising smile. 'With all due respect, it was a tad more sophisticated than that. We had to push the envelope on a fair-few protocols to get your editor at the *Bugler* on board, while website construction was something of a stretch, given the timescales. And managing the risks around engagement with the local constabulary was no easy task, I can tell you!'

'The police were in on it as well? I begged them for help and ended up getting arrested. All I really needed was protection!'

'Which is precisely what we provided for you.' Fotherbridge, gestured towards Ollie and Rupert. 'These gentlemen are the department's premier, close-quarters detachment - unobtrusive, discreet and so forth.'

'Fat lot of use they've been! Where were they when those gangsters came after me and Fred at OT's, to say nothing of what went on outside the Pig this afternoon?'

'It was difficult,' muttered Rupert - Ollie mumbling something about Felix's 'chaotic lifestyle'.

'And how about that Wild West show last Sunday?' continued Felix. 'My girlfriend's never going to speak to me again after what you did to her.'

Rupert shifted uncomfortably, while Ollie appeared to have developed a nervous twitch.

Felix's dad looked surprised. 'I didn't know you were dating, Son?'

'I'm not, Dad, not anymore. She took a header into the boating pond because of these two numpties, and now she's blaming me. And the worst of it is, she's a model!'

'A model? Blimey - I thought that was more our Freddie's department!'

The Mi5 boss interrupted the exchange. 'Permit me to express our condolences, Felix. You must appreciate, we couldn't allow anything to compromise your safety, given the rapport you'd established with the target.'

Felix plonked himself down on the settee, arms folded across his chest.

'Items of immeasurable importance have been stolen,' Fotherbridge continued. 'With your assistance, we believe we can apprehend the perpetrators and conclude a successful recovery.'

'He's up for it, aren't you Son?' Felix's dad added.

The Mi5 chief's brow furrowed. 'If you don't mind, *Brian*, I really do need to hear it from the boy.'

'Of course - silly me.' He sat back, miming the zipping of his lips.

'Now, Felix,' Fotherbridge began, 'I know you've been through a lot these past few weeks, and things are still a tad raw, but when you hear the backstory, I'm confident you'll grasp the importance of what we're trying to achieve here.'

The briefing was crisp and to the point. The diamonds had been stolen in Johannesburg from under the noses of the South African government, who were deeply embarrassed by what had happened. Local intelligence pointed to the involvement of the notorious *Quesos Grandes* gang from Venezuela. Despite the South African's best efforts, the trail had gone cold, but following an incident in a south London hotel, Mi5 had been drawn into the search. They'd quickly secured evidence that placed Themba firmly in the frame and had been tracking her ever since. It was Mi5's agents who'd detained her at Preston station, although their interrogation had drawn a blank and they'd had to let her go. The following evening, the monitoring team at GCHQ spotted the posting on HB's *Braking News* site. After that, it was simply a matter of heading for Lancashire and waiting for things to fall into place.

'Surely the police, should be handling this kind of thing,' said Felix. 'Aren't you lot meant to be focussed on national security issues?'

'Which is precisely what this has turned into,' replied Fotherbridge. 'I'm afraid things have become somewhat *political* over the past few weeks. Let's just say, certain senior figures in Her Majesty's Government would be delighted if the diamonds were to be recovered and retained within these shores. Terribly sorry but I can reveal no more than that at this stage.'

'All a bit hush-hush, eh?' Felix's dad chipped in, tapping the side of his nose.

'Indeed,' chimed The Mi5 chief, sweeping his fingers back through his hair. 'And now Felix, as a loyal British subject, all we ask is that you do the *right thing*. We need your full cooperation if we're to ensure that Operation Perfect Storm bears fruit.'

Felix gave him a puzzled look.

The Mi5 chief chuckled. 'I'm sorry, we do love our code names in the department - dramatic effect, mainly. Put simply, Felix, your brother will be hosting the City of Culture event tomorrow evening. You will, of course, want to be there to support him in his endeavours and we're here to make sure that happens safely. Naturally, we'll do everything we can to maintain a sense of calm normality throughout this whole process.'

'Calm normality - with Fred on stage?' Felix spluttered. 'Why they chose him to host this thing is beyond me.'

Fotherbridge smiled. 'I must say, the Got it All! Bid Team did take a bit of persuading on that particular front, but everyone has their price.' His eyes strayed to Felix's dad.

'Oh... of course! Trenton was just saying before that the government have got this special Nether Regions regeneration funding,' Felix's dad said. 'It's worth millions, apparently! Wouldn't it be great if some of that cash found its way to Frecklesall to sort out the lido? I know how worried you've been about the state of the place since you torched it a couple of years back.'

'I didn't do that, Dad!' snapped Felix. 'You know it wasn't me!'

'Best not crying over spilt milk, eh?' Fotherbridge said, soothingly. 'What's done is done and so forth. Suffice to say Her Majesty's government will be *extremely* grateful for any assistance provided in this matter. But perhaps we might return to that later?' He sat back in his chair. 'Now, Felix - I'm sure you've seen our posters, and the web content, publicising Freddie's central role in forthcoming proceedings?'

Felix's brow furrowed. 'That was you?'

'We had to find a way of placing your brother centre-stage, as it were. The fact is, the Venezuelans still believe he has at least some of the diamonds about his person. By letting everyone know he'll be hosting the show tomorrow night, we all but guarantee their appearance at the town hall, giving us the opportunity to make an interception.'

Felix shook his head in disbelief. 'Operation Perfect Storm? - I get it now. You're using our Fred as bait! Come on, Dad, you know this isn't right.'

Felix's dad shrugged. 'We all need to do our bit for the country, Son. Anyway, Freddie's up for it. He's been talking about this witness protection thing - thinks it could help him and Themba to make a fresh start.'

'Might as well stick a target on his chest and let them take pot-shots,' muttered Felix. 'So, what's Mum saying?'

Fotherbridge intervened. 'Rest assured, your immediate family are all safely under the department's care and protection - or they will be, soon enough. We've moved your brother to a safe house, not far from here, and your sister's staying at your aunt's. Unfortunately, your mother isn't at the address she provided, but our agents will track her down soon enough.'

Felix winced. So much had happened over the past few days, he'd almost forgotten about the car crash that was his parents' marriage. His mum was supposed to be staying at her friend Norma's house - if she wasn't there, where the heck was she?

'You do know you're too late, don't you?' he said. 'Themba's probably back home in Lesotho by now. If you ask me, you'd be better off looking for that Sir Hubert Montague-Dunk guy. I'm pretty sure the two of them have been working together on this. I'd probably be handing over the diamonds to you right now if you hadn't stopped me going to the Isle of Man.'

The Mi5 Chief stroked his chin, thoughtfully. 'The department is well aware of your theory *vis-a-vis* this Sir Hubert *slash* Colin Anderton character, Felix. We've run the checks but as I explained to you over the telephone, there's absolutely no connection. On a more positive note, however, we've recently intercepted some very interesting communiqués from our Latin American friends. It appears our little ruse has had the desired effect and they're planning to pitch up at the town hall tomorrow evening. Furthermore, we understand that *Themba* as you call her, will be there as well, carrying the real diamonds.'

Felix laughed. 'No chance!'

'Think about it,' mused Fotherbridge. 'Where better to conduct the trade than at a public event in a dead-end backwater like Frecklesall-on-Sea? There are risks of course, but she knows full-well the Venezuelan's will pay top-dollar for the haul. Once she's trousered the proceeds, she'll go dark - invisible, as it were - either that or we'll find her mutilated body dumped on a remote patch of wasteland somewhere nearby.' He pulled out a laptop from his briefcase. 'I sense you're still harbouring doubts, Felix. I hadn't planned on showing you this, but as time is now of the essence...'

He flipped opened the computer and as his fingers began to tap across the keyboard, Felix could see the now-familiar Mi5 logo and the 'Top Secret' header on the screen. After a few more clicks, the security chief turned the laptop towards him. The image was a scanned copy of what looked like a military identity card, the photograph instantly recognisable.

'So she *was* in the army!' Felix exclaimed. 'I knew it! She had this way about her. And she was so cool in a tight spot.'

'Not just the army,' Fotherbridge said. 'She's a former member of the elite South African Special Forces Unit - a somewhat pale imitation of our own SAS. Have you spotted the names yet?'

Felix gasped as extracts from different identity cards flashed up in quick succession. There was Nafula Magatos from the South African military, Themba Kigelle - a student from Lesotho, a visa issued by the UK Border Force to someone called Kefie Ngwane, and an Irish passport in the name of Barika Shokoya. The hairstyles and outfits were different but the face told the same story.

'So… who is she really?' he asked.

'That's classified intel I'm afraid, but what I *can* tell you is that back in May, she was part of the diamond retrieval operation, working on behalf of the South African security services. They managed to track down the Venezuelans but before they could organise the interception, she'd disappeared into thin air, taking the diamonds with her. It's no coincidence that immediately afterwards our Latin American friends were at each other's throats, and she was hot-footing it out of the country. She's a rogue agent of the most dangerous kind, Felix - charming, beautiful… and a trained assassin. We'd never have found her if she hadn't left such a mess behind in London.' He clicked another key.

'Whoa!' shrieked Felix, as he set eyes on the photo of the body, bundled up in a shower curtain and crammed into a tiny bath-tub. The image was headed 'London Metropolitan Police Evidence File: Room 6 Majestic Hotel, Rotherhithe 20.10hrs - 18 July'.

'Stabbed, then had his neck snapped for good measure,' said Trenton, in a matter-of-fact tone. 'One of our chaps I'm afraid. Left a wife and two sprogs back in East Grinstead. Occupational hazard, I guess.'

'What... what makes you think she did this?'

The Mi5 chief clicked open another file. The CCTV footage was not the best advert for the Majestic Hotel - the reception area looked bleak and soulless, the wallpaper stained and peeling. Dressed in jeans and T-shirt, a courier bag slung over her shoulder, the girl with the cropped afro loitered by the desk before cutting back to the lift, opposite. After waiting impatiently for a few seconds, she headed towards the stairs at the side, glancing up at the camera on the way. Fotherbridge froze the frame and zoomed in on her face.

'Look familiar?' he asked.

Felix didn't reply - he was too busy reading the display at the bottom of the screen: '19.30hrs - 18 July' - the recording made just forty minutes before the police photographer had taken the shots of the murder victim.

Suddenly, it seemed like all the air had been sucked out of the room.

'I... I just need to clear my head,' Felix mumbled, as he made for the back door.

Standing out on the patio, the chill night air began to bring him to his senses. Themba or Nafula or Kefie, or whatever the hell she was called, really *was* a cold-blooded killer. He felt sick at the thought of what she'd done in that hotel bathroom, to say nothing of the other murders she must have committed over the years. And to top it all, she'd spent the past week as guest of honour at their house!

He was furious with Trenton Fotherbridge. Apart from the NKI con, Operation Perfect Storm had put his whole family at risk. And he was pretty sure that if something actually *had* kicked off, Mi5 would have simply stood back and watched it happen. A couple of weeks earlier he'd have been desperate to find out why they were involved - which senior politicians were lurking in the shadows and what the heck the *Saydoss/Seetoo* mystery was all about - but that seemed like an irrelevance now. Someone had been killed and more would surely follow unless he did something to help bring Themba to justice.

'*It's family. Nothing is more important*' - Doreen's words, which had been playing on a continuous loop in his head, suddenly began to fade into insignificance.

He wandered back inside. It seemed odd, knocking on the lounge door in his own home, but for some reason he felt a degree of formality was required. The Mi5 chief looked up as he entered the room.

'You said everyone has their price, Mr Fotherbridge,' Felix began, struggling to keep the nerves out of his voice.

A smile eased its way onto the Mi5 man's lips. 'I'm sure that Nether Regions regeneration funding will go a long way towards transforming Frecklesall lido into the splendid attraction it once was, Felix. You're definitely doing the right thing.'

'I hope so. But there's one other favour I need from you before I can agree to anything.'

Fotherbridge laughed. 'You certainly drive a hard bargain! How may I help?'

Felix glanced at his watch. 'I need you to speak to Jeremy Grindrod at the *Bugler*, and it has to be right now, please. There's something important I want him to do for me.'

The Mi5 chief reached forward and as they shook hands, Felix felt a jolt run through his body. It was as if his soul had suddenly decided it was time to jump ship.

He had a terrible night, tormented thoughts careering around inside his head like fairground bumper cars. By the time he eventually dropped off, the first glimmers of morning light were creeping beneath the bedroom curtains. When he surfaced again, his befuddled mind was almost convinced he'd woken up to just another ordinary Saturday morning. The presence of his little sister, waiting impatiently at the bottom of his bed, suggested otherwise.

'It's afternoon,' Flo announced. 'You need to get up.'

Felix was still struggling to open his eyes. 'What are you doing here? Aren't you meant to be at Doreen's?'

'She's got a darts match at the Pig, so Dad brought me over in a taxi this morning. The good news is that they've tracked down Mum. She's been rehearsing at the club most of the night. It's this new routine for the culture show.'

He breathed a huge sigh of relief. 'Thank God for that. I was really worried about her.'

'Me too - the sooner this is over with, the better. Anyway, Aunty Doreen asked me to have a word. It's about Themba. She want to know if you're on board.'

Felix could hardly believe what he was hearing. 'How did you find out about this?'

'I'm not stupid,' she replied. 'It was obvious you and Themba were up to something, what with you chucking those diamonds all over her bedroom floor that time, and then trying to palm me off with that ridiculous *Saydoss* story. I had a chat with Aunty Doreen last night and everything's finally beginning to fit together.'

'She told you what's been going on?' he spluttered. 'That's ridiculous!'

'Coming home to find the house crawling with Mi5 spooks was a bit of a giveaway but to be fair, I'd already picked up most of it from your mate, Naz.'

'What?'

'Me and Saj have been working on this jewellery start-up. I popped round to see him yesterday and got lumbered with his brother... And I thought you were wet!' She let out a sigh. 'So let's get down to business, shall we? What are you going to do about Themba?'

Felix could hear his heart pounding. Once Flo found out about his deal with Mi5, he was dead in the water.

'I've still got the phone Doreen gave me,' he said. 'I haven't dropped her in it, if that's what you're worried about.'

His sister looked unimpressed. 'Aunty Doreen can take care of herself - it's Themba who needs our help.'

He levered himself up onto an elbow. 'Listen Flo, they're saying she's got the real diamonds and is going to sell them to the Venezuelans at the show tonight. They reckon she's just been killing time with us, waiting for the chance to do the deal.'

'Except there is no deal. The diamonds have been in her family for years. There's no way she'd ever sell them.'

'That's just another of her stories, though, isn't it? You can't believe a word she says. She *murdered* someone. I saw the photos - he was a British agent.'

'That's rubbish,' said Flo. 'The dead guy was a friend of hers from the South African security services. He tried to help her out and ended up getting killed by the Venezuelans for his troubles.' Seeing the look of disbelief on her brother's face, she tore off a sheet from the notepad on his desk and started writing. 'Zaaia Bakuba - that was his name. You can check out his obituary in the *Johannesburg City Press* if you don't believe me.'

'They told me he was from East Grinstead...'

Flo was struggling to hold back her irritation. 'Who are you going to trust on this, Felix - me and Aunty Doreen, or that slimeball Trenton Fotherbridge, and his toadies?'

'I'm… I'm not sure of anything anymore,' he replied. 'Anyway, Dad's all for it.'

'He would be, wouldn't he? He's been promised a new car if he helps them out. He's downstairs now, drooling over the brochures.'

'Oh… But there's this other stuff as well - she's got these secret identities.'

Flo rolled her eyes. 'She's from the South African Special Forces Unit - it's how they work! Listen, I'm not saying I agree with everything she's done, but she saved Freddie's life. Surely that's got to count for something?'

Felix's torment was cut short by their dad's shout from downstairs.

'Just coming!' Flo yelled back. She turned to her brother. 'It's time you got off the fence, Felix - made a decision for once in your life. Have you thought about why Mi5 might be putting so much effort into this?'

'It was to do with these diamonds getting stolen, they said. And now the government are interested. I... I didn't really follow that bit, to be honest.'

His sister glanced across to check the door was still closed. 'When I was with Naz the other day he told me about the message you saw on the mirror in HB's flat. "*Colinan... Diamon..*" - I've been doing some digging and I'm pretty sure it's got nothing to do with that Sir Hubert character.'

Felix snorted. 'It's definitely Colin Anderton, Flo - it has to be him. He was out in that boat on his own with the bag, and that's when he did the switch.'

She shook her head. 'You always moaned to me about HB being a useless journalist - about how he couldn't spell and never listened. So how would it be if he *thought* he heard them say *Colinan*, but what they actually said was something else?' She moved across to the desk to scribble on the sheet of paper again. 'Everyone knows about the *Cullinan* diamonds, that's a no-brainer. It's how they link to Themba's story that's the problem.'

Felix looked confused. 'I don't want to sound stupid, Flo–'

'Check it out, you idiot! Oh, and there's something else you need to know. I phoned Ramón from the dance club when I was trying to track Mum down last night. He's the only person I know who speaks Spanish, so I asked him about that *Saydoss* word. He got it straight away.'

'Got what?'

'It's obvious, when you think about it - *Saydoss* and *Seetoo* are the exact same thing.'

Felix looked at her, incredulously. 'How come?'

'What does *dos* mean in Spanish?'

'*Uno, dos, tres,*' he replied, hesitantly. '*Dos* is the number two, isn't it?'

She nodded. 'And according to Ramón, "*say*" is how the Spanish pronounce the letter C, from the alphabet. A, B, C is *Ah...Bay...Say* - are you with me? Which means that in English...'

'*Saydoss* is C2 - which is... *Seetoo*!' he exclaimed. 'So where does that get us?'

His sister shrugged. 'You tell me...' Their dad was shouting up the stairs again and she started towards the bedroom door. 'I've got to go now. What do you want me to tell Aunty Doreen?'

'I... I don't know. They've got all this evidence. And I still think Sir Hubert is involved, somehow.'

'On your head be it,' she said brusquely, before disappearing out of the room.

Felix slumped back into his bed. After hearing the front door slam, he got up and grabbed the piece of paper Flo had left on his desk. A couple of website addresses had been carefully scribed in her best handwriting, but the name written across the middle of the sheet had been printed out in huge capitals.

CULLINAN

16

'But why won't you let me go online?' Felix whined. 'You said you wanted things to seem normal. If I'm not messaging my mates before a big night out like this, they're bound to get suspicious.'

'Absolutely out of the question,' replied Trenton Fotherbridge, who was tapping away on his laptop. 'We'll reconnect the router and return your smartphone as soon as this operation has been concluded. In the meantime, why not try something old-fashioned, like reading a book or engaging in some intelligent conversation?'

Felix moved the appeal on to his father. 'Come on Dad, give me a break!'

His dad's dinner jacket and bow tie combo seemed strangely out of place in their tiny lounge. Felix had tried to persuade him to go for a more casual look but he'd insisted on showing solidarity with Freddie, who was required to don formal evening wear for the cameras. With his newly shaven head glistening, and white dress-shirt straining at the buttons, Felix's dad looked more bouncer-gone-to-seed than James Bond-*Casino Royale*.

'Trenton has a point, Son,' replied his dad. 'We've only an hour to wait. Can't you find something else to do?'

'How about we run through the drill, one last time?' Vikki DeBrett suggested, doing her best to calm the situation. 'So, at 19.30 hours the three of us will travel down together in an unmarked department car. We arrive at the town hall at 19.40 hours, gaining access via the Tootell Street entrance, which is conveniently located for our rendezvous with Freddie. You'll have a few minutes to catch up together and then at 19.55 hours we take up our positions in the auditorium. We'll have a full surveillance team in place but even so–'

Felix groaned. 'I know - I have to stick with you and if anyone asks, you're an old family friend from down south. You do realise no one's going to believe a word I say, don't you? If you'd just let me message some of my mates, I could set things up nicely.'

One look at the Mi5 chief's face was enough to convince him he was wasting his breath.

They sat together in silence while Felix felt his blood coming to the boil. It was ridiculous - he'd already agreed to cooperate so why was Fotherbridge being such a pain? And after the way he'd stitched him up with the NKI scam as well! In the end, he decided he'd had enough.

'Actually, I do have a couple of questions, Mr Fotherbridge, if you don't mind?'

The Mi5 chief looked up from his laptop.

'It's about my ex-boss, Howard Brake,' Felix continued. 'He went missing about ten days ago and I'd like to know what you've been doing to find him.'

He saw a flash of concern cross Vikki's face.

'Mr Brake's wellbeing is of the highest possible concern to the department,' Fotherbridge replied, curtly. 'We're currently pursuing a number of lines of enquiry and so forth.'

'I've read about this kind of thing,' said Felix. 'If HB ends up getting killed because of Operation Perfect Storm, is that something you'd class as "collateral damage"?'

'Absolutely not! I don't know what's got into you, but if it's because we won't allow you to access your social media channels for a few hours, I suggest you grow up, and fast.'

With nothing to lose, Felix went straight for the jugular. 'To be honest, I'm still a bit puzzled by this *Saydoss* thing. I told Vikki about it earlier, but none of you lot seem interested. It's odd really, because when I mentioned it to Themba, and the Venezuelans for that matter, they totally freaked out!'

The Mi5 chief would not be drawn. '*Saydoss* is a made-up, meaningless word,' he snapped. 'As is this *Seetoo* nonsense you've picked up from somewhere or other. And if I may be candid, Felix - things will run a lot more smoothly if you'd leave the investigative work to the professionals. All we need you to do is concentrate on getting through this evening without fouling things up.'

'Yeah, well that would be a lot easier if you'd tell me what's really going on...' His voice trailed away as he sensed a tingling against his right thigh. Grabbing for his pocket, he felt the outline of Themba's mobile through the cheap denim of his jeans. 'I've got to go,' he mumbled, getting to his feet. 'Upstairs. Got to... err... sort out something to wear.'

'Are you alright, Felix?' asked Vikki. 'If anything's the matter, you must let us know.'

'No worries,' he replied. 'It's all good.'

He thundered up the stairs to the backdrop of raised voices from the lounge. Shutting the bedroom door, he pulled the mobile from his pocket, struggling to focus on the text message he'd just received.

Makinson's Quay @9.45 tonight.

Come alone. Use bike. TK

Felix stared at the sheet of paper Flo had left, for the umpteenth time. It was hopeless - no internet connection and absolutely no way of checking anything she'd told him. And anyway, even if he did decide to help Themba, how on earth could he shake his Mi5 minders and make it the four miles up the coast to the remote Second World War jetty at Makinson's Quay, without setting off a full-scale security alert?

He was agonising over it all when he was hit by a blindingly obvious bolt from the blue. Mi5 had confiscated his phone, but if the one Doreen had given him really was 'clean'… He grabbed at the mobile and clicked onto the text again. Themba's details had been withheld so there was no way he could call her. Before he had time to think up an excuse, he was punching in Naz's number. His friend picked up after a few rings.

'Naz, it's me,' said Felix. 'Listen, my phone's out of action and our internet's just died. I need you to check out some stuff for me - it's pretty urgent.'

'Is everything alright?'

'It's fine. Have you got a pen and paper?' Felix ran through the details Flo had provided, painstakingly spelling out the names and website addresses. 'Print whatever you find and bring it to the show tonight. But the most important thing I need from you is a search on this name. Flo reckons I might have got that Colin

213

Anderton thing wrong. She says what HB was trying to write on the mirror was something else - *Cullinan* - and that it might be linked to the diamonds in some way.'

Naz hesitated. '... Actually, that does kind of ring a bell. I've got the laptop up now, if you can just wait a sec.'

Felix listened to the patter of his friend's fingertips on the keyboard.

'It's here,' Naz said, moments later, 'although I reckon your sister's got her wires crossed for once. There's no way–'

'What is it? What have you got?'

'Wait your hurry, mate - this is pretty heavy reading.'

Felix hung on, pacing up and down his bedroom, listening out nervously for any sign of Vikki coming up the stairs. 'Come *on* Naz,' he muttered, 'I haven't got all day.'

It seemed to take an age but eventually his friend came back on the line.

'It's saying that the Cullinan diamond was the biggest in the world when it was discovered in South Africa, way back in 1905.'

'Blimey!'

'Hang on, it gets better... So in 1907, the government down there gave it to King Edward VII as a birthday present. He was Queen Victoria's son - reigning UK monarch from 1901 to 1910, and succeeded by–'

'Naz... please!'

'Oh. Sorry. Anyway, the diamond was uncut, meaning it was still in one big chunk - more or less as it was found. So the first thing they did when they got it over here was to have it shipped off to Switzerland where it was cut and polished into finished diamonds -

nine of them all in. It's quite a specialised process, actually. There are only a few places–'

'Thanks for that, Naz,' Felix interrupted him a second time. 'Does it say where these diamonds are now, or if any of them are missing?'

His friend took a deep breath. 'I think everyone would know about it if they'd been stolen, Felix.'

'Why's that then?'

'They're locked up in the Tower of London. Basically, it's the crown jewels we're talking about here.'

It took a few seconds for Naz's words to sink in. It was crazy - there was no way he'd had the crown jewels stashed under his bedroom floor and anyway, they were all fakes. None of it made sense.

'I need you to talk to Flo,' Felix said, eventually. 'She's been doing some digging on this. See what she's found out, will you?'

'I'm really sorry, Felix, Naz said, sheepishly. 'I know I shouldn't have said anything to her but she was relentless. She just wouldn't stop with the questions.'

'Don't worry about it, mate - been there, got the T-shirt. Oh, and there's one more thing you and Bernie can do for me…'

The town hall dressing rooms were buried deep in the basement - musty and windowless, they were a suitably bleak setting for the reunion of the Haythornthwaite boys and their father. Freddie looked pale and gaunt - the exact opposite of someone who'd spent the previous five days living it up on the French Riviera, or even St Helens for that matter. The ill-fitting dinner suit jacket hung untidily from his rounded shoulders, crumpled trousers partly covering a pair of scuffed brown boots. His lank, greasy hair had been tied back into a ponytail and the newly forming goatee beard was still very much a work in progress.

Felix's appearance was in radical contrast. Trenton Fotherbridge had questioned his choice of the garish Born to Boogie! shirt, and the purple Got it All! baseball cap. Felix had waved away all objections, assuring the Mi5 boss that this was what he always wore on a big night out. For once, Ollie and Rupert had backed him up, recalling his unique styling from the time they'd rescued him at Freddie's flat.

As soon as the formalities were over, their dad made his excuses and headed for the bar. With close-quarter protection lurking in the corridor outside, the brothers were able to enjoy a few minutes of quality time together.

'They told you what's going down tonight?' asked Felix.

Freddie grunted.

'It'll be fine,' Felix said, as reassuringly as he could. 'These guys seem to know what they're doing.'

'S'pose.'

Freddie looked suicidal, his monosyllabic replies sucking all hope out of the room. Felix had never seen him looking so low before a gig.

'Come on, Fred!' he urged, clapping his hands together. 'You're live on national TV in a few minutes. OK, they're going to arrest your girlfriend and there's a bunch of Latin American nutters out there who want to kill us both, but think of the publicity!'

'I'm not bothered about that stuff no more,' mumbled his brother. 'There's something else vexing me.' He gestured towards a white plastic bag, dumped in the corner of the room.

Felix walked across and peered inside. 'Bloody hell!' he exclaimed, pulling out the family's stainless-steel colander. 'It must be nearly a week now. What's going on?'

'Nowt!' wailed Freddie. 'It's like sitting on a time-bomb!'

Felix tried to keep things upbeat. 'A week? What's another hour or two between friends? Once you've done the show you can grab something from the chemists. You'll be right as rain after a good clear-out.'

Freddie pulled a face. 'I mentioned it to those FBI dudes, didn't I? They took me down the Sultan for a curry last night, then gave me a couple of pints of prune juice for breakfast this morning. When that didn't do the job, they made me take these.' He reached into his pocket and handed over a small pack of tablets.

'Blimey Fred - Dyno-Lax Blockbusters?' Felix exclaimed. 'Things must be serious if you've taken this stuff and you're still bunged up.'

'Yeah, well... they said to double-up on the dose, just to be on the safe side.' He pointed at his stomach and winced. 'From the vibes I'm getting, things are definitely on the move down there, but there's no end product yet. I'm telling you, Bro, this diamond's doing my head in! If I could just squeeze it out, that Trenton dude promised he'd get the Feds to back off. Themba and me could make a fresh start - witness protection programme, new identities, that kind of thing.'

'I've told you before, that diamond's a fake - they all are!'

There was a knock on the door and a young woman walked in, carrying what looked like a toolbox.

217

'Makeup!' she announced, cheerily. 'Got to get you looking lovely for the cameras, Freddie. My, you're looking as white as a sheet - I might need to send out for some more foundation!'

Felix edged out of the room. Given what he'd just heard, he was keen not to be around his brother for any longer than was absolutely necessary.

The corridors were packed with punters scurrying to their seats, clutching pints of beer and packets of crisps. Felix was on first name terms with most of them so despite Vikki's best efforts, their progress to the Lancastrian Suite, the town hall's grand ballroom, was slowed by countless high-fives, slaps on the back and slurred words of encouragement.

As they approached the main doors, Felix noticed the gathering a few metres away up a gloomy service corridor. He spotted Bernie and Naz straight off but it was only as they got closer that he clocked who they were with - Zoe, Neesha… and Dannii.

Vikki sensed his hesitation. 'What's wrong, Felix?'

'It's her,' he hissed. 'My "ex".'

'We can go straight in, if you'd prefer?'

'No, we should say hello. They'll get suspicious if I ignore them.'

They joined the circle but before he could introduce everyone, Bernie had dragged Vikki over to talk with Zoe. Felix was doing his best to avoid eye-contact with Dannii, when Naz sidled up next to him.

'I've got the intel, mate - it's total dynamite,' he whispered. Nodding towards an unmarked door on the opposite side of the corridor, he mouthed the words, *'In there.'*

Suddenly, Dannii popped up at his side, looking as if she'd been crying. Before he could ask her what was wrong, she was pulling him towards the door. Vikki intercepted them in just a couple of strides.

'The show will be starting soon,' she announced firmly. 'We really should be getting to our seats.'

'Just let them have some private time together, Vikki,' pleaded Bernie. 'They've got a lot of things to catch up on after all the stuff they've been through recently.'

Vikki shook her head. 'I'm sorry, Bernard, that's just not a possibility.'

But then Zoe pulled her aside. Felix couldn't hear what she was saying but he saw the look of surprise on Vikki's face as she glanced across to Dannii, who was now wiping tears from her eyes. Moments later the Mi5 agent disappeared into the store room, emerging just seconds later.

'Five minutes, that's all,' she said to Felix in a low voice. 'And I'm only doing this because of the baby. I have to say I'm really disappointed - I thought you were both better than that. Becoming parents at your age is... well, it's *completely* irresponsible.'

He went into shock, but before he could say anything he'd been shunted forward and was following Dannii into a narrow, walk-in store, with tall metal shelving racks on either side. The door closed behind them and in an effort to buy himself some time, he shuffled over to peer through the window at the far end of the room. From his vantage point, up on the first floor, he found himself looking down over Tootell Street where he could see his bike, still chained to the rack from his trip into town the day before.

Heart sinking, he turned to face the music. 'Listen, I'm really sorry about what happened on the Prom the other day, Dannii. It was just a crazy accident.'

There was a moment of pained silence, and then she burst into life. 'Can't believe you're still wearing that shirt. No offence, babes, but it's a total minger!'

'Sorry,' he mumbled, folding his arms across his chest. 'Fashion's never really been my strong point.'

'Felix babes, you totally crack me up!'

'Is everything alright?' he asked, hesitantly. 'Only, you looked so upset before. And... and Vikki seems to think you might actually be *pregnant*. You're not, are you?'

Dannii threw her head back and roared with laughter. 'Bernie came up with that one... And as for the skriking - I was acting, wasn't I? I tried it out on him earlier and he's like, "You're so good, Dannii - you should be in *Corrie*", and I'm, like, "Bernie, babes, no way am I doing a career change - not when the modelling's about to take off".'

'Really? That's awesome! Have you had some good news, then?'

'Bee-have willyer! So, what do you reckon - have I put weight on?'

He looked her up and down, self-consciously. 'No... absolutely not. You look great!'

It was another transformation, her hair - now cropped and a kind of silvery colour - had been shaped into a sharp bob. The black cocktail dress was like something off a fashion catwalk, the tailored strapless top held in place by forces Felix could never begin to understand. The bottom half was short, bubbling out below the waistline into a ruffled frenzy which showed off her shapely legs and patterned white tights. The black ankle boots added about six inches to her height.

'Aw, that's so sweet!' she shrieked, shoving her hand down her cleavage and rummaging around.

Wondering what the heck was going on, he did the gentlemanly thing and turned away. When he looked again, Dannii was thrusting a fistful of crumpled papers at him.

'Only, carting this lot about hasn't exactly done much for my figure,' she continued. 'Special delivery from your mate, Naz.'

Felix grabbed the printouts and began working through them while Dannii emptied the contents of her handbag onto a shelf and set about fine-tuning her makeup. Flo had done a brilliant job, highlighting the most important sections so he could skim through the sheets at pace. He instantly recognised the images of Chief Nomalanga Magatos III, from his recollection of the black and white photo he'd found in Themba's wallet. And there was no mistaking the stunning smile of the old man's granddaughter, captured in the photograph on the front page of the *Lesotho Times*, where the two of them were featured together at the launch of a new farming project.

He felt a jolt of dismay when he spotted the picture accompanying the obituary of Zaaia Bakuba, in the previous week's *Johannesburg City Press*. A devoted father and grandfather, only recently retired from the South African security services, the piece confirmed that Zaaia had been brutally murdered in a south London hotel room while on holiday in the capital. So much for Fotherbridge's line that the body discovered in the bathroom at the Majestic had been 'one of our chaps'.

Dropping each sheet to the floor after he'd scanned it, he turned to the last few pages which majored on the Cullinan diamond - the fluorescent yellow of Flo's highlighter guiding him through a potted history. But it was the photos of the finished stones that really grabbed his attention - mainly because they just didn't fit. The original Cullinan had been cut into nine diamonds, but the wrap in Themba's bag contained only six. More importantly, the fakes he'd seen were a completely different shape to the priceless royal gems pictured in the printout. It was obvious, even to Felix's untrained eye that if the actual diamonds bore any resemblance to the replicas he'd found in Themba's bag, they definitely weren't part of the crown jewels.

That much was a relief, but his heart sank as it dawned on him that he was no closer to finding the answers he was looking for.

The final sheet in the bundle was a scanned copy of an old newspaper article, the print quality poor, the typeface dense and difficult to follow. It was a cutting from the *New York Times*, from way back in 1909. Felix held it up to the light to get a better look.

The headline alone, took his breath away:

Where is the Cullinan's Other Half?

Diamond rumours are once more flying about South Africa, this time to the effect that the missing portions of the great Cullinan Diamond have been found. When the diamond that is now known as the Cullinan was discovered four years ago in South Africa's Premier Mine, it bore every evidence that, huge as it is, it is only a portion of a much larger stone, the original form and size of which can only be approximated. Experts estimate the dimensions

of the 'lost Cullinan' to be in the region of 4,323 carats.

The mine officials immediately instituted a thorough search for the missing pieces but up to the present time, the search has been fruitless.

While the existence of the lost diamond is disputed by mine owners, it is worth noting that in the case of the slightly smaller 'Excelsior' diamond, the stone was picked up by a native mine-worker while loading a truck and it took many days before its presence was discovered.

One of the rumours now in circulation comes from the African newspapers which claim that the other half of the Cullinan is in the possession of the Magatos tribe of the Butha-Buthe region.

'Bloody hell!' he exclaimed, steadying himself against one of the shelving units.

'Is that good news then, babes?' asked Dannii.

'Yes… no… I mean, I'm not sure. Maybe Themba was telling the truth, after all! Those secret service guys showed me some of her fake identity cards and *Magatos* is one of the names she uses.' He waved the article in Dannii's face. 'According to this, it might have been someone from the Magatos tribe who found this extra chunk from the original Cullinan stone, back in the day. It all adds up, sort of, but I still can't see how any of it links with this C2 thing they're all so wound up about.'

Dannii gave him a funny look. '*Really?* 'Cos I was only talking about that with this random guy the other night.'

He looked at her, incredulously.

'Girls' night out - so me and Portia were down OT's,' Dannii began. 'These old fellas were trying to chat us up - they must have been thirty, at least. Gross - *eughh*!' She pulled a face. 'So Portia's giving me the "let's get out of here" look, but my guy's droning on about this really important job he's working on, and he won't quit with the yappin', even though I'm yawning my head off–'

Felix interrupted her. 'This is really interesting, Dannii, but can we talk about it later? We need to tidy these papers up. If Vikki comes in–'

'So he's telling me he's with MFI or summat like that,' she continued. 'And this project he's on is totes secret squirrel. So Portia's like, "It's just a lame chat-up line, *stoopid* - let's do one!" but the more I'm trying to ditch him, the more he's banging on about it. So I'm thinking of tipping my Malibu and Coke over his head, when he mentions this Cullinan thing.' She snorted loudly. 'Like I was gonna be impressed! I didn't have a clue what he were on about.'

Felix stood there with his mouth hanging open. 'What... what did he say, Dannii?'

'Well, it were a bit like you were telling me before, babes. The Cullinan is this super-spesh diamond, innit? Belongs to the Queen, apparently. So, him and his mates have given it this *stoopid* code name - "C1", he said. And then he's like, there's this second bit that might have fallen off it somewhere and got lost. And guess what? That's where the "C2" thingy comes in! *So* original, I said. Anyway, he reckoned even that was worth a fortune and they got a tipoff it might be stashed around here, somewhere. So, I'm telling Portia about it and she's like, "If you fall for that one Dannii, you want your bumps feeling, you mare"–'

She was interrupted in mid-flow by a knock on the door.

'Just a minute, Vikki!' yelled Felix, his mind in meltdown.

Dannii had barely paused to take a breath. 'So then I'm like, "Make sure you let me know how that turns out for you, Ollie, cos if you find it and suddenly you're like, totally minted, we should deffo meet up again… *Not*!".'

'*Ollie*? His name was *Ollie*?'

'Yeah, Ollie - and his mate was called something like Roop, I think. Just a couple of chancers up from London, thinking they're God's gift. You know how it is?'

They both heard the second knock, much louder this time.

'We absolutely must take our seats, Felix!' Vikki shouted through. 'I'm coming in.'

'No!' he shrieked. 'It's really not a good time!'

The two of them looked at each other, the illicit purpose of their meeting still strewn across the floor for all to see.

And then the door began to open.

17

'I'm sorry, Felix, but I must insist… Oh!' Vikki DeBrett's words faded away as she stumbled across the couple rolling about on the grubby vinyl flooring, tangled together in the most passionate of clinches.

Dannii lifted her head, yelling indignantly, 'Excuse *me*! Can't a girl get a bit of privacy around here?'

'I'm so sorry,' Vikki mumbled as she backed out of the room. 'I… I had no idea.'

Dannii kicked the door shut with an outstretched foot. 'I should think so, too!' Extracting herself from Felix's clutches, she got to her feet, dusting herself down and straightening out her dress. 'Did the job, didn't it, babes? I don't think she saw owt, and it's my way of saying thanks.'

Felix gawped at her, blankly.

'Bernie said you'd landed yourself in a spot of bother and needed a hand,' she continued. 'And I'm like, "No way, Bernie, babes, not after what's gone on" and he's like, "Everything happens for a reason, Dannii". And I know he shouldn't of told me 'cos it was supposed to be a surprise but… I'm *so* excited, I can't wait! We *have* to get together on Tuesday when it comes out. Whaddya say?'

'What? You mean… like a date?' Felix mumbled, wondering when the dream was going to end, and hoping it wouldn't.

'Yeah, why not?' she replied, gathering up the sheets from the floor. 'But I'm telling you right now - there's no way August's *Bugler Belle* is gonna be seen around town with you in that *stoopid* shirt. And the hat's gotta go as well!'

A few minutes later, Felix and Vikki squeezed into their front row seats on the edge of the ballroom. The Lancastrian Suite had been specially kitted out for the occasion, the stage bookended with towering speaker stacks and backdropped with what looked like a giant cinema screen. Got it All! and UK City of Culture banners were hanging everywhere. High above, the tangle of purple streamers cascading from the hefty Victorian chandeliers, wafted in the warm air like the broken threads of a giant spider's web.

It was to be a live broadcast with simultaneous events taking place in each of the cities and towns on the City of Culture shortlist. Well-known BBC arts correspondent, Quentin Thesaurus, was running the show - his job, to link everything together while guiding the viewers at home on a whistle-stop tour, visiting each of the finalists in turn as they gave one last pitch for the big prize.

The concept was ambitious, its success dependent on cutting-edge technology, split-second timing, and total professionalism on the part of the local hosts. With the heady cocktail of a drunken audience infiltrated with Mi5 officers, the likely appearance of a band of Venezuelan diamond smugglers, and a constipated heavy metal DJ recently overdosed on industrial-strength laxatives, Felix sensed the evening might not end up going quite as well as the Got it All! Bid Team were hoping.

After narrowly surviving a lecture from Vikki on the perils of teenage pregnancy and the importance of safe sex, he was mightily relieved to see his dad rolling up from the bar, bow tie askew, the beads of sweat on his bald head glistening in the TV lights.

'Two minutes and counting,' he slurred. 'Hey - I don't know about you, Son, but I've got a really good feeling about this!'

Moments later, the crowd cheered loudly as Freddie wandered onto the stage. His dad jumped up, waving his arms about enthusiastically.

'Sit down please, Mr Haythornthwaite!' urged Vikki. 'Think of the security risk.'

'Oh, right,' he muttered, taking his chair again. 'What's that he's got there, Son?'

Any hopes that Freddie might have made use of the town hall's toilet facilities were dashed by the presence of the gleaming stainless-steel kitchen utensil, tucked under his arm.

'Dunno, Dad,' Felix replied. 'It's probably one of the trophies he has to hand out - Best Local Act, that sort of thing.'

'Wouldn't it be fantastic if he ends up presenting it to Mum? Handy as well - our colander went missing a few days ago.'

The screen at the back of the stage burst into life and suddenly the giant face of Quentin Thesaurus was beaming down at them from behind a pair of heavy, square-rimmed glasses. Handsome enough, in a middle-aged sort of way, his pelmet of straight, shoulder length hair hung limply from the sides of his bald pate, lending him a vaguely clownish appearance. The burgundy velvet jacket, Paisley cravat and white shirt with oversized cuffs, oozed unwatchable late night TV arts shows.

'Good evening,' he began in the fruitiest of tones, 'and welcome one and all to the grand finale of this year's UK City of Culture competition! My name is Quentin Thesaurus and I'm speaking to you live from our London studio, here on the Southbank. Tonight, it will be my absolute pleasure to guide you, the viewers at home, through a veritable smorgasbord of the finest in British culture. Over the past few weeks our five finalists have been pulling out all the stops, impressing the judges with a cultural cornucopia: opera, extemporary dance, performance arts - from Puccini to Punk, from Brecht to Bacon.

'But, alas, all good things must come to an end,' Quentin continued. 'Tonight, we learn which of our five cities and towns has the *Zeitgeist*, the Wow! factor, the *Je ne sais quois*? if you will, to secure the ultimate accolade. Even as I speak, preparations are underway at gala events around the country, showcasing our finalists' claims for the coveted title of UK City of Culture! Through unique simulcast technology, we'll be sampling the delights of each in turn before returning to the studio, here in London, for the announcement of the winner.

'So, without further ado, let's make our first house call - *King Lear*: act three, an interpretation in the style of the seventeenth century Japanese *Kabuki* theatre. Sound interesting…? You bet! Come in Darius Guyler, over there in Milton Keynes… Darius - is that a concrete cow I hear mooing in the background?'

There were cheers as the big screen blanked out, leaving the way clear for the local action to get underway. Up on the town hall stage, Freddie looked awkward and out of sorts. His microphone clunked noisily as it slipped through his fingers and dropped to the floor.

'Everyone oreet?' he muttered, grunting as he bent down to retrieve it - at least, most audience members assumed it was a grunt. Having shared a room with his brother for many years, Felix knew better.

The silence that followed was broken by a single, whooping response.

'Go for it, Son!'

Peering out into the audience, Freddie shielded his eyes from the spotlight's glare. 'Oh… thanks Dad. OK you guys - I guess I'm, like, your host for tonight.'

'We know what you are, you pillock!' someone heckled. 'Gerron with it, mate!'

'Cool. That Quentin dude will be back for our showcase act, which is going out live on the national telly in around twenty-five minutes. We've got a pile of local stuff to get through before then, so best get a wiggle on, eh?' He pulled a sheet of paper from his pocket and glanced down at it. 'First up, it's the East Frecklesall Dog Obedience Society and their version of the Gene Kelly classic - *Singing*… Oh, sorry guys, that should be *Barking in the Rain!*'

A dozen mutts wearing purple Got it All! jackets cantered onto the ballroom dance floor, dragging their owners along behind them. The opening bars of the classic number were greeted with a tuneless howl from the choral section, while the dancing pooches scampered along, crisscrossing and running around in circles. Sadly, the kilos of chocolate drops invested in the routine were undermined by the dance floor's polished surface. Back legs slipped and slithered, sending dogs and humans tumbling like skittles.

No one laughed louder than Felix's dad, whose enjoyment of the spectacle was aided by a seemingly endless supply of drinks. No sooner had he downed one than another would appear on the table in front of him. Felix overheard the words of any number of well-wishers.

'All the best Brian, lad. Great to see you out and about again. You can beat this thing!'

'Don't fret about the hair, Bri - it'll grow back thicker than ever, soon as you've done with the chemo.'

'Stay strong, mate. No surrender. We're all rooting for you!'

Felix looked at him, accusingly.

His dad shrugged. 'I didn't say anything, Son. They just, kind of, assumed.'

Vikki remained as alert as ever, constantly scanning the room and talking quietly into the two-way radio tucked under the lapel of her jacket. Felix checked his watch, a shiver running down his spine at the thought of what lay ahead.

The musical mutts were replaced by the Edelweiss Rest Home's armchair aerobics group, followed by the town's rugby league club and their distinctly limp version of the All Blacks' *haka*. In between times, Freddie's announcements were becoming less and less coherent. At one point, during the Frecklesall-on-Sea AmDram Society's extract from *Run for you Wife*, he crouched down at the side of the stage, clutching his stomach. From where Felix was sitting it looked very much like things were about to get serious.

Vikki leaned forward to have a word with Felix's dad. 'Do you think he's alright, Mr Haythornthwaite?'

'He'll be fine, love,' came the slurred reply. 'It's probably just part of his warm-up routine.'

No sooner had he spoken than Freddie grabbed hold of the colander and dashed from the stage.

'Good news!' announced the Mi5 agent after picking up a message on her radio a few minutes later. 'Freddie's gone to the toilet. Must be the nerves, I guess. He'll be back soon.'

'I hope so,' said Felix, 'because that Quentin's up on the big screen again. It's Frecklesall's turn to go live to the nation and Fred should be on stage, introducing our showcase act.'

Quentin Thesaurus was beaming down at them now and as the am-dram troupe trudged off, he launched into the wrap-up for the previous showcase number: 'Marcel that was simply stunning! Who amongst us could fail to be moved by the haunting sounds of the Tibetan nose-flute, a fitting accompaniment to Ballet de Chipping Norton's unique interpretation of Picasso's masterpiece - *Homme à la banane.*'

Back at Frecklesall town hall, things were going from bad to worse. Earphone-wearing techies were rushing around in blind panic and a young production assistant standing centre-stage, looked like she was about to burst into tears.

'And now we turn our attentions "oop north" as it were,' Quentin announced brightly. 'The Lancashire resort of Frecklesall-on-Sea is not a place hitherto renowned for its cultural offering - or anything else, for that matter - although that is surely set to change tonight! Self-styled "arts guerrilla" and some-time presenter of Frecklesall FM's iconic *Metal Mania* radio show,

Freddie "DeeJay FoF" Haythornthwaite, joins us now to introduce the town's showcase offering. DeeJay FoF - I believe you have something rather intriguing in store for us this evening?'

The picture on the big screen switched to the Frecklesall live-feed and the now-deserted stage, the camera panning about to pick up the empty dance floor and the drunken audience crammed in around it. There was an agonising pause in proceedings before Quentin got the message.

'Apologies, ladies and gentlemen,' he announced, 'it appears that our north of England cultural correspondent, DeeJay FoF, is temporarily indisposed.'

'HE'S STUCK ON THE LAVVY, QUENTIN, LAD!' yelled Felix's dad as he jumped to his feet, his bald-headed image glinting on the town hall's big screen and TV sets across the nation. 'HE'S BEEN A BIT BUNGED UP LATELY. HE'LL BE BACK AS SOON AS HE'S HAD A GOOD CLEAROUT!'

'Indeed. Thank you so much for that clarification, sir,' simpered the arts correspondent. He paused to cup his hand over a hidden earpiece. 'Well, I'm afraid we really do have to press on, which means that the honour of introducing our token northern contribution must rest on my own unworthy shoulders.' His focus moved to the side of the camera as he read from the autocue. 'Ladies and gentlemen, live from Frecklesall-on-Sea town hall, somewhere up there in deepest, darkest Lancashire, I give you... Krissy and Micky from the Salsatastic Sensations Dance Academy, in the world premiere of their fusion piece, *Tango-a-Go-Go!*'

There were whistles as the spotlight picked out the entwined couple, stranded in the middle of the ballroom dance floor. It was only as the pair prised themselves apart that Felix realised the woman wearing the incredibly high heels, a ton of makeup, and the slinky silver skirt split to the thigh, was his mother.

Her hair was piled into a towering platinum-blonde beehive - although this didn't last very long. Reaching back behind her head, she pulled out a huge hair pin, sending her tresses tumbling down across her shoulders. In the next instant she was marching purposefully towards her dance partner, the pin glinting as it was thrust, dagger-like, towards his neck. The man seemed distinctly unperturbed by the threat. Grabbing her by the arm, he span her around, the weapon falling to the floor as she swooned theatrically into his arms.

Micky was most definitely toy-boy material. Somewhere in his mid-twenties, he was square-jawed and handsome. His skin was pale, his neatly trimmed red hair glistened with oil, while a slim pencil moustache added to his film-star good looks. The ruffled front of his orange silk shirt was unbuttoned to the waist, revealing a powerful, waxed torso. The audience could only guess at how he'd managed to shoehorn himself into the tightest of white trousers, which emphasised every wiggle of his hips. And there was a heck of a lot of wiggling going on.

Felix watched through the gaps in his fingers as the pair glided around the dance floor, like competitors in an Olympic three-legged race. After any number of twirls and gyrations, they appeared to have another falling-out, mincing away from each other, lips pouting, heads thrown back. Alas, their separation was short-lived. Drawn together again by the sheer magnetism of their passion, Felix's mum drew further gasps as she ran towards her partner and leapt high into his outstretched arms.

'Fair play to the lad,' remarked someone nearby, 'that Krissy's no lightweight.'

It was slick and polished and while Felix was in the process of dying of embarrassment, the crowd were lapping it up. Suddenly there was a ruction immediately in front of him, and the one person in the room who was finding the routine even more painful viewing than he was, had clambered on top of his chair.

'Hey Micky!' Felix's dad yelled. 'That's my missus you've got your mitts all over! Lay off her, right now or so help me, I'll come over there and punch your flippin' lights out!'

Vikki DeBrett's pleas for calm fell on deaf ears.

'I hope you've got a good dentist, lad, 'cos you're going to need one after I'm done with you!'

The dancers were oblivious to the threats - perfectly synchronised, they only had eyes for each other, the driving Latin rhythm turning the heat up from 'simmer' to 'sizzle'.

The young Mi5 agent eventually succeeded in talking Felix's dad down from the chair, but his heckling continued and people began turning around to see what was going on.

Felix decided it was time to lend a hand. 'Come on Dad,' he pleaded, 'they're only dancing.'

'I'm not having this… Oww!' his dad yelped as Vikki twisted his arm up behind his back. 'It's bang out of order, Son, that's what it is!'

'Our control pod is reporting an imminent intervention,' Vikki said urgently. 'It isn't safe - you really must return to your seat immediately, Mr Haythornthwaite!'

'But that's my wife over there!' Breaking free, he made a pathetic attempt to gyrate his hips. 'Christine,

I'm here for you, love!' he yelled. 'I can do that sexy boogie too, y'know!'

An incandescent Trenton Fotherbridge burst onto the scene from out of nowhere. 'What the hell's going on, DeBrett? We've just escalated to a Code Red and you let Homer Simpson here, off the leash? It's unbelievable!'

Felix's dad rounded on him. 'Steady on, Trenton lad - the girl's doing her best.'

'Well it's not bloody good enough, is it? Sit down this instant or I'll have you arrested, and you can say goodbye to our deal!'

Felix was about to tell Fotherbridge where to get off, when something caught his eye. The dancers were shimmying towards them now, hips wiggling, arms waving around above their heads. Their cheesy smiles made him want to heave, but it was something else that set the alarm bells ringing. Micky's hands were fluttering about all over the place - the left one looked fine, but the right...

'Have you seen his hand?' Felix yelled, grabbing the Mi5 chief by the shoulder. 'Take a look now, for God's sake!'

Fotherbridge brushed him aside.

He tried again. 'The right one - the top half of his middle finger is missing! It's been covered with a skin-coloured dressing!'

'What the hell's that got to do with anything?' snapped Fotherbridge.

'I told you earlier. When that pie blew up in Fred's flat, there was this... this *thing* by the side of the fridge. It must have been *Micky's* finger I saw on the kitchen floor. He's one of them! He's one of the *Quesos Grandes* gang!'

The Mi5 man was having none of it. 'Just another stupid distraction ploy,' he snarled. 'I personally vetted everyone involved in this freak show, so I know what you're suggesting is–'

His words were interrupted by the raucous cheer which greeted Freddie's reappearance on stage. Looking like the weight of the world had been lifted from his shoulders, the DJ was grinning manically as he grooved away to the music. Within seconds the crowd were on their feet, laughing and yelling encouragement - many of them doing their own drunken versions of the Latin steps. Buzzing from the reaction, Freddie bowed theatrically and after throwing in a few spins, began wiggle-walking towards the tower of speakers on the left-hand side of the stage.

Felix sensed something bad was about to happen but no one around him seemed that interested in what his brother was up to. Vikki was listening to updates on her earpiece, while Trenton had climbed onto a chair and was peering back over the heads of the crowd. Felix's dad was on another planet, transfixed by the sight of his wife in the arms of her young partner.

'Dad, we've got to do something!' yelled Felix.

'You might just have a point there, Son,' his dad replied.

Felix spotted the crazed look in his father's eye. 'No, Dad, please! Calm down, will you?'

Back on stage, a second spotlight illuminated Freddie's antics as he began clambering up the speaker stack. Moments later, he was balanced precariously on top of the swaying tower, waving his arms around as if conducting the music. And then he delved into a jacket pocket.

Felix knew what was coming next but his despairing cry of, 'NOOOOO!' was lost in the cheers of the crowd. In the next instant, bullets of light were pinging around the Lancastrian Suite as Freddie thrust the fake diamond high above his head.

The dancers stopped dead in their tracks. Felix's mum, who'd been hanging upside-down, courtesy of a leg gymnastically hooked over her partner's shoulder, shrieked as she was dumped to the floor like a sack of potatoes. Ignoring her squeals, Micky rummaged around in the billowing orange satin of his shirt, before sprinting, full-pelt, towards the stage. The tiny silver pistol gripped in his hand pointed unerringly at Freddie's cowering figure.

The effect on the audience was instantaneous - screams giving way to a mad scramble as chairs were sent flying and the elderly and infirm were trampled underfoot. Freddie was frozen in terror on top of the speaker stack, but Felix's more immediate concern was for his dad. Roaring like a lion, Brian Haythornthwaite had shoved his youngest son aside and was thundering headlong onto the dance floor.

Micky never stood a chance. As he steadied himself to take aim, the older man slammed into him with the force of a herd of stampeding wildebeest gate-crashing a vicarage garden party. Locked together in a life-or-death struggle, the pair rolled about on the floor, Felix's dad desperately trying to wrestle the pistol's aim up to the ceiling.

Seizing the moment, Freddie jumped for it, but as he crashed to the stage the diamond slipped from his fingers. Felix caught the flickering glint of the fake stone as it bounced off the boards, pinging up to arc through the spotlight's beam before skittering across the dance floor. It came to a halt just a few metres from the grappling figures.

Trenton was toppled from his chair in the crush while Vikki had to dive for cover when Micky's pistol wafted crazily in their direction. Felix was already lying flat-out under the table and while he couldn't help wondering whether Micky would have been quite so keen to get his hands on the gem if he'd known where it had just come from, he kept his head down, the side of his face glued to the grubby carpet.

The ear-splitting 'CRACK!' of a pistol shot signalled the end of the *Tango-a-Go-Go* backing track.

Felix's dad lay motionless in the centre of the dance floor. Still clutching the smoking gun, his adversary was trapped beneath the dead weight of the older man's lifeless form. Felix could only watch on, helplessly, as Micky prised himself free and began crawling towards the fake stone.

And then, somehow, Felix's dad stirred. Grabbing the younger man's foot, he began hauling him back. Micky thrashed about, kicking furiously, but to no avail. Cursing in Spanish, he twisted around, the pistol glinting in the spotlight as he took aim.

Felix's cry was drowned out by the loud creaking noises suddenly echoing around the ballroom. Chunks of plaster began thudding onto the dance floor, exploding in spectacular powdery starbursts around the grappling pair. Distracted for an instant, Micky glanced up towards the hefty crystal chandelier, now swinging crazily from its broken fixings, directly overhead.

The Venezuelan saw what was heading his way but could do nothing to stop it.

CRASH!

The monster light-fitting scored a direct hit, spewing chunks of cut-glass in all directions.

While everyone froze, turning to try to see what had happened, Felix scooped up his baseball cap and ran for his life.

18

With the town hall fire alarm clanging noisily in his ears, Felix was swept along in a jostling crush of elbows, fists and knees. A few chaotic minutes later the pressure began to ease and, just before he was spewed out onto the street along with everyone else, he managed to break free. Darting up the deserted service corridor he landed outside the store room where he'd met Dannii, an hour or so earlier. He dived inside, slumping back against the door to catch his breath.

'We thought you'd bottled it, mate!'

He nearly jumped out of his skin as Bernie emerged from the bottom shelving unit.

Naz rolled out from the other side. 'Are you alright, Felix?'

'I'm fine,' he replied. 'It's madness out there. Is… is Dannii OK?'

'Yeah - she got out, no problem,' said Naz. 'How about your dad? He was amazing!'

'I'm pretty sure he made it,' replied Felix. 'Can't say the same for Micky, though. That chandelier made a right mess.'

Naz already had his sweatshirt halfway up over his head, revealing his Born to Boogie! Hawaiian number, underneath. 'Are you absolutely sure about this?' he asked. 'I mean, it's all extremely high risk. Wouldn't you be better following Mi5's instructions?'

Felix was unbuttoning his own Boogie! shirt. 'No way,' he muttered, 'not after what they've done to us.'

'But you've dragged me into it now,' Naz moaned. 'I'm an accessory to a crime. I could be prosecuted for aiding and abetting.'

'Stop flapping and get on with it! You know what we agreed.' He tossed his shirt to Bernie, straightening out the sleeveless Led Zeppelin top he had on underneath, liberated from his brother's side of the wardrobe earlier that afternoon.

Bernie screwed up his face. 'Eeughh, it's soaking! I should never have agreed to this.' Grimacing, he all but disappeared in the billowing polyester of Felix's Boogie! shirt, so long on him it looked like he was wearing a mini-skirt. 'I hope the paparazzi aren't out there - I'd hate my fans to see me like this.' He flipped his friend's Got it All! baseball cap onto his head and pulled a face.

'Yeah, they'd make a fortune selling the shots to *Morris Dancing Weekly*,' quipped Felix.

'Come *on*, you two!' pleaded Naz, donning his own purple headgear. 'We need to get outside before things start to calm down. Bernie, you go left and once you're on the street, head for Felix's house. I'll go right, then down to the Prom. And don't forget, the aim is to get noticed. Those Mi5 guys will be on the lookout for this hat and shirt combo.'

'Even those numpties couldn't miss us in this lot,' grumbled Bernie, gesturing at his new, ill-fitting outfit. 'What were your mums thinking when they bought you these shirts?'

Naz ignored him. 'And you,' he said, turning back to Felix, 'if there's any sign of trouble - anything at all - promise me you'll get the hell out of there and call the police.'

They split after the briefest of huddles and Felix was left on his own in the relative calm of the store room. He spotted a lone stick of chewing gum, still in its green wrapper, up on one of the shelves. Dannii must have left it there when she'd emptied her handbag to do her makeup. He couldn't stand the stuff but he shoved it in his pocket, hoping it might bring him luck. Where he was heading, he was pretty sure he was going to need it.

After checking the coast was clear, he took a deep breath and climbed out through the window onto the stone sill. Gingerly manoeuvring around, he clung onto the bottom of the window frame as he lowered himself down, feet first. He dropped the last metre and a bit onto the pavement, and moments later he'd unlocked his bike and was on the move.

Sprinting along the Prom, past the wreckage of the burnt-out lido, he lost count of the number of police cars and ambulances tearing towards the town hall. The plan had been for Bernie and Naz to act as decoys, creating enough of a distraction to give him a clear run, but the emergency services seemed to be making a pretty good job of that on their own. All Felix knew was that if he was going to get to Makinson's Quay in time, he'd have to keep his head down and turn the pedals faster than he'd ever turned them before.

After speeding around the rusting remains of the Big Lamp, he laboured up the climb to Top o'th' Moor. Opting for an off-road shortcut, he slung the bike onto a shoulder and clambered over a rickety stile, landing on the narrow footpath that tracked the edge of a recently manured potato field. The surface looked decent enough so he hopped on board and got back up to speed, until a cunningly concealed tree root sent him flying over the handlebars. Luckily, the damage was limited to his pride and he picked the bike up once more to continue on foot.

The path burrowed into a small copse and he had to ford a narrow, angry-looking stream, deep within the trees. Soaked to the knees, he emerged from the woods and after a dash across another field, arrived at Tinkler's Street, a single-track lane bounded by high hawthorn hedges. He hoped they might provide him with some level of cover but had second thoughts when he spotted the police helicopter clacking noisily overhead.

Felix hit the last mile at full gas. The bike's fixed wheel was a pain going up any kind of hill, but out on the flat, unburdened by gears and brakes, he could really make it shift. With sweat stinging his eyes and legs burning, he arrived on the main road directly opposite the track down to Makinson's Quay, more or less on schedule. It felt like he'd won a stage in the *Tour de France*, but there were no cheering crowds to greet him at the finishing line. As he crossed the road and began wheeling his bike along the rutted pathway, the doubts began crowding into his head.

The old concrete pier at Makinson's Quay is an isolated spot, tucked away in a tiny valley between two steeply sloping headlands. Felix had been there on bike rides when he was younger and knew that if anything bad happened, the only witnesses would be the seagulls wheeling lazily overhead on the late evening breeze.

The sea was calm in the shelter of the bay, but just offshore, the monotonous grey was tinged with the flashes of white-crested waves. It looked like the wind was picking up out there and from the accumulation of angry-looking clouds on the horizon, it was obvious a storm was brewing.

Felix dumped the bike and edged away from the path to check out a tiny corrugated-iron shed at the foot of the jetty. One side was completely covered in a grey, lichen-like growth, the other, a brilliant, glowing orange, its crumbling metal sheeting the victim of decades of attack by the salt-laden air. He peered in through one of the gaping holes, but apart from a few empty beer cans and some cigarette butts there was nothing to be seen.

It was getting close to ten o'clock and his mind was turning to the possibility that the text message had been another of Themba's stupid games, when he spotted something moving around the headland. Although he was aware of the sheer scale of the craft, he couldn't make out any detail - it was pitch black and with no lights visible, the whole thing seemed to be dissolving into the late evening gloom.

He was walking to the end of the jetty to try to get a better view, when the mobile in his pocket burst into life. Pressing the handset to the side of his face, he heard a confusion of voices.

'Themba, is that you?' he asked. There was a lengthy pause before he caught her reply.

'...Felix?'

'Speaking! I'm here - I made it! So, what happens now?'

'You must do exactly what I say,' she said, her voice tensing. 'It is a trap! Save yourself - get away while you still can!'

He hesitated, trying to make sense of her words. 'What's going on, Themba? Are you alright?' He heard shouting in the background - men's voices - and then he was sprinting back along the jetty, struggling to keep upright on the uneven surface.

He must have only travelled about twenty metres when a loud 'WHUUMPPF!' heralded the sudden explosion of the old tin shack at the side of the path. He dived for cover as shards of rusted corrugated-iron sprayed into the air.

'Bloody hell!' he screamed into the phone. 'What are you trying to do to me?'

'Make another move like that and it will be your last.' It was a man's voice, deep and menacing - every last syllable spoken with a spine-tingling precision. 'Stand up and retrace your steps.'

Felix picked himself up but was trembling so much it was a struggle to put one foot in front of the other. 'I'm not frightened of you, whoever you are,' he said, sounding absolutely petrified. 'What's to stop me calling the police, right now?'

The voice on the phone cracked into laughter. 'It may be an unfortunate coincidence, *Señor* Haythornthwaite, but those making the mistake of involving the authorities in their dealings with *Los Quesos Grandes*, often find themselves falling prey to unexpected health concerns. Your chest complaint, for example?'

'What do you mean? My chest is fine - I haven't had a cough in…' The words faded on his lips as he looked down at the piercing dot of the red laser beam, now resting directly over his heart.

'Kalashnikov AK12 - laser sights, night vision, a superb piece of precision engineering. And opportunities for live target practice are so rare these days.'

'Who are you?' asked Felix. 'What do you want with me?'

'My name is Alfonso Llanero Guayanes del Manchego - although for your purposes a respectful *Señor* Manchego, will suffice. And what I want, *mi amigo*, is for you to follow my instructions, precisely. Understand that your life depends upon it.'

'If this is about the diamonds, I don't know where they are. I've got nothing that could be of use to you.'

'Let us both hope that proves to be incorrect,' said Manchego. '*Los Quesos Grandes* has invested heavily in this venture and my associates would be understandably disappointed should it prove to have been a waste of their time. And talking of time, we really must make progress. Please be so kind as to walk to the end of the jetty and untie the rope you find there.'

One glance at the laser beam, still burning a hole in his rib cage was enough to convince Felix that he should do as he was told. He found the rope knotted around a rusted iron loop.

'*Bueno*,' Manchego purred as Felix untied it. 'Now drop it over the side, *por favor*.'

It seemed an odd request but he did as he was told and within seconds, sensed something moving on the water behind him. He turned to see the nose of a small, grey inflatable dinghy, complete with tiny outboard motor, poking out from beneath the concrete platform.

'You will join us as our guest, here on my yacht, *La Calabres,*' announced Manchego. 'Please accept my apologies for the rudimentary nature of the transportation. Rest assured you will receive the warmest of welcomes upon your arrival. Naturally, we will be observing your progress closely. Any transgressions, no matter how minor, and not only will it be the end for you, but for your friends also.'

'Friends?'

The question was met with silence.

As he pulled the dinghy from its hiding place, Felix realised it was also tethered at the back. He was about to jump down to untie it, when Manchego's voice stopped him in his tracks.

'Petty theft is such a curse on your British way of life, *Señor* Haythornthwaite. I could never forgive myself if your bicycle were to be stolen while you were enjoying our hospitality. Perhaps you should bring it with you?'

Felix looked out towards the yacht, a malevolent presence fading into invisibility as the night took hold. 'Why?' he asked. 'What's my bike got to do with anything?'

A blinding beam of blood-red light, flashed into his eyes.

'No more questions!' growled Manchego. 'Bring the bicycle!'

After lifting the bike into the inflatable, he untied the rear mooring rope. He had to heave on the starter cord three or four times before the outboard eventually wheezed into life. The dinghy puttered gently away from the jetty and Felix gazed back at the deserted quay, wondering whether he'd ever set foot on dry land again.

Ten minutes later, he was guided towards the low-slung metal platform at the yacht's stern, by two familiar faces. Scarface and his gold-toothed sidekick grinned as they welcomed him on board with rasping sound effects and shouts of, '*Hola*! *El Pedorro*!' before dissolving into fits of laughter. Following a body search, the mobile Doreen had given him was dropped over the side and he was escorted below deck. After bouncing along endless corridors, they arrived at a steel-plated door. Heavy-duty security bolts were slid back to reveal a small, rectangular cabin with a tinted glass porthole, through which Felix could see the lights of Frecklesall, slipping away towards the horizon.

The cabin contained a small table with four high-backed chairs. Although the lighting was dim, he instantly recognised the slim, elegant figure, now facing him.

'Themba - are you alright?' he asked.

Her face showed only the briefest flicker of recognition. As his eyes adjusted to the gloom he spotted the heavy chain running between her ankles.

'*Xavier speaks a little English*,' she whispered. '*Hernandez - the scar - has almost nothing.*'

Felix was pushed into the chair next to her while Xavier secured the bike to the cabin wall with a couple of straps. As the leg-irons were snapped into place, he realised that someone else had been invited to the party. Slumped face-down across the table, the stained pink shirt, red braces and greasy flop of dandruff-ridden hair, could only mean one thing.

'HB, is that you?' he asked, hardly able to believe his eyes. 'I thought you were dead!'

'I wish I was,' groaned his ex-boss, prising his head up to gawp listlessly at the new arrival. It was a shocking sight - his face was skeletal, his skin sickly pale. With over a week's worth of patchy stubble on his chin and bloodshot eyes sunk deep into his skull, he looked like something out of a horror movie. 'It's been a nightmare, Haythornthwaite,' he said, 'but d'you know what's been keeping me going?' His expression cracked into a leering grin. 'I'll tell you, my friend - it was knowing that sooner or later these guys were going to reel you in, and when that happened, I'd be able to sit back and watch you suffer the same torture I've had to go through these past two weeks.' Burping loudly, he lowered his head back onto the table.

'Ohmygod, they tortured you?' Felix shrieked. 'What was it - multi-sensory deprivation? Waterboarding? Themba, we've got to do something. We can't let them get away with this!'

'Sitting opposite this fool has, indeed, been a form of torture for me,' she said calmly, 'but in truth, our captors have been remarkably attentive.'

'I can't take it any longer!' moaned HB, his eyes now closed. 'Hernandez, kill me - kill me now!'

'Are you sure, Themba?' Felix asked in a low voice. 'Only, he seems a bit *mental*.'

She slid a packet of tablets across the table. 'He has developed an addiction to these. They are for the treatment of sea-sickness. They confuse him, but make him sleepy also, which means we are able to enjoy at least some respite from his constant moaning.'

Felix eyed the packet of Kwell-Eaze pills with suspicion.

'I am so sorry,' she continued. 'This is not how it was meant to be. Manchego gave me his word that we would all be set free once the transfer was complete.'

'What transfer?' he asked.

'The diamonds, of course.'

'I haven't got them. Really. I don't know where they are! Doreen said–'

Hernandez marched over and shook him roughly by the shoulder. '*Silencio*! *Silencio, ahora*!'

An uneasy hush descended. Staring blankly through the porthole, Felix watched the white crests sliding by on the oily black waves, wishing he was anywhere other than on this godforsaken boat. He hadn't wanted to play the hero but as usual, he'd done exactly what his great aunt had told him to. If he ended up dead because of this, it would be all her fault. Not that that would be much consolation, of course.

As mighty as the *La Calabres* had seemed when he'd first set eyes on her, she was soon being tossed around like a cork, the steady roll of the earlier swell now replaced with sudden, violent lurches. In no time, the cabin was heaving back and forth, the sea welling up to wash across the porthole before falling away to reveal the desolate blackness of the night sky.

Despite the howl of the wind, HB had quickly fallen into a deep, Kwell-Eaze-induced coma, the drool of saliva from the corner of his mouth now oozing steadily across the table. Themba was sitting bolt-upright, her eyes closed. Felix could only hope that she had a plan, because the indisputable fact remained that he didn't have the diamonds and when Manchego got around to asking him for them, there was going to be big trouble. Drained and exhausted, he eventually found himself sinking into a dark and troubled slumber.

Felix had no idea how long he'd been out of it, but when distant voices edged their way into his consciousness, he began to come-to. At least the roll of the yacht had eased slightly, and the wind seemed to have died down a bit, although how long he'd be around to worry about the state of the weather remained to be seen. With his eyes still shut, he could hear HB snoring loudly, but it was the pungent whiff of aftershave that now overloaded his senses. A whispered conversation was going on beside him. Themba's voice was instantly recognisable but he had no idea who she was talking to.

'I really should be making tracks, sweetie.' It was a man's voice, high-pitched, English and well-to-do. 'I was feeling simply ghastly before, but I do believe I'm perking up now. And it's all thanks to you - my very own Florence Nightingale!'

'Please, Gerald, it was nothing,' simpered Themba. 'And thank you so much for the Champagne. It was such a lovely surprise.'

'A beautiful young lady such as yourself deserves the finest things in life,' replied the man. 'From now on my job is to make sure you have them, in limitless supply!'

'I am so grateful for your representations to *Señor* Manchego,' she said, her voice cracking with concern, 'although I fear it may not be enough.'

'Oh, come now, my darling! His methods may be a little unorthodox but he's not such a bad egg. He's given me his word - once this little piece of business is done and dusted, it's full steam ahead to the beautiful holiday island of St Lucia, where you and I can enjoy some proper "us" time.'

Themba sighed. 'That would be lovely, Gerald. You have been so kind... I do hope you understand my concerns?'

'Of course! Don't you worry your pretty little head, sweetie - Gerald's here now!'

'In my home country we have an old tradition,' she said. 'If two lovers share the last glass from a bottle, their wishes must always come true.'

Felix heard the fizz of Champagne as it glugged into a plastic beaker.

'How quaint!' Gerald said. 'Couldn't have held it down twenty minutes ago... My word, that's rather a lot. One could get quite squiffy polishing that off on one's own!'

Felix was livid - Themba was trying to swing some kind of escape deal and unless his ears were deceiving him, he and HB weren't on the guest list. He wanted to confront her, to ask what the hell she was playing at, but something kept him pinned to his seat, eyes shut tight. He waited while they slurped their way through the Champagne and as they said their goodbyes, risked the sneakiest of peeks. Short and chubby, with a scrubbed, moon-shaped face, the visitor's white slacks and nautical-themed jumper were the outfit of a sad, middle-aged man, dressing to impress. Felix knew that under normal circumstances there was no way Themba would be interested in a loser like Gerald. He glared accusingly at her and for once, she was the one avoiding eye contact.

As the first signs of dawn appeared through the porthole, the cabin door was flung open, Hernandez and Xavier marching in to unlock the leg-irons and haul them to their feet. HB's mood had not been improved by a fitful night's sleep and he staggered around the cabin, loudly demanding another dose of Kwell-Eaze.

After struggling up numerous flights of stairs they were bundled out onto the open loading deck, Xavier following on with the bike slung over his shoulder. Felix didn't want to think about what might be coming next but HB seemed totally oblivious to the danger, standing there with his mouth hanging open, dribble running down his chin.

Their captors were a motley bunch - eight of them all told - slouching about and muttering as they lit their early morning cigarettes. Felix knew that Themba could handle herself in a tight spot but seeing the arsenal of semi-automatics wielded by the *Quesonistas*, guessed that even Wonder Woman might have thought twice before chancing her arm. Anyway, she wasn't going to be putting herself out for him or HB, now that 'us' time with Gerald in St Lucia was on the cards.

The doors onto the deck swung open and the gang members snapped to attention in honour of their leader. Manchego was in his early seventies, his handsome suntanned features framed by expensively trimmed silver hair. The tailored blue suit must have cost a small fortune while his white, open-necked silk shirt revealed a chunky gold chain and cheese-shaped medallion - an upmarket version of the ones Felix had seen Hernandez and Xavier wearing. The gang boss was surprisingly short, probably no more than five-foot-six, but his eyes were his most striking feature - a startling icy blue. Even from a distance, they looked cold and soulless.

'I am used to exercising control,' he announced, 'but as ever, I find my well-laid plans compromised by your miserable British weather. We should be in international waters by this time, but the storm has put paid to that. It is of no real concern - indeed, in my experience, the deferral of pleasure makes moments like this all the more enjoyable.'

'I think there's been a bit of a misunderstanding, Mr Manchego... err... *señor*,' said Felix. 'Y'see, I haven't actually got the diamonds on me at the moment. I've a pretty good idea where they might be, though. So if you wouldn't mind dropping me and Howard off somewhere - on dry land, preferably - I'd be happy to nip back to Frecklesall and have a look for them. I can send them on, later. Don't worry about the postage - I'll cover the costs.'

'Liar!'

He turned to find HB pointing accusingly at him.

'You're a liar, Haythornthwaite!' his ex-boss screamed. 'He's got those diamonds, Mr Manchego, sir. He's trying to trick you!'

Felix was incensed. 'Shut up, you plank! If you hadn't stuck those pictures on your stupid website, we wouldn't have got into this mess in the first place!'

'It was your bag - you're the one who started it–'

'*Caballeros*!' Manchego shouted over them. 'Let us not spoil the beauty of this moment with such petty disagreements. *El Cullinan Perdido* - the Lost Cullinan, or "C2", as it is known to your security service, has been our quest for many years. I am ashamed to say, that even I doubted its existence until earlier this year, when its most exquisite offspring came into our possession. Alas, our joy turned out to be all too brief.' He gave Themba a dirty look.

Hernandez rushed forward with a white hand towel which Manchego used to dab his brow, the smile quickly returning to his lips.

'Happily, those dark days are behind us,' he continued, 'for it is now that we, the humble *Quesonistas,* are to be reunited with what is rightfully ours! *El Cullinan Perdido es nuestros*!'

A loud cheer went up from the gang members.

'Actually, *Señor* Manchego… Ow!' Felix doubled over as a gun-barrel was jabbed into his ribs.

Xavier delved into a metal storage locker at the side of the deck, emerging a few seconds later with a vicious-looking angle-grinder which hummed ominously as he clicked it on. Teeth glinting, the henchman wafted the lethal power tool's spinning circular blade just inches from Themba's face.

She didn't flinch.

Manchego fixed her with his chilling gaze. 'My dear, you have provided me with certain assurances. Should these turn out to be false, the consequences for you will be *most unpleasant.*'

Felix closed his eyes as Xavier thrust the angle grinder's blade either side of his head, knowing that one false move would result in something a lot worse than a dodgy haircut.

'You say you do not know of the diamonds' whereabouts, *Señor* Haythornthwaite,' continued the gang boss. 'This loss of memory is *most unfortunate*, but I believe my dear friend, Xavier, may be able to help aid your recollection.'

Powerful arms grabbed him from all sides. He tried to break free but it was no use. Grinning broadly, Xavier turned the angle grinder towards HB, who was clearly still surfing the wave on planet Kwell-Eaze.

'*El abrazo izquierdo o derecho*? *Tu decides*!' the gangster shouted gleefully, before continuing in barely intelligible English, 'The arm of left or right?'

Felix struggled for all he was worth. 'No! You can't do this! You've got to believe me - I don't know where the diamonds are and hurting him isn't going to help!'

Manchego's barked command cut across his plea. '*Ahora, Xavier. Vamos*!'

Felix screwed his eyes shut, but was powerless to block out the dreadful screech as the blade's razor-sharp teeth cut deep.

will appreciate that for a connoisseur such as myself, comparisons between the peerless beauty of *El Cullinan Perdido* and worthless tin coins, stamped with the faces of second-rate English footballers, might be considered a grave insult.'

The gang members stirred, uneasily.

'But happily, your story is an irrelevance,' Manchego continued. 'The sixth diamond - your *Wayne Rooney* - is already in our possession.'

Felix couldn't hide his surprise.

'I anticipated that you might split the stones with your brother,' the gang boss said, 'So as a contingency, I despatched a "sleeper" into your midst. He is the most loyal and skilled of my *Quesonistas* - a master of deception, fluent in many languages and unflinching in his willingness to make whatever sacrifices are required. When we secured intelligence that your brother was to host last night's event, and would be carrying one of the diamonds about his person, it was a simple task to activate our plan.'

'This sleeper character,' asked Felix, 'was his name Micky, by any chance?'

Manchego laughed. '*Miguel*, to be precise - hair dye, skin lightener, a set of false papers, and who would know? Least of all, the swooning English housewives who throw themselves at him wherever he goes.'

'So… you reckon he's got the sixth stone, then?'

'It is being flown back to Caracas even as we speak, although I am sorry to say, Miguel's success has come at a terrible price.'

'Why? What happened to him?' asked Felix, the awful image of Micky's body, crushed and broken beneath the shattered chandelier, looming large in his mind's eye.

You could have heard a pin drop.

The gang boss pulled out a handkerchief to dab away a tear. 'We can never repay the debt we owe dear Miguel,' he announced solemnly.

'Was he badly hurt?'

Manchego paused. 'It is worse than that - much worse. He had to make the ultimate sacrifice.'

'You mean he's...?'

'I mean,' the gang boss replied, his face breaking into a sparkling smile, 'he had to perform that most sensuous of dances - the tango - with your mother! The poor boy may never live it down!'

There were howls of laughter and raucous shouts of '*Tu madre!*' but before Felix could respond, the door onto the deck banged open noisily. Hernandez dashed forward to prop up the bedraggled and confused-looking new arrival.

'Geraldo!' Manchego greeted the pyjama-clad Englishman, who was blinking in the morning light. 'You must join with us in our celebration, but first, there is a simple task you have agreed to perform, *sí?*'

Felix was taken aback by Gerald's appearance. His pyjama top was buttoned up wonkily and he was only wearing one slipper. His hair, so neatly coaxed into place for his date with Themba, was all over the place, while his eyes seemed unfocussed and distant.

Manchego beckoned Hernandez to one side, leaving Gerald swaying precariously in the middle of the deck. '*Está el enfermo?*' he asked, quietly.

'*No, es el mareo,*' Hernandez replied, shielding his mouth with his hand. '*Todo es bien.*'

Staggering slightly, Gerald gave Themba a twinkly wave as he was led across to the diamonds. 'Papa's here, sweetie. Don't you worry your pretty little head.'

She smiled, coyly.

'Allow me to introduce one of your compatriots,' Manchego announced, grandly. 'This is Sir Gerald Farquharson OBE, of Knightsbridge, London.' He patted his guest on the back. 'I understand you may be a little out of sorts as a result of the inclement weather conditions, Sir Gerald. Please accept my apologies for this regrettable state of affairs. I take it your judgement remains sound and unimpaired?'

'I should say so, Alfonso - absolutely and unimpeachably peachy!' Gerald replied. Glancing down at the diamonds, his expression cracked into a crazed, lopsided grin.

Manchego turned to his three captives. 'Sir Gerald is personal adviser to the British royal household, in the field of precious stones. His knowledge of the crown jewels is unparalleled, making him ideally placed to authenticate the package you have so kindly brought to us.' He paused for a second, a cruel glint returning to his eye. 'And mark my words, *Señor* Haythornthwaite, should these diamonds prove to originate from anything other than the bona-fide Lost Cullinan stone, my wholly inadequate consolation will be to pull the trigger of the gun which will be pointing… just… here.' He lifted his hand, pointing his forefinger at the side of Felix's head.

'Yeah Haythornthwaite, that's unless I get you first!' added HB.

Manchego turned to the scouser. 'Rest assured, *Señor* Brake, you will be the next to die.'

HB dissolved into a blubbing mess.

A magnifying lens was passed to the royal adviser and he held it to his right eye while a chubby hand skipped across the five diamonds.

'*One potato, two potatoes, three potatoes four...*' He squinted at one of the smallest stones through his left eye, before realising the lens was in the other one. 'Oops, Gerald - you're such a silly Billy!' Switching the lens, he studied the fake, long and hard. There was a 'Goodness gracious' and an 'Oh my giddy aunt', and even a 'Wowzer!' but as he placed it back onto the wrap, no one was any the wiser.

The expert greeted the largest gem with a cry of 'Come to daddy, big boy!' but predictably, it was the single, mid-sized diamond - the damaged half of Freddie's home-made earring project - that proved decisive. After examining it for just a few seconds, Gerald pressed his hands together and looked up at his audience.

'That's it, gentlemen - I have arrived at my decision!'

Felix filled his lungs with the fresh sea air, determined to make the most of his last few mortal breaths.

'Well, Geraldo?' Manchego asked. 'In your expert opinion, do these beautiful gemstones genuinely and definitively originate from the fabled Lost Cullinan?'

'*Señor* Manchego, *caballeros, mademoiselle*,' the diamond expert began. 'I, Sir Gerald Farquharson, personal adviser to Her Most Majestic Queen Liz, will now tell you what's what, without further *adoobee, doobee, doo.*' He smirked as he swept his hand over the fakes. 'You have asked, *señor*, whether the provenance of these magnificent sparklers links directly and unequivocally to the fabled *Lost* Cullinan stone.' He paused again to dab his brow with a pyjama sleeve. 'Well, I can exclusively reveal, right here, right now, and without fear of contraception, that in my humble opinion, it most definitively does... NOT!'

The stunned silence was broken only by the solitary pop of a wayward Champagne cork, followed by a loud wail from the Braking News Corporation's Chief Executive. And then Themba was struggling to break free. Four of the *Quesonistas* pounced on her, pinning her arms behind her back.

Felix felt numb with shock. He was about to die, but weirdly, all he could think of was Dannii. He'd spent years dreaming about dating a girl as beautiful as her and now he'd finally cracked it, here he was, stuck out in the middle of the ocean, waiting for a bullet to the head. 'Unfair' was the understatement of the year!

His thoughts were interrupted by a high-pitched shriek.

'Friends, Romans, crunchymen! *Tranquillo per favore*!'

It was like pressing 'pause' on the remote in a game of musical statues. All eyes turned back to the diamond expert.

'Ahem! In response to this most unexpected of brouhahahas, and for the avoidance of gout,' Sir Gerald continued. 'Please permit me to re-postulate my previously postulated postulation. All I am *trying* to say *vis-à-vis* this Cullinan thingamajig, is simply… Now that you've *found* the blooming things, how the heck can they possibly be described as *lost*?'

Everyone looked at each other, Manchego's forehead creasing as if he'd been struck down by the world's biggest migraine. It was Felix who found his voice first.

'So… *Geraldo,* I mean, Sir Gerald - correct me if I'm wrong here, but I think what you're trying to say is that if we renamed these stones the *Found* Cullinans, you'd be happy?'

A gust of wind caught the royal adviser's hair and for a moment he looked like a jolly public schoolboy from the 1950s who'd just been presented with a large bag of gobstoppers. '*D'Accord*! Yes indeedy!' he replied. 'Because these babies are slam-dunk on the *dinero*, my dahhlings!' He turned to Manchego. 'Congratulations Alfonso, you may now kiss the bride!' And with that, his knees buckled and he crumpled to the deck.

It was great while it lasted - the *Quesonistas* launched into a spontaneous salsa version of the hokey-cokey and even Manchego joined in the fun, flashing his dazzling smile and wiping his hands with painstaking care after each high-five. The mood was so buoyant, Felix's hopes of a last-minute reprieve were in danger of being rekindled. But Themba didn't seem to have caught the mood. She was arguing in fluent Spanish with one of the crew members, and while Felix assumed it was because Xavier had led a celebratory conga line right over her beloved Gerald's unconscious body, the real reason soon became apparent.

Felix watched in dismay as the tiny inflatable dinghy from the night before was lowered into the swell. And then Manchego extracted himself from the party to call for silence.

'Alas, all good things must come to an end,' he announced, solemnly. 'We must make progress if we are to avoid unwanted interference. So, on behalf of all of us here at *Los Quesos Grandes*, I offer thanks to our three guests for their invaluable assistance, and wish them *bon voyage.*'

His words were greeted with polite applause, after which Felix, Themba and HB were shoved at gun-point into the tiny boat.

'You'd never have got the diamonds back without me, Mr Manchego!' pleaded HB. 'A man of your standing deserves more recognition. Have you thought about developing your platform - an authorised biography perhaps, or maybe even a feature in *Lancashire Life*? I can make totally make that happen and my rates are very reasonable.'

Xavier tossed a packet of Kwell-Eaze down into the well of the boat and laughed as HB scrambled after it, hungrily stuffing a handful of the pills into his mouth. Grim-faced, Themba had already positioned herself by the outboard motor while Felix crouched down at the side, observing the swell rolling around the *La Calabres'* stern with trepidation. The battered little tender may have been fine for pootling around sheltered bays along the coast but out on the high seas, exposed to the full force of the elements, he knew their chances of survival were less than slim.

Hernandez pulled out a short, hook-bladed knife, and sliced through the mooring rope.

'*Adios amigos*!' Manchego shouted after them. 'Your place in our history is assured. And as a token of our gratitude, please accept this parting gift.' The faintest of nods to Hernandez and the knife flashed once again. Felix watched, open-mouthed, as a quick-fire stab sent air hissing from the boat's front compartment.

The gang boss turned and walked off across the deck without so much as a backwards glance as the superyacht's engines roared into life, churning up a bubbling wake that all but flipped the inflatable over.

Themba dived forward, desperately trying to stem the air loss with her fingers.

'This is all your fault, Haythornthwaite!' shrieked HB. 'One of my associates just happens to be a top level legal eagle and if we all end up dead after this, you'd better lawyer up, my friend, 'cos your life won't be worth living!'

Felix jumped to his feet. 'Shut up, you moron! One more word and you'll be swimming home.'

'We are losing air!' Themba shouted over their bickering. 'We need some tape, or a patch - something that will stick. Quickly!'

'Didn't your lovely *Geraldo* make sure you had a puncture repair outfit before he waved you on your way?' Felix screamed back at her. 'Tell you what - don't worry your pretty little head about it, *sweetie*, I'm sure I've got one on me, somewhere or other!' Incandescent with rage, he rammed his hands into his pockets and pulled the linings inside out.

'What was that?' Themba said, as a small green object flew over the side.

Felix did a double-take. 'Ohmygod! That's it!' In the next instant, he'd jumped overboard, spluttering back to the surface a few metres from the boat. He hauled an arm up over the side and thrust Dannii's soggy stick of gum into Themba's hand. 'Keep your finger over that hole and get chewing!'

20

A frantic search of the dinghy's storage compartment led to the discovery of a single, ancient-looking lifejacket and a small, foldable plastic paddle. Felix sat alone at the front of the boat, his mood plummeting. Being stranded out on the open sea with his obnoxious ex-boss was the stuff of nightmares - throw in the woman who'd got them into this mess and done everything she could to abandon them to their fate, and it had all the ingredients of a Channel 5 fly-on-the-wall documentary.

At first, Themba focussed on trying to get the outboard going. It was only when she gave up on the motor, and Felix jumped in to salvage its top cover before she dumped it over the side, that they finally found themselves face to face. The row that followed was epic - accusations layered on top of insults that would have made even Doreen blush. In the end it was HB who begged for a timeout and the shock of his zombie-like appearance was enough to drag them into an uneasy ceasefire.

Twenty minutes later, with HB snoring loudly and the chewing gum patch still holding up, Themba broached the subject again.

'We are wasting valuable energy with these unnecessary arguments,' she said quietly.

Felix blanked her.

'You have to believe me,' she continued. 'I was playing Farquharson in the hope it might create an opportunity for us.'

Felix laughed. 'For you, more like. I didn't hear you putting in a word for me and HB when you were off on your pathetic "Flirty-Gerty" routine.'

Themba didn't rise to the bait. 'I risked everything to help this *fool*.' She gestured dismissively towards the comatose body lying in the well of the dinghy. 'Tell me - having placed my own life in such peril, why would I suddenly decide to abandon him, or you for that matter?'

'I don't know - probably because when push comes to shove, all you're really interested in is saving your own skin,' he replied. If lover-boy *Geraldo* hadn't messed up so badly, me and HB would be floating face down in the Irish Sea by now, while you'd be swanning off to the beautiful holiday island of St Lucia for some "us" time. You must be gutted with the way things have turned out.'

'He is a world-renowned diamond expert. The marks on that replica stone were obvious, even to someone like you. Why do you think he missed them?'

'We got lucky, I guess.'

Themba shook her head. 'Sometimes we must make our own luck, Felix.' She picked up the soggy packet of Kwell-Eaze from the water slopping around their feet. 'I persuaded Gerald to take some of these pills to help with his seasickness last night. You should read the instructions on the back.'

He snatched the packet from her and scanned the guidance notes with an air of indifference.

Kwell-Eaze

Recommended adult dose one tablet. May cause drowsiness and impairment of mental capacity. If taken, do not drive; do not attempt to use heavy machinery

UNDER NO CIRCUMSTANCES MIX WITH ALCOHOL

Suddenly, he was feeling about as small as the print he'd just struggled to read. 'You mean… you drugged him?'

'How was I to know he would be drinking alcohol so soon afterwards?' she replied, innocently. 'Or, indeed, that he would end up consuming almost the entire bottle?'

On the verge of death by embarrassment, Felix toyed with the idea of jumping overboard for a second time.

Ten minutes later, after checking that HB was still out of it, Themba tried again. 'I understand why you might think ill of me, given everything that has happened. If we are to die out here, it is important to me that you know the truth.'

Still overflowing with awkwardness, all Felix could manage was a faint nod of his head. Themba leaned forward to tell him her story.

'My ancestors were warriors,' she began, 'but they could never win their war against the colonialist oppressors. By the early years of the twentieth century, my great, great, great grandfather, Chief Bonokwane Magatos, had lost everything. Every able-bodied Magatos tribesman, and those from every other tribe in the province, had been coerced into the camps surrounding the diamond mines. It was forced labour - slavery in all but name. Life was cheap, conditions brutal, and nothing could be allowed to disrupt the exploitation of the land we had once called our own.

'He was working at the Premier Mine in Pretoria when the Cullinan stone was discovered. It was the biggest diamond in the world and the mine owners celebrated for many days. The following week he was heading back across the compound at the end of his shift, when he stumbled across an odd-shaped piece of rock, partly buried in the dirt.'

'The Lost Cullinan?' asked Felix.

'The colonialists called it that,' she replied, 'but for us, the treasure Chief Bonokwane found that day will always be known by another name.'

Felix listened to the story in awe. Taking his life into his hands, Bonokwane smuggled the precious stone out of the mine compound, hiding the newly named Magatos diamond in a secret place. The southern cape was awash with stories about a lost segment rumoured to have split from the original Cullinan, and everyone was looking for it. But Bonokwane was too smart for the authorities and while there were a couple of close shaves, it was never found.

The story of the Magatos diamond was quickly absorbed into local folklore, becoming a symbol of defiance which somehow helped give the tribespeople the strength they needed to get through those dark years. When the mines closed, those that survived returned to the land and began rebuilding their lives.

When Bonokwane grew old and frail, he shared the secret of the stone with his eldest son. The knowledge was passed on through the generations, eventually resting with Themba's grandfather, Chief Nomalanga III. Because Themba's father had died when she was young, the proud old man placed his faith in his grandson - Themba's older brother, Dakarai. And that's when things turned sour.

Dakarai hatched a plan to smuggle the stone to Johannesburg, determined to finally unlock the glittering secret lying within its rocky shell. He took it to one of the city's top gem cutters, walking away a couple of weeks later with six exquisitely finished diamonds. The following day, when he tried to have them valued, he was politely informed that each and every one was a high-quality fake.

The complex sting operation had cost a small fortune to set up, but now *Los Quesos Grandes* were heading out of South Africa with the biggest prize of all. Dakarai went into hiding, unable to face his grandfather's grief.

'Brothers, eh? And I always thought our Fred was a liability!' Felix joked.

Themba didn't see the funny side. 'Like so many before them, the South African Government had doubted the existence of the Magatos diamond, regarding the story as little more than a myth,' she said. 'But when they received credible intelligence confirming the switch had taken place, they decided to investigate. They had their reasons of course, but I knew these had nothing to do with the return of the diamonds to my family. As a recent recruit to their Special Forces Unit, I was able to reach out to a contact - an old family friend who was already involved in the tracking exercise. It did not take long for him to locate the Venezuelans, and from there we took matters into our own hands.'

'If you'd told me this when we first met, I'd have done what I could to help,' Felix said. 'Why didn't you say?'

'I could not be certain of your reaction,' she replied. 'There are many within your country who believe that as part of the original Cullinan stone, the Magatos diamonds belong to Britain, or more specifically, to your Head of State.'

'You mean the Queen? I reckon she's got more than enough trinkets to be going on with, already! But what about that poor guy who was murdered in the hotel? Mi5 showed me these photos and this CCTV footage. They said you did it.'

'My dear friend Zaaia is the real hero of this story,' she replied, her face downcast. 'He is the one who tracked the gang, risking his life to make the interception. Soon afterwards we realised that the Venezuelans were closing in on us and with all routes into Lesotho being carefully monitored, we were obliged to separate and flee South Africa. We had an agreement that when things had cooled off a little, Zaaia would make his way to London where he would transfer the diamonds to me. I was then to find a way of securing their safe passage back to Lesotho.

'He was murdered in cold blood before I could get to the rendezvous point at the hotel. They left his body in the bath, wrapped in a shower curtain - I saw it with my own eyes.' She paused to wipe away a tear. 'Those *Quesos Grandes* animals may have killed him but they left empty-handed. I will always regret arriving too late to save Zaaia's life but somehow, in the midst of that most awful tragedy, I discovered where he had concealed the diamonds. To this day, I am still not sure how I was able to extract them, and myself, from that hotel room, given the close attention of your Mi5 agents.'

Felix sighed. 'They're not *my* agents, Themba.'

She smiled and shook her head. 'My intention was to travel to Stranraer on Scotland's west coast, where I could board a ferry to Northern Ireland. I knew that security would be less problematic over there, and I could travel down to Dublin, and more easily catch a flight back to Lesotho. So I headed north with the fakes concealed in the lining of my rucksack - the real diamonds were hidden within the bicycle. I had to change trains at Preston and, of course, this is where we first met.'

'If I'd known what was in that bike frame...' Felix said, blowing out his cheeks.

Themba shrugged. 'The Mi5 operatives who detained me at the station interrogated me for many hours. I told them nothing and eventually they had to let me go. After I caught up with you and was taken in by your family, it was simple enough to switch the real diamonds from the bicycle frame, with the replicas you discovered in my bag. Perhaps you will recall that early morning visit I made to your garden shed?'

'I knew someone had been messing with my bike. The saddle was all over the place,' Felix said, glumly. 'I had no idea it was you, though. Sounds like I might owe my dad an apology... if I ever get to see him again.'

'Of course, I still needed time to arrange the transfer out of the country,' she continued. 'Being aware of your suspicions, I was obliged to manufacture certain distractions to keep you occupied while this process was underway. After I hacked your mobile phone, I quickly discovered your collaboration with the so-called NewsKwest agency. This was most unhelpful.'

Felix could feel his face beginning to flush. 'I'm really sorry about that, Themba. I didn't know they were setting me up. I was gutted when I found out.'

'These people are highly skilled at finding a weakness and manipulating it to achieve their objectives,' she said. 'I had my doubts about NKI but by the time I became certain it was a front, the diamonds were already in transit.'

'So why hang around then? You got what you came for - why not go home?'

'Because HB's fate weighed heavily on my conscience. The text message I intercepted when I was visiting your aunt, offered one last opportunity to save his life.'

'How on earth did you think were you going to get him off that boat in one piece?' asked Felix. 'It was a suicide mission!'

'My plan was to pass off the fake stones as the originals, trading them in return for his life,' she replied. 'It was a high-risk strategy - even more so as one of them was missing, thanks to the stupidity of your brother. Then, when I discovered you had taken my bike on your trip to the Isle of Man, together with the remainder of the replicas, I had to think again.'

'But you went ahead anyway?'

'I had no choice. I decided to surrender to Manchego and try to convince him I could persuade you to bring him the bike, complete with the diamonds hidden in its frame. I feared you might not respond positively to a direct approach from me, so I channelled my request through your aunt. I know the respect you have for her, and that you will always do whatever she asks of you.

'Manchego gave me his word that you would not have to set foot on board the *La Calabres*,' she continued, 'that the transfer would take place on the quayside and once the "diamonds" were in his possession, we would all be set free. The moment you arrived at the rendezvous point it became clear he was lying. By then it was too late.'

'So, where are the real diamonds now?' Felix asked. 'You might as well tell me - it's not like there's anything I can do about it, stuck out here, is there?'

Themba gazed out across the endless ocean swell. 'Most are back in Lesotho by now - the others are, let us say, in transit. I can tell you no more until their safe arrival is confirmed.'

'OK, so how did you pull it off? I was shadowing you all the time, and those Mi5 guys were watching you like hawks.'

She smiled. 'The story of the original Cullinan diamond is a most intriguing one. I believe there is saying in your country - about history, and how sometimes it can repeat itself?'

'What does that mean?'

Their exchange was interrupted by the sounds of retching from the well of the dinghy as HB began to stir. Themba held a finger to her lips, making it clear the conversation was at an end.

There was little they could do but sit and hope. The chewing gum patch was holding up, after a fashion, but they were still losing air and shipping water at an alarming rate. Felix was exhausted - he and Themba had taken it in turns, using the cover from the outboard motor to bail out as best they could. HB's contribution had consisted of an endless stream of moans and groans.

By early evening, things were getting desperate. At first, Felix convinced himself they had a chance - surely they'd been through too much to end up in a watery grave, somewhere in the middle of the Irish Sea? But as the hours passed the wind began to whip up again and with exhaustion, hunger and raging thirst kicking in, dark thoughts began crowding into his head. He pictured himself flailing in the freezing water, powerless against the ocean's grasp. Spiralling downwards, his final breath spent, he was coughing… choking… drowning - his body fighting on for just a few short seconds before the final surrender.

Sitting there, waiting for the inevitable, he began to think a bullet to the head from Manchego's gun might have not have been such a bad deal after all.

'We've got to do something!' HB shrieked, as if he'd been reading Felix's mind. 'There's no chance of anyone spotting us once it gets dark!' The boat lurched to one side as he struggled to his feet.

'Howard, sit down please!' urged Themba. 'It is not safe.'

'Who cares?' he screamed, picking up the paddle and waving it high over his head. 'Help! Anybody out there… Please! You've got to help me!'

'I'm warning you, HB - sit down or you'll flip us over!' shouted Felix.

'It doesn't matter - we're all going to die out here!'

The inflatable lurched again as Felix launched himself at his ex-boss's midriff. HB was flung backwards, his head splatting into the soggy grey blancmange of the dinghy's front buoyancy compartment with a dull 'Whumpf!' Groaning, it took him a second to come to his senses.

'You've just broken my neck, Haythornthwaite. You're going to pay for this!'

Themba crawled forward to assess the damage. 'You are fine, Howard,' she announced, after the most cursory of examinations. 'You can move your arms and legs. There is nothing the matter with you.'

HB's scrawny body writhed around in the seawater slops, but his head remained motionless, as if glued to the front of the boat.

'My head's stuck!' he wailed. 'I'm paralysed from the neck up!'

A look of alarm flashed across Themba's face. 'You must stay still, Howard,' she said urgently. 'Please, I beg you!'

But it was too late.

'Oww that hurt!' HB yelped as he jerked his body forward. Sitting up, he rubbed furiously at the back of his head, immediately spotting the sticky grey mess smeared across the palm of his hand. 'That's my brain leaking out! You've fractured my skull!'

'It is the patch!' shouted Themba. 'Felix, the chewing gum is stuck in his hair. Hold him down - we must try to retrieve it and secure it over the puncture once more!'

But Felix didn't respond. Still on his feet, he was gazing, transfixed, towards the horizon. 'I… I think there's something over there,' he mumbled, fearful he might be hallucinating. A handful of red lights twinkled back at him through the evening gloom. Now he was the one in danger of capsizing the boat. 'I don't know what it is, Themba, but… I can't believe it!' he yelled, jumping in excitement.

Seconds later, she'd confirmed the sighting and taken control. 'Everyone is to remain calm!' she ordered. 'We must work together as a team. HB - get to the front and do what you can with the puncture. I will take the paddle - Felix, you use the motor cover.'

It was the longest hour of his life - arms and shoulders screaming in pain, it felt like his back was breaking, but nothing, not even HB's constant whining, could distract them from their mission.

The giant sentinels of the offshore windfarm rose majestically from the sea - thirty white columns towering above the horizon, their massive rotor blades circling steadily, despite the blustery conditions. But even as the single red beacon crowning each turbine beckoned them onwards, a more immediate concern threatened their hopes of salvation.

The boat was sinking.

For once, it wasn't HB's fault. He'd been doing everything he could to hold things together but the wind had picked up and the swell was increasing by the minute. To make matters worse, the dinghy's front compartment had almost completely collapsed. Water was flooding in over the bow, forcing them to cling to the stern of the boat as they struggled towards their target.

As they inched closer, they could see that each of the towers had a mini-platform, complete with railings, suspended a few metres above sea level. To Felix's eye, they didn't look like they offered much in the way of shelter, but it was infinitely preferable to drowning. Head down, he gritted his teeth and paddled for all he was worth.

They were no more than a couple of hundred metres away when they were caught by a sudden gust of wind that sent them lurching sideways. And then the wave hit, spilling them into the water. Gasping from the cold, Felix spluttered to the surface, vintage life jacket in one hand, a packet of Kwell-Eaze in the other. He watched on as what remained of the inflatable careered off beyond his reach.

He eventually spotted Themba. Rising and falling with the swell, she had hold of HB and was struggling to keep his head above water.

'He cannot swim!' she shouted.

Mercifully, the lifejacket burst into life as Felix squeezed the emergency gas canister, and then he was doggy-paddling towards them with all the energy his exhausted body could muster.

'*Ahoy there, on the starboard side! Worse things happen at sea, what?*'

The bizarre greeting blew past on the wind. Felix could only guess that he was in the grip of some kind of Freddie-esque near-death experience.

'*Reminds me of the time I had to abandon off the Cape back in '53! Not so many great whites this far north, but still a rum do!*'

Stuffing HB's head into the lifejacket, Felix wiped the water from his eyes and tried to focus on the bearded, windswept figure in the stained combinations, who was waving at them from the platform of the nearest turbine.

Minutes later they dragged themselves up the slimy, seaweed-coated ladder, before sprawling, coughing and spluttering, across the cold steel deck. Somehow, they'd made it, and the buzz of adrenalin was like nothing Felix had ever experienced before

'Welcome aboard, shipmates, I've been expecting you!' Rear Admiral Sir Hubert Montague-Dunk (Retired) greeted them warmly.

Felix's heart sank as it dawned on him that of all the people they had to bump into, out here in the middle of the ocean, he couldn't think of anyone who would be of less use. 'We've met before, actually, Sir Hubert,' he said, half-heartedly. 'It was on the beach at Frecklesall, a couple of weeks back - just before you set off.'

The old sea dog did a double-take. 'Well I'll be blowed! Aren't you that young whippersnapper from the *Lancastrian Bugler*? Remarkable! I've half a mind to offer you an exclusive interview given the effort you've put into tracking me down. First things first, though - tea anyone?'

The three of them listened in disbelief to the familiar sound of a kettle whistling as it came to the boil.

'Force ten blew in last night,' Sir Hubert continued. 'The dear old *Diamond Queen* was shipping water at a rate of knots, God bless her, so it was a case of any port in a storm. Luckily, I managed to salvage most of the essentials.' He shuffled off to the other side of the turbine's broad metal column, returning moments later with a fully laden tray.

'Now, that you're all safely stowed,' he said, handing out the steaming mugs of tea, 'what say you, we call on some assistance?' He pulled up his sleeve to reveal a chunky, futuristic-looking watch, and began pressing a sequence of buttons on its side.

'What is that thing?' asked Felix.

Sir Hubert grinned. 'This, young man, is state of the art global positioning technology, complete with an emergency call facility. God willing, every vessel within a fifteen-mile radius will have picked up our Mayday message by now.'

'That's amazing! With all due respect, Sir Hubert, I wouldn't have thought–'

'With all due respect to you too, my boy,' the old man interrupted him, 'I may have the misfortune to suffer from early stage dementia - Alzheimer's, the quack calls it - but I'm not bloody stupid. Now, Mars Bar anyone?'

21

Totally exhausted, they huddled together in the cramped cabin of the *SS Alexandr Solzhenitsyn,* the grubby Russian trawler that had been first to the scene. They'd been given blankets, food and hot drinks, and after persuading Sir Hubert that they weren't the victims of some sinister Soviet kidnap plot, they settled down for the hour-long trip back to Dundalk, on Ireland's east coast. It wasn't the most comfortable of journeys, the stench of rotting fish and acrid diesel fumes catching in the backs of their throats.

Themba and Felix went out on deck to watch the approach into port. She gave him a hug, kissed him on the cheek, and thanked him for his help. Eventually, he headed back inside, leaving her chatting away in Russian with a member of the crew.

A few minutes later they were greeted at the quayside by the port police, who insisted on a full search of the vessel. They turned the old tub inside-out but found nothing. It was only as they were being ushered into the back of the *Garda* Land Rover up on the quay that Felix realised Themba had disappeared.

'Come on Son, cheer up will you?' his dad said, breezing into the lounge in his dressing gown, even though it was well into the afternoon. 'Learn some lessons from your old man - move on, seize the day!'

'Dannii hasn't returned any of my calls, Felix replied forlornly. 'We'd arranged to go out on a date tonight…'

It was Tuesday, and the yearning anticipation of seeing Dannii and maybe even picking up where they'd left off on the floor of the town hall storeroom, three days earlier, was the one thing that had kept him going through the ordeal of his Mi5 de-briefing. The endless questions from the long line of stern-faced suits had been torture, but his final encounter with Trenton Fotherbridge made all of that seem like a walk in the park.

'The PM's beside himself.' The Mi5 man spat the words out angrily. 'Thanks to your rank stupidity we've lost the diamonds, and worse still, I'm the one getting it in the neck! I've told them in no uncertain terms about your role in proceedings but they're not having it. I'm facing a disciplinary panel in the morning and if I get through that, they've said they're posting me to the bloody Falklands Islands on junior diplomatic duties!'

Felix's laughter was cut short by Fotherbridge's final words as he was frog-marched from the room by a couple of burly security guards.

'That lido funding is off, Haythornthwaite - it was never a thing anyway. And after you'd reneged on our deal, I managed to get a call through to your editor. I made sure your pathetic *Bugler Belle* request is totally null and void. You've got no chance with that girl now - you never did, you loser!'

Felix had been in a state of torment ever since. Even word of HB's blubbing collapse after learning of the double-whammy of his dismissal from the *Bugler* and the court order sectioning him to a secure addictions unit for treatment of his Kwell-Eaze habit, had done nothing to lighten his mood. All he wanted was the phone to ring, or a text - even a letter would do - but if Fotherbridge really had scuppered his late-night request to Jeremy Grindrod, it was over with Dannii before it had even begun.

Under normal circumstances he wouldn't have gone anywhere near the BBC News24 channel, but since landing back at Scundale Chase he'd been glued to the TV and had watched nothing else. The '*La Calabres* Incident' had quickly gone viral and as the plucky youngster at the very heart of the maelstrom, Felix knew that every media outlet in the country should have been beating down his door to get the inside story. Alas, this was anything but the case. He'd not come across the Official Secrets Act (1949) before, but after a series of terrifying alternatives were spelt out to him by an unsmiling official from the Crown Prosecution Service - kicking off with the threat of a lengthy prison sentence if he so much as breathed a word of what had really happened to another living soul - he'd had no choice but to sign up.

Which meant he was gagged for life.

Amazingly, his dad had happily put his name to a similar agreement, and the delivery of his new car had been supplemented by a heart-warming good news story, specially crafted to throw the press pack off the scent. Suddenly, he was the hero of the hour, and he'd been milking it ever since. The *Daily Scorcher* captured the mood of the nation, perfectly:

Dad of Three Tackles Kylie-Crazed Killer in Dirty Dance Cult-Fest Showdown

Lion-hearted Brian Haythornthwaite (46) has been hailed Frecklesall-on-Sea's very own 'have-a-go hero', after single-handedly tackling a crazed gunman at the Lancashire resort's City of Culture showcase finale on Saturday night. Armed only with true British grit, the used caravan salesman wrestled deranged Latin psycho, Miguel Iglesias (25), to the ground, after the Venezuelan tried to gun down his son, DJ Freddie 'FoF' Haythornthwaite (19). The dramatic incident was captured live on prime-time national TV, shocking viewers around the country. In a bizarre twist, Brian's curvaceous wife, Christine (39), had thrilled an audience of millions with a raunchy sexy-boogie routine in the arms of the very same would-be killer, just moments before the attack took place.

'I knew Miguel was a wrong 'un from the start,' the mum of three told *The Scorcher*, 'but I had to go through with the Salsatastic routine for the sake of the town's Culture bid. I know people round these parts are gutted with the way things turned out, what with Frecklesall's disqualification, but why should I be bothered about that when I've landed the best prize of all? It's such an honour to be married to the bravest man in Britain - my gorgeous husband, Brian!'

Iglesias's deadly dance floor dash was all Brian needed to spring into action. As bullets flew and terrified audience members fled for their lives, the heroic dad risked severe hernia complications to launch a flying tackle so devastating, division two (north) rugby league outfit, the Slaidforth Sluggers, have offered him a trial.

'I guess all those hours spent working out in the gym finally paid off,' Brian told *The Scorcher*. 'Iglesias chose the wrong family when he decided to mess with the Haythornthwaites. I knew the lad was packing heat but the only thought going through my head was - threaten my boy, and I *will* take you down!'

Extracts from Iglesias's social media pages reveal how he became obsessed with exacting a terrible revenge on the controversial heavy-metal DJ for 'disrespecting' foxy Australian songstress, Kylie Minogue, after he refused to play her latest single on his Frecklesall FM radio show. Airlifted to Blackpool General Hospital the gunman, who entered the country on a forged visa, has already been extradited back to Venezuela where he is wanted for a series of cheese-related offences.

Kylie Minogue was unavailable for comment.

'They're not still banging on about that stupid yacht, are they?' Felix's dad asked, blocking his son's view by standing directly in front of the TV. 'People couldn't care less if some billionaire's boat gets sunk. What they really want is human interest stories - like me and your mum, for instance. Did I mention, we're meeting the mayor next week?'

Felix rolled his eyes - he'd heard the same line three times that morning.

'We've got a telephone interview with Radio 5 this afternoon,' his dad continued, 'and they're running a special feature in today's *Bugler*. But the best bit is that your mum can't get enough of me now!'

Felix shooed his dad away and turned his attention back to the news channel, where an earnest young reporter in a blue anorak was battling the elements on a windswept road next to a sea loch.

'Witnesses claim to have heard the explosion from here in the tiny village of Dunfanaghy on Ireland's North West coast, four miles from the spot where the multi-million-pound yacht went down,' the reporter began. 'The Caracas registered *La Calabres* was owned by Venezuelan billionaire, Alfonso Manchego, a controversial figure with links to the notorious *Quesos Grandes* crime cartel. Royal Navy Search and Rescue have confirmed that only one survivor has been picked up so far - British citizen, Sir Gerald Farquharson OBE. Police believe that Sir Gerald, a renowned gemologist and principal adviser to the Royal Collection Trust, was the target of an audacious kidnap plot. Senior sources have advised the BBC that a ransom note delivered to his exclusive Knightsbridge office on Saturday evening, offered his safe return in exchange for selected items from his personal precious stone collection. Our cameras were on hand when Sir Gerald was discharged from hospital, earlier this morning.'

The picture cut to a gaggle of reporters crowding around the hospital's main entrance. Gerald emerged in a white dressing gown, blinking in the confusion of flashlights. As soon as he spotted the journalists, he scuttled back inside with a shriek of, '*No commento!*'

The shot cut back to the reporter. 'Preliminary reports of an explosion in the yacht's engines have been questioned by some local fishermen who claim to have seen a mysterious white trail speeding through the water towards the vessel in the moments before she went down. Specialist Navy diving teams are now engaged in a painstaking search of the seabed to try to piece together just how the *La Calabres* met her untimely end.'

Felix knew exactly why Royal Navy divers were scouring the ocean floor, and it had nothing to do with finding out how the *La Calabres* had sunk. In his Mi5 debriefing, Sir Gerald had been adamant that the diamonds he'd examined out on the loading deck, just hours before the incident, were most emphatically, most genuinely, 'and without fear of contraception', the fabled Lost Cullinans. When quizzed on the matter, Felix could only agree. After all, who was he to question the expert opinion of the Queen's personal gemologist?

And so, as far as Her Majesty's Government was concerned, there was definitive proof that the Lost Cullinan diamonds really did exist. The problem was, they were swilling around somewhere on the bottom of the Atlantic Ocean, which meant the underwater search would continue until they turned up - something that Felix knew was never going to happen.

Having spent the best part of a day in the company of a series of over-excited junior intelligence officers, it hadn't been too difficult for him to piece together the events of that fateful Sunday morning.

After weathering the storm and outrunning the Royal Navy's finest, the *Quesonistas'* getaway had seemed assured - until something rather unexpected happened. The order, direct from Number 10, had been crystal-clear - the *La Calabres* was to be captured and escorted to the nearest UK port, the C2 diamonds retrieved and flown to London under armed guard. Unfortunately, in the heat of the live mission scenario, things had become a little confused.

The Spearfish torpedo, launched from the Trafalgar Class submarine lurking in the depths off Ireland's northwest coast, was intended as the classic shot across the bows. Alas, the combined impact of *La Calabres'* evasive manoeuvrings and the collective hangover endured by the crew of HMS *Invincible*, following the previous night's drunken screening of *The Sound of Music* (singalong version), resulted in an explosive end for the yacht.

For all of Mi5's attempts to waft a smokescreen over the story, the media reaction to the sinking had been like dropping a bloody leg of lamb into a tankful of peckish piranha. Questions were being asked and so far, the answers sounded less than convincing.

'So... I know we're not supposed to even mention her name, but any word on Themba?' Felix's dad asked. 'Only, your aunt Doreen's been asking after her.'

'Even if Mi5 knew where she was, they wouldn't say,' Felix replied, grumpily. 'Anyway, she'll be fine - it's you I'm more worried about.'

His dad looked at him, questioningly.

'The cover-up has been text-book,' Felix continued, 'but now the press are on the trail, you need to tread really carefully.'

'All I know is what my mates at the ministry told me,' his dad said, brightly. 'I'm a national treasure, everyone loves me *and* I've just taken delivery of a brand new 2.0 litre Mondeo Vignale!'

The rattle of the letter box sent Felix's dad springing from the settee and he returned, moments later, clutching a copy of the day's *Bugler*. His wife came in from the kitchen and the two of them snuggled up next to each other, giggling as they read through the write-up of the weekend's dramatic events.

Felix was delighted that everything was back on track with his parents' marriage, but their lovey-dovey displays of romance were beginning to get on his nerves.

Mercifully, things were cut short by the ring of the landline.

Felix's mum picked up the call. 'Hello, who's speaking?' she asked between giggles as she tried to wriggle free of her husband's clutches. '*Brian, will you behave please…*? Who do you want...? I'm sorry, you'll have to speak up.… *Brian, stop it now - there's a time and a place...*' Untangling herself from his arms, she placed a hand over the mouthpiece and turned to her son. 'Felix, it's for you. He says his name's Danny but if you ask me, *he* sounds a bit more like a *she.*'

'Give me the phone!' Felix yelled, jumping from his chair. 'No, hang on a minute, let me see the paper first!' He snatched the *Bugler* out of his dad's hands and rifled through its pages before ripping out the fashion supplement. It took a second or two for things to register.

'Ohmygod, it's her!' he shrieked.

'Who? What?' his mum asked.

'It's Dannii - that girl I was telling you about. Her picture's in the paper! She's August's *Bugler Belle* and she wants to speak to *me*!'

His dad grabbed the supplement from him and studied Dannii's photo carefully. 'By the 'eck, lad,' he remarked, 'you're punching above your weight there!'

The afternoon passed in a blur - a long shower was followed by a dousing in Rampant and a series of wardrobe visits to check out any number of outfits. With twenty minutes to go, he'd finally cracked it. The skinny white trousers found screwed up under Freddie's bed, were a bit on the half-mast side, and he'd always thought the striped lime-green shirt he'd been given the previous Christmas was way too much - but that was before fashion had become such an important part of his life. The tartan scarf knotted loosely around his neck was the icing on the cake. Freshly shaved, sockless, and with hair jelled into razor sharp spikes, he was looking good. He was admiring his reflection in the mirror when his sister wandered in.

'Do you have any idea what you look like?' she asked.

'It's a style thing,' Felix replied dismissively. 'You wouldn't understand.'

Flo rolled her eyes. 'You do realise there's no way you're going to cop off with someone like Dannii, don't you? The two of you have nothing in common, and when she finds out the only reason she got her picture in the *Bugler* is because you did a dodgy deal with those Mi5 spooks, and by the time they tried to pull the plug the fashion supplement had already gone to print, do you think she'll be quite so impressed?'

He instantly regretted confiding in his sister - not that he'd had much choice in the matter. 'Yeah, well... She doesn't need to know about that, does she?'

Flo smiled sweetly. 'So, where are you taking her tonight?'

'She's getting a lift over here, which is a bit of a worry, to be honest.' He winced at the memory of his previous encounter with Dannii's dad.

'Well?' Flo asked, impatiently.

'Sorry... I'm thinking we might head into town and grab a curry down at the Sultan. Then there's this 'Nineties Nite' on at OT's.' He started preening his hair again. 'Now, if you don't mind, I need to finish off getting ready.'

'I'll leave you to it, then,' she said, pausing in the doorway. 'I just thought you might be interested in hearing how she did it.'

'How who did what?'

'Themba, you idiot! You never did work out how she got those diamonds back to Lesotho, did you?'

Felix sighed. 'OK, but make it quick. Dannii will be here soon.'

Flo settled in on the end of the bed. 'Did Themba ever get you to take a package down to the post office for her?'

'What's that got to do with anything?' Clocking his sister's disapproving glare, Felix began to backtrack. 'Oh… Sorry, Flo. No, she didn't, actually. But now you mention it, I heard her ask Fred once. She said she was sending a present home to her granddad. Pretty stingy if you ask me - I know how I'd feel if someone sent me a Frecklesall-on-Sea fridge magnet for my birthday.'

'I took something down to the post office for her on the day she left,' said Flo. 'Dad did the same, the day before. Doreen told me she dropped off a parcel for her as well.'

'So what? She's got a big family - they'll all have their fridge magnets by now, won't they?'

Flo rolled her eyes. 'You do know about the original Cullinan diamond, don't you? How it was gifted to King Edward VII for his birthday, back in 1907?'

Felix groaned, he didn't need another history lesson.

'They had to get his lovely birthday present all the way from South Africa to London,' his sister continued. 'Obviously, air travel wasn't much of a thing back then then and the journey overland would have taken weeks - months even. They were so worried about getting ambushed on the way that they hired hundreds of security guards and set up this special armoured train to take the diamond to Cape Town, down on the coast. Then they loaded it onto this fully armed steamer, which had a navy escort all the way back to London. It cost them an absolute fortune.'

'It was pretty valuable, to be fair,' her brother said, getting up to admire himself in the mirror for the umpteenth time. 'What's your point?'

'My point,' replied Flo, 'is that the Cullinan diamond didn't get anywhere near that armoured train, or the ship for that matter. The package those security guards escorted half way around the world was full of worthless chunks of glass.'

Felix stopped his preening and turned to look at her.

'It was a *decoy,*' she announced, brightly, 'a set-up to throw everyone off the trail!'

'So... how *did* they get it over here, then?' he asked.

Flo was grinning now. 'In the exact same way Themba got the Magatos diamonds safely back to Lesotho... In the post!'

'What? You mean those trips to the post office...? We did it for her...?' Felix spluttered. 'Those diamonds are worth millions, maybe more! Why would she take the chance?'

'They were stuffed inside that bike for long enough and considering the way you looked after it, that was way riskier!' Flo replied. 'Themba mentioned something to you about history repeating itself, didn't she? Well, that really is how they got the original Cullinan diamond to London back in 1907 and it worked out fine then - so why not now? Think about it, Felix - if she'd sent them home in one big package, she'd have lost the lot if it had been intercepted. She knew they were watching her every move, so she hung around here and had us do the job for her, one piece at a time - with a bit of help from the Royal Mail, of course!'

'That's amazing! I can't believe it.'

His sister's laughter was cut short by the sounds of shouting from the front garden and she jumped up to look out the window. Recognising their dad's voice, Felix made straight for the stairs.

'I don't care who sent them!' his dad was yelling. 'Get those bloody animals away from my car - that's a top of the range Mondeo Vignale! It's got pearlescent paint *and* leather seats… No - not on the lawn, for God's sake! I only trimmed the edges yesterday!'

Felix arrived at the front doorstep to see his dad squaring up to a middle-aged, ruddy-faced man dressed in wellies, brown corduroy trousers and a crumpled check shirt. The two of them were surrounded by an ambling, mooing, sea of black and white cows. A herd of Friesians had invaded the front garden of 21 Scundale Chase, leaning their substantial flanks against the new car, churning up the grass with their hooves and chomping the blooms off the prize hydrangea - and that wasn't even the worst part. It was unclear whether it was down to the excitement of their new surroundings or something they'd eaten on the way, but all the animals appeared to be suffering from an acute case of bovine diarrhoea.

'Felix!' his dad shouted over the sounds of liquid manure squirting onto the driveway. 'Get inside and call the police, now!'

'What's going on, Dad? Where have these cows come from?'

'I don't want no trouble,' said the visitor, pulling a piece of paper from his jacket pocket. 'Just sign this chitty and I'll be on me way.'

One of the cows had mooched across to sit on the Mondeo's bonnet.

Felix's dad made a grab for the guy. 'Look what that thing's doing to my car!' he shrieked. 'You're going to pay for this, you idiot!'

'Come on Dad, that's not going to get us anywhere,' Felix pleaded, his trainer sliding through a particularly loose cow-pat as he jumped in to separate the two men. The next thing he knew, he'd lost his footing, dragging the pair down on top of him. An untidy wrestling match followed, the three of them rolling around on the muck-splattered lawn while the herd sauntered off to check out snacking opportunities in neighbouring gardens.

The impatient toot of a car horn called a halt to proceedings.

Felix scrambled to his feet and staggered towards the sporty white hatchback parked at the end of the drive. Plastered in cow diarrhoea and with a smell to match, he made a half-hearted effort to spruce up his hair, only succeeding in smearing more of the stuff across his forehead.

'Dannii... I can explain,' he gasped, as the car window whirred open to reveal August's *Bugler Belle*, resplendent in all her finery. 'Just give me a minute to... err... Wow! You look stunning, by the way.'

The expression of horror on her face said it all.

He leant forward to peer inside the car and was confronted by her dad, who glared back at him.

Felix, extended an excrement-stained hand. 'Hello sir. A pleasure to meet you properly at last–'

His greeting was interrupted by the sound of a nearby cow, ripping out a humungous fart.

'Look at the state of you!' shouted Dannii's dad. 'This place is a madhouse - cows running wild, grown men mud-wrestling in front gardens, and *you,* covered in all that *filth*!' He turned to his daughter. 'I should never have let you talk me into this, Dannii!'

'It's not how it looks!' wailed Felix. 'Things just got a bit out of hand. I know I'm not looking my best, Dannii, but if you could just give me five minutes to freshen up...'

Her dad was jabbing a finger at him now. 'If you think I'm letting a moron like you anywhere near my girl, you've got another thing coming. Now clear off before I get out of this car and do something *you* might regret!'

The car screeched away, roaring off up the close. Felix gave chase, but it was no use. Head bowed, he trudged back to the house, pausing only to peel a soggy, badly stained piece of paper from the driveway block paving. It was a delivery note, from Pear Tree Farm, Over Wyre. The Scundale Chase address was right enough, and there was no mistaking the presence of the pedigree cows - all six of them - but it was the printed message it contained that caught Felix's attention.

A gift for the Haythornthwaite family: with many thanks for the help and support you have given my beloved granddaughter, and for your extraordinary bravery over the past weeks. I will always be indebted to you for her safe homecoming and the return of that which is rightfully ours.

Yours, in eternal gratitude,

Chief Nomalanga Magatos III,
Butha-Buthe, Lesotho

Acknowledgement

With special thanks to:

Scott Cockerham, for a great cover design.
Karen Bradbury, for fabuloso Spanish translation services.
Clive Barker (exploding tinned pie survivor), for awesome proof-reading and relentless encouragement over too many years to mention.
Darryl Lawrence, for jaunty Morris Dancing consultancy services and excellence in melodeon playing.
Sharon Pimbley, for invaluable technical and moral support
Chorley & District Writers' Circle, for the laughs, continuing inspiration and a drip feed of grammatical and layout tips which have led to me re-editing this novel hundreds of times (and it still won't be right!).
The Guinness Partnership, for keeping the wolf from the door.
Kimberly 'Hitch' Hitchins from Book Nook (Arizona), for her generous trans-Atlantic support on KDP technicalities and for cheering me up when I was at a low ebb.
Richard Branson and the Virgin Trains West Coast Main Line team, for a fast-moving writing environment, with the occasional tilt.

Susan Yearwood from SYLA, for a clandestine meeting at Euston station and for pushing me to get on and write this thing.

Lindsey Fraser from Fraser Ross Associates Literary Agency, for preliminary editing advice and encouragement.

Susanne Holt from Runshaw Writers, for arming me with the basics, and early advice and encouragement.

Jenni Rickard for last minute punctuation consultancy services.

The *New York Times* for their kind consent to using the 'Lost Cullinan' article from 1909 (only slightly tweaked to fit the plot).

The *Chorley Guardian*, *Lancashire (Evening) Post*, and *Lancashire Life* - for inspiration.

Wikipedia.

Franz Kafka, for devising my editing strategy.

My wonderful sister Kathryn Ramsay, for her ongoing encouragement, support and hyphenation expertise.

And most importantly, my lovely Louise, for everything, really.

About The Author

Al Ramsay

Al lives with his wife, Louise, in the beautiful Lancashire market town of Chorley. Until the recent call of the pipe and slippers, he worked for a national housing association, helping build affordable homes across the north of England. His career objective was to solve the UK housing crisis, and in this, he failed. Some say he may even have made things worse - although that never stopped him from trying. Travelling all too frequently by train, between Wigan and 'that London' as part of his job, The Felix Haythornthwaite Series was conceived during down-time on board the Virgin Trains' Pendolino fleet (quiet carriage 'A'), the creative process fuelled by way too many bacon rolls.

Al now spends his time riding his bike, writing and getting mildly disheartened (and sometimes overly excited) by the travails of his three favourite football teams: Everton, Leyton Orient and, of course, Chorley. He's a member of the Chorley Writers group and a regular contributor to the town's literary festival, 'What's Your Story, Chorley?' His lifetime ambition is to appear in *Lancashire Life*.

alramsay2@gmail.com

December 2021

The Felix Haythornthwaite Files by Al Ramsay

Underground

When Felix Haythornthwaite's on-line news blog, the *Frecklesall Exposer*, is picked up by billionaire energy mogul, Donald Kincaid, it seems the sky's the limit. But after Felix is cajoled into welcoming Donald's wayward son onto his team, and crosses swords with visiting delegates from the Russian GulaGaz energy corporation, things quickly get out of hand. And then legendary ladies' man, and mainstay of Felix's dad's ManShed male support group, Archie Crowfoot, dies. The police say it's from natural causes but after teaming up with a bunch of militant feminist eco-warriors, Felix stumbles across unexplained goings-on at Archie's remote farmhouse and suddenly he's the one at risk of ending six feet under. But who would want to kill Archie, and why? And could there be a connection between his death and some of the weird things that have been happening in the area?

Mislaid novelty underpants, low-flying offal and a publicity-hungry celebrity undertaker on a mission to put the 'FUN' back into FUNerals are woven into a fast-moving plot of dodgy dealings, international duplicity and environmental calamity, where nothing is quite what it seems. Anglo/Russian relations may never be quite the same again.

Published as an Amazon Kindle ebook May 2021
Paperback available from May 2022

The Free Lunch

Nothing ever happens in Frecklesall-on-Sea, an unremarkable Lancashire town, located on the road to nowhere, beyond the back of beyond. So when an ambitious new mayor takes control of the council and announces that things are going to change, the locals can't believe their luck. But for wannabe investigative journalist and discredited school newspaper editor, Felix Haythornthwaite, there are questions to be answered. When he starts asking them he's dragged, kicking and screaming, into a murky world of corporate greed, corrupt politicians, extortion and kidnapping. With the action played out against the glamorous backdrop of the world's greatest bike race - the *Tour de France* - one hapless teenager, his stupid big brother and six donkeys, are all that stand between their hometown and total oblivion. It should be no contest, but *Le Tour* has never visited anywhere quite like Frecklesall-on-Sea before, and on this showing, never will again!

Due for publication on Amazon Kindle in ebook and paperback format in September 2022.

Printed in Great Britain
by Amazon